20,000 LEAGUES REMEMBERED

EDITED BY

STEVEN R. SOUTHARD AND KELLY A. HARMON

Pole to Pole Publishing
Baltimore

The Ghost of Captain Nemo ©2020 J. Woolston Carr
Water Whispers ©2020 Gregory L. Norris
At Strange Depths ©2020 Jason J. McCuiston
The Maelstrom ©2020 Maya Chhabra
The Game of Hare and Hounds ©2020 Stephen R. Wilk
Recruiter ©2020 Andrew Gudgel
Nemo's World ©2020 James J.C. Kelly
The Silent Agenda ©2020 Mike Adamson
Fools Rush In ©2020 Allison Tebo
An Evening at the World's Edge ©2020 Alfred D. Byrd
A Concurrent Process ©2020 Corrie Garrett
Homework Help from No One ©2020 Demetri Capetanopoulos
Leviathan ©2020 Michael D. Winkle
Last Year's Water ©2020 Nikoline Kaiser
Farragut's Gambit ©2020 M. W. Kelly
Raise the Nautilus ©2020 Eric Choi

Editors' Note: This volume of work was edited using the *AP Stylebook* and *U.S. Navy Style Guide*. For this reason, ship and boat names are not italicized.

20,000 LEAGUES REMEMBERED

"Professor Aronnax," the Canadian said, "...You talk about some future day...I'm talking about *now*."

~ Ned Land, in 20,000 Leagues Under the Sea

Table of Contents

Forward

*O*ne hundred and fifty years ago, Jules Verne launched a novel now regarded as a classic, translated and reprinted in countless book versions, transcribed for stage and screen, and transformed into video games and a theme park ride. *Twenty Thousand Leagues Under the Sea* has inspired innumerable submariners, undersea explorers, and ship designers, not to mention armchair adventurers.

I'm one of them. More than anything else, that novel prompted me to major in Naval Architecture in college, to join the submarine service, and much later to write fiction of my own.

When I realized the sesquicentennial of Verne's masterwork approached, I felt it deserved a worthy commemoration. I pitched the idea of this anthology to my friend, Kelly A. Harmon, the Senior Editor at Pole to Pole Publishing. As I'd imagined then, I'd contribute a story to a book she'd edit and publish. Kelly imagined things differently: "It's *your* idea. *You* edit it."

That sparked a new experience for me, one that became a marvelous odyssey. So many fine writers submitted excellent stories, each exploring a different facet of *Twenty Thousand Leagues*, each capturing its nautical wonder and literary power. I loved reading them all, but could only select a few for this volume.

Many have never read the novel and only saw one of the movies based on it. Each of those films took liberties with the Nautilus and with the characters. But the authors of the stories in this volume took their cues from Verne's text, not from film adaptations.

Four of these tales include high adventure, set in or near the time of Verne's novel. Author Stephen R. Wilk had long envisioned a different ending for Jules Verne's later novel, *The Blockade Runners*, so he ties the two books together in his lively story, "The Game of Hare and Hounds." Former submariner M. W. Kelly will enthrall you with an ironclad, an airship, and Mark Twain in "Farragut's Gambit." Author J. Woolston Carr brings back John Strock, Verne's American detective in *Master of the World*, to investigate strange maritime reports from Baltimore in "The Ghost of Captain Nemo." Perhaps the Nautilus lay intact, waiting until World War I to be salvaged by the British; read Eric Choi's "Raise the Nautilus" to discover if they succeed.

A quartet of other stories, also set in the past, are more thoughtful and exploratory in nature. When you read "The Silent Agenda" by Mike Adamson, you'll see why translations of Verne's works into English got so horribly botched. What if Professor Aronnax met up with Cyrus Smith of *The Mysterious Island*? Alfred D. Byrd answers that in his thought-provoking tale, "An Evening at the World's Edge." "The Maelstrom" by Maya Chhabra is a fascinating take on Captain Nemo's origin story, and how his early years influenced some climactic scenes in Verne's novel. In "Recruiter," Andrew Gudgel gives us Nemo's method for gathering his initial crew together and obtaining new crewmen in later years.

If you prefer stories set in our present time, you'll enjoy four other tales in this volume. Perhaps the Nautilus still exists, and maybe its secrets can change humanity forever, as imagined in "Nemo's World," by James J.C. Kelly. For a captivating coming-of-age story set in Greenland, we present "Last Year's Water" by Nikoline Kaiser. A young boy might just receive the help he needs from Captain Nemo in Captain Demetri Capetanopoulos' "Homework Help from No One," a masterful problem-solving tale. The investigation of a mysterious UFO leads to a surprising discovery in "A Concurrent Process" by Corrie Garrett.

Four other stories defy easy categorization and stand on their own. In Jason J. McCuiston's "At Strange Depths," you'll discover what adventures Captain Nemo, along with one of his more mysterious crewmen, experienced after Professor Aronnax and his companions departed. In a humorous take on Verne's novel, the delightful "Fools Rush In" by Allison Tebo presents quirky criminals attempting to steal Captain Nemo's riches. Verne wrote a chapter about the Nautilus attacking sperm whales—cachalots—and in Michael D. Winkle's "Leviathan" you'll explore an alternate version, from a whale's point of view. The tale of Nemo and his Nautilus can inspire an outer space adventure, as you'll see from Gregory L. Norris' "Water Whispers."

In their correspondence with us, the authors mentioned how much they enjoyed re-reading Verne's novel, conducting research for their story, and writing it. That enthusiasm shines through in every tale. Each one is a labor of love, an admiring tribute to one of history's greatest authors. I think Jules Verne would have been pleased.

Steven R. Southard
June 20, 2020

The Ghost of Captain Nemo

J. Woolston Carr

Inspector John Strock searched for mysteries in a world where technology was prying through the keyhole of the cosmic door concealing the universe. Only six months previous the 1904 World's Fair debuted in St. Louis. Exhibits showcased the marvels of a new age with automatic telephony, telegrams sent from typewriter to typewriter and electric cars easily capable of traveling at forty miles an hour. But even while people were amazed at machines using x-rays to see inside human bodies, Strock feared the existence of maniacs who devised terrifying machines beyond modern comprehension.

John Strock, Head Inspector of the Federal Police Department in Washington DC, found himself 40 miles northeast in the city of Baltimore pursuing a rumor. His fellow inspectors had scoffed at him, because Strock was known as a man to chase ghosts and theories.

It had been less than a year since his encounter with the fantastic vehicle of Robur. Robur the Scientist. Robur the Conqueror. Robur the Madman. Strock had witnessed the man and machine both plunge to their destruction in a storm-ravaged ocean, but strange sightings in the Baltimore harbor whispered of the mad inventor's return.

Strock was a plain man. His simple, dark colored suit and patent leather shoes had been ordered from a Sears Roebuck catalogue. No jewelry embellished his hands. His one exception was a stiff, wool homburg hat from the Stetson Company, constructed with a soft satin lining and a black shiny silk hat band, decorated with a clipped red peacock feather pinned to the side. His immigrant mother had told him a well-made hat was the sign you had arrived.

The hat drew attention to a hard, square face fixed with a penetrating stare. A trim moustache crowned his lips, set in a compact line rarely revealing a smile or frown. If he ever played cards, it would have been a superb poker face. Yet the city of Baltimore caused the tinge of a grimace. Strock covered his face with a handkerchief, trying to smother the odor of charred wood, mold and decay.

A great fire had burned through the city, a disaster surpassed only by the Chicago fire of 1871. Now scorched remnants of buildings leaned precariously as diligent workers continued to repair the seaport.

Strock prowled the easternmost portion of Baltimore harbor. Fells Point was a poor neighborhood on a thin little finger of land projecting out of the harbor that had escaped the fire, but maybe it shouldn't have. Years ago the shipbuilding industry moved further downstream, replaced by the reek of canneries, the lure of brothels and the obscurity of shady dives.

He followed the winding cobbled streets to the docks, following the curve of the waterfront. Red brick buildings squeezed together among narrow alleyways. He passed Polish and Italian immigrant women and children, busily peeling shells from crabs and rinds from fruit.

He kept his head down and his attention vigilant. It was difficult to tell if the bar he finally discovered had somehow succumbed to the fire or simply to poor management. He half-expected the door to come off its hinges when he opened it. Inside swirled the acrid odor of beer, urine and sea. No one acknowledged his entrance, and he felt the scrutiny of men who preferred anonymity.

Strock sat at the bar as a man wiped a space off the counter with a tattered rag, clearing away little of the grime.

"What'll you have?" asked the bartender.

"Miller High Life," said Strock. Then he laid a five-dollar bill on the stained wood. "And some…advice."

The bartender, a tall, gangly man with unruly hair and a surly expression, stared at him. The money disappeared; his rag more effective at removing the bill than the filth.

"I'm looking for someone with this insignia," said the Inspector.

He laid a piece of paper on the counter where the five-dollar bill had been. On it was drawn a single letter—a calligraphic *N* illustrated with swirls and curves. Strock did not know what it meant, but an informant assured him it was connected to the mystery in the harbor.

The bartender shrugged. "I seen it, on a flag. This man, he brings this small flag and sets it on his table while he drinks alone. Not here now, but he'll be here, comes regular. Big man, looks like a sailor, someone who's been at it for a long time."

"Is he a hard drinker?" asked Strock.

"Funny you mention it. He was for a while. Now he's stopped. Just comes in and orders a cup of tea. Sits and acts like he's waiting for someone. But no one comes. He goes home, comes back the next day."

Strock pursed his lips. A man stops drinking only when he has a reason to.

Strock sipped his beer and waited. After a few hours a big, thick-set man entered, moving with the odd wobbling gait of a seaman on land. He sat down and ordered a drink, planting the miniature flag at the edge of the table.

Strock approached him.

"Mind if I join you?" Strock nodded to the man.

The man shrugged, broad shoulders indicating permission. Stamped with a look of ruggedness, he had attempted to groom his white, thinning hair, strands pasted to the side of his head.

The inspector sat, and ordered a coffee. He knew it was fruitless to pretend friendship or interest other than his purpose.

"My name's John Strock. I work for the Federal Police in Washington."

He waited for a response. The man shrugged again as he spoke.

"Everyone's got to have a job, no matter how dull, ya?" He chuckled at his own joke. The accent was odd to Strock, one he couldn't quite place, maybe eastern European. The sailor's expression was bold and purposeful. Strock could see the scars where the beard had been removed, revealing a wrinkled but clean-shaven face.

"The name's Kessler," said the sailor. He didn't offer to shake hands.

Strock pulled out another five-dollar bill. "I need your help. I can pay."

"I ain't lookin' for that kind of work," said Kessler.

"What kind of work are you looking for?"

The man remained quiet for a moment, thoughtful, sorting his words.

"*Nautron, nautron respoc lorni virch.*"

Strock didn't understand. It was no language he had ever heard.

The sailor shook his head and spoke again. "The kind of work with a purpose. You know what I mean?"

"I do. That's my kind of work, dull as it is. But right now the Baltimore harbor seems a shabby place to look for work with a purpose."

"Ya, maybe so. But it's about more than making a dollar," Kessler continued. "There's meaning to the life I want, beyond just being at sea. You ever been at sea?"

"Not of my own free will. I prefer to stand on something solid."

"Sure. Land is predictable. Land is boring. The sea, it has its own personality. A great man once described it as a desert, but one where yer never lonely, 'cause you feel life all around you. It's liberating; you got yer independence with no rules."

"No rules? Surely you realize nations occupy the sea and control it with great fleets?"

"Oh, I know. But I'm talkin' about below. You go just a few feet under the water, and suddenly you are in a land that has no restrictions, where no one can follow, no laws but of nature. Beneath the sea, she's pure. Not tainted by the hand of man. See, long ago when I was but a swabbie, the Captain took us to places no one ever set eyes upon. I seen under the ice at the North Pole. I seen vast fields of seaweed growing enough food to feed a whole country. Why, do you believe I even seen Atlantis!"

Strock thought of Robur's exotic ship, how it could travel anywhere—in the air, on the water...or underneath it. The idea of submarine ships was no longer a wild theory. American and British navies were in the business of building them, though skeptical of their use beyond harbor defenses. Submarines would never replace a good battleship during war, and most nations considered the limited submersibles only for inferior navies. Even the most modern submarines could not carry a man to the distances the sailor described. If someone were able to build such a vessel, arm it and man it with a large crew, he would be of great interest to powerful governments.

"You've been aboard such a vessel, one that could take you to those places?" asked Strock as he ordered more tea for his companion. He believed the sailor. This was no drunken wretch, or an unhinged member of a cult.

"Ya. It was no ordinary ship, and no regular captain. To be part of his crew, and to have a purpose. Not something every fish can claim."

The sailor settled back quietly. His tone became muted as he sipped his tea. "You ever had dolphin liver?" Kessler asked.

"That's not something Mother made for Sunday dinner."

"Course you haven't. The captain, he said it tasted like some sort of pork ragout. Good with sea cucumbers," the sailor said as he licked his lips.

"Hmm...I'm not sure that makes it more appetizing. This captain, who was he? Is he still alive?"

Kessler held up his cup in tribute.

"A great man. Maybe more than a man. A man that cannot die, I think. Or he's died more'n once, and returned from the grave each time. The Captain, he knows the sea, top and below. Knows its value, knows its limits. He must be more than a man. Gotta have a brain, savviness, better than you or me or any other human. Ya, we all would have risked our lives for that man, and we doubted not he would do the same for us."

"But if he's not dead, what happened to him? Why did you abandon him?"

"He suffered greatly," answered the sailor in a grave tone. "You could see it in his eyes, like great storms at sea. There were rumors his family had been murdered by some great nation, but he never talked of it. Ya see, he did not hide in the ocean, he escaped to it. But he finally realized the ship, it would not protect us forever. Sharks and men, eh? So he let us go, and he disappeared. But maybe, maybe he's ready to return."

"You're being very forthcoming to an officer of the law."

"It don't matter. You and your inspection agency from Washington DC, you won't have no authority where I'll be going, and you'll not ever find me. I been without purpose for near 30 some years, but now..." Resolve returned to his face. "Now I get another chance to be redeemed."

"It sounds like you are waiting for the second coming of Christ," said Strock.

"Christ walked on the water. My savior walks beneath it."

Strock ran a finger along his moustache, pinching the pliant wax used to keep it neat.

"You think he's here, this captain. What was his name?"

"Didn't say. Just nobody." He laughed as if he had made another joke.

Strock spoke directly. "I came here because of strange sightings outside the harbor in the Chesapeake Bay, reports of a large sea creature. But I've learned the manipulation of man is usually behind the pretense of unnatural phenomena. There's a mystery ship here, and it's meant to attract you and others you sailed with. The flag you display is a ticket, a symbol to allow you back in. Does the name Robur mean anything to you?"

When the sailor leaned towards Strock as if to whisper an answer, a bar window shattered and a glowing ball darted through the air. It struck Kessler and exploded. He stood as his body convulsed, the scent of electricity and scorched flesh pervading the room. The sailor fell backwards, as charred as the city of Baltimore.

Strock ran to the window and caught a glimpse of a person running away. He looked back at the bartender, who stared in horror at the electrocuted body.

"Should...should I call a doctor?" he asked.

Strock shook his head and returned to Kessler, A closer examination revealed a red blistering bruise the size of a silver dollar on his chest, now red and blistered, smelling of burnt flesh.

The other customers were standing and staring. More mysteries confronted the inspector. Why kill this man?

"Is it safe to touch him?" asked the bartender.

Strock didn't speak. He searched the floor, and found the steel ball that had struck the sailor. Strock shook it, and could hear bits of shattered glass rattling inside.

"What is that?"

"I don't know, but it electrocuted the man. Curious." Strock put the ball in his pocket to study later. Spying the black flag fallen to the floor, he retrieved it as well.

The bartender tightened his mouth critically.

"Evidence," said Strock. "Call the police."

"I thought you were the police?"

"I'm a Federal Inspector," he replied.

Strock studied the sailor and his wide-eyed grimace of death. Kessler spoke the truth. He was going someplace where the Federal Police Department in Washington had no authority.

Inspector Strock had changed out of his usual apparel. Despite it being a warm day for October he was dressed in the bulky clothing of a longshoreman's attire, with baggy trousers, a pullover knitted sweater and canvas coat. His homburg was gone, replaced by a white cotton cap, shadowing vigilant eyes. Most important, he carried the sailor's flag. The workman's outfit concealed a diving suit made of vulcanized rubber. It forced Strock to walk stiffly and awkwardly, making it appear as if the clothes didn't properly fit.

He discovered other deaths by electrocution had occurred in the city of Baltimore. Most were attributed to accidents, but they had all been sailors. He had made no connection between these and the strange bay sightings until now.

Strock found a different bar along the same wharf and settled in. Patience was a key element to being an inspector, and he sat for several days talking to the bartender and other patrons as if he were a sailor looking for work. He flashed the flag. He imitated the speech of the sailor Kessler as much as possible, and his perseverance paid off. On the third day, as he left the bar, a familiar whoosh of air shrieked, followed by a ball striking him and exploding. An electric charge crackled around Strock's body and he collapsed to the ground. A figure approached, a hat slouched over the head, a scarf wrapped around the face. The person reached down towards the prone Strock and lifted his hand holding the flag. Strock opened his eyes and grabbed the arm.

The figure tried to pull away and the scarf fell to reveal the face of a startled woman.

"What...how?" she gasped.

Strock rolled, trying to pull the woman down. The killer was unexpectedly agile, though, and twisted as they reeled along the street, freeing her arm. She dropped the rifle and began to run.

Struggling to his feet, Strock retrieved the abandoned gun and pulled a round projectile from the firing chamber. Stuffing it in an interior pocket, he pursued the assassin. She dashed down an alley at a good pace, while Strock was frustrated by his cumbersome clothing. He still managed to chase her to the wharf. At the end of a short dock the woman leapt in to a small motorized launch. With a trembling cough, the engine stirred as she cranked it, causing the three-bladed propeller to slowly churn in the water.

Strock ran along the dock, fearing he was going to lose her again. With a prodigious leap, made awkward by his outfit, he launched himself from the dock to the boat. Reaching the edge of the craft with a splash, the force of the landing briefly knocked the air from his lungs. It also tipped the woman so she lost balance.

She recovered her footing and grabbed a pike to strike at him, but he had enough time to pull himself up and block the blow, then roll into the boat. Abandoning her pike, the woman withdrew a pistol from a nearby box. Strock stared brazenly at a grim face scarred with middle age and grief.

"How did you survive the Leyden ball?" she asked, the gun leveled.

"The what?" replied Strock, gasping for air as he slumped back in the boat.

"The Leyden ball. It should have electrocuted you."

"Oh, the electric bullet from the air rifle." Strock opened his jacket and pulled up the sweater. Underneath was a set of clothing insulated with a thick layer of rubber.

"A vulcanized rubber suit," he said. "It's designed for flotation, but I thought it might protect me from your electrified projectiles." Strock held up a calming hand. "Before you shoot me, I'm not a sailor. I'm a Federal Inspector." He carefully produced a badge.

The woman kept her gun steady, but refrained from pulling the trigger.

"Who do you work for?" Strock asked. "Is it Robur? Why are you killing these seamen?"

She scowled. "Work for? I work for myself. I have no quarrel with you, and I will prove to you the justness of my actions."

She sat with one hand on the tiller and the other with the pistol trained on Strock. He didn't move.

They cruised away from the city, past the flapping flag atop Fort McHenry and towards the rippling blue waters of the Chesapeake Bay. Strock became worried his captor was looking for a likely spot to throw him overboard.

After a period of quiet, she spoke.

"Are you a man of history, Mr. Strock?"

"Are you asking if I know my history? I can tell you the difference between the Enlightenment and Romanticism, and Napoleon was defeated at Waterloo in 1815. Would you like a chronological list of our Presidents?"

"Have you ever heard of a ship called the Abraham Lincoln, commanded by a man named Farragut?"

Strock shook his head.

"It was an American military vessel some 38 years ago. It spent six months searching for an elusive sea serpent."

"Wait, I *have* heard of it," said Strock. The woman's scorn turned to surprise as he continued. "That would be 1866, when the sightings of some mysterious sea creature dominated the news. You see, I make it a point to keep abreast of the unusual." Strock smiled and continued. "Several ships had been mysteriously damaged, and the Navy sent a frigate out to investigate. Was it the Abraham Lincoln? It chased what some scientists considered to be a giant narwhal, a sea creature with a long horn."

"It is more of a tusk or tooth, but you are basically correct."

"Really? Interesting. At any rate, I know the Abraham Lincoln was disabled in an attack. I'm afraid I don't remember learning about anything after."

"Then let me educate you, Mr. Strock. It was no sea monster the Abraham Lincoln sought, but a ship, a submersible boat called the Nautilus. You are not skeptical?"

"I've seen worse."

"There is nothing worse than the great evil named Captain Nemo. Nemo and his crew were merciless, and obsessed with wreaking havoc on the civilized world. They are the ones who crippled the Abraham Lincoln. Other ships met disastrous fates at the hand of Nemo, but Commander Farragut never again found his quarry. His relentless pursuit to exterminate the Nautilus cost him his life."

Strock was perplexed. This did not sound like the same captain he had learned about from Kessler.

"I had a long talk with the sailor you…executed," said Strock. "He described his captain as an explorer and a man of science. Perhaps guilty of a certain swagger and pride, but hardly a monster. Under the command of this Nemo it was an idyllic and peaceable life, a captain to be envied for his leadership and devotion from his men."

"Devotion? No, fanaticism," the woman insisted, temper flushing her cheeks. "Do not be deceived by some romantic story of life under the sea. Nemo was a hypocrite, decrying the tyrannical rule of nations on land, while he proclaimed himself master of the seas. Those who served him were not men seeking knowledge. They were pirates, and they too deserve the sentence of death as murderers. There is no denying Nemo's purpose was to ruthlessly kill. Does a man of peace build an engine of destruction with a prow designed for ramming into defenseless ships? Does he create weapons such as the Leyden gun with the power to kill an elephant? These are machines of violence, not instruments of science. He was a butcher, a terrorist. Nothing more."

"This was nearly 40 years ago. You must have been a child. What could possibly inspire you to seek out these men and kill them?"

"Not inspiration, but obligation. Commander Farragut was my father. As a little girl I watched him descend in to his delirium, not understanding, only knowing he was lost to me as a parent. His fixation on Captain Nemo left no room for the love of a wife or a daughter. His tantrums finally had him discharged from the Navy, and with no means to pursue Nemo, I watched as his heart burst in a furious, frustrated rage. When I was older, I resolved to take over his quest for Nemo. I would become a huntress, and his Leyden gun a fitting form of retribution."

"And now that's become your purpose, don't you find it ironic?" said Strock, hoping to find some method of reasoning with the bitter and vindictive woman. "The sailor I spoke with, he told me Nemo was motivated to seclude himself to the sea because his own family was murdered. Aren't you becoming that which you despise? If your story is true, you have the opportunity to offer mercy and prove yourself better than Nemo."

The gun in her hand quivered. Strock knew the rubber suit would not stop a lead bullet.

"Do not try my patience," she whispered, returning to the navigation of the boat without further utterance.

The motorboat zipped along the water, down the Patapsco River and into the middle of the Chesapeake Bay. They passed the narrower confines between Kent Island and Annapolis. Only a few miles separated them from the island, where unhelpful crabbing boats hugged the shoreline. Rather than making for some clandestine port, the woman maintained a path in the middle of the bay. The sinking sun had disappeared in the horizon, leaving a dim mantle of blue skies to illuminate their route. Barely visible in the dark water, the motorboat slowed near a black and white buoy. The woman checked her watch, and waited for only a few minutes.

It rose like some leviathan, water cascading off its hull. Long and thin, over 100 feet from stem to stern, with a menacing prow and a control tower ascending like a steeple on a church whose congregation prayed for revenge. Strock found his sea monster.

The woman motored to the rear of the submarine, locking in the small launch.

"This is the Nemesis, Inspector. I married a feeble but wealthy aristocrat, and when he died, I poured all my resources into building this ship to take revenge on Nemo and the Nautilus."

An airlock clanged open, discharging a man in a blue uniform and a round flat hat. He moved with the discipline of an experienced seaman.

"My crew is like me, seeking revenge for the misery to their families caused by the Nautilus. That is the legacy of Captain Nemo."

The woman jumped lithely aboard, and Strock was taken below.

They stood in a cramped control room, Strock hunched over in the narrow space crowded with iron pipes, hissing air pressure gauges and men scooting by shoulder to shoulder with military precision. Inside it felt damp, and stank from diesel oil. Valve wheels of various sizes were clustered on both sides, all illuminated by sputtering electric lights protected inside steel cages. Colorful knobs and switches extended from an electric switchboard. Through a rear oval bulkhead door, Strock could see more compartments, none of them any more spacious or inviting. The forward door revealed a glimpse of long tubular underwater missiles cradled in secure shelves. This was no luxurious ship of travel as he supposed the Nautilus had been, nor a submarine designed solely for coastal defense. This was a machine meant to seek and destroy.

"She is a match for the Nautilus in every way," the woman said proudly. "The Nemesis is propelled on the surface by diesel engines, but electrically operated when we submerge, reaching speeds of 40 knots. Though I understand she is smaller than the Nautilus, I believe it makes her more nimble. She is armed with two forward tubes firing self-propelled torpedoes. Ah, what I would give for the opportunity to engage the Nautilus, I would blast her to the bottom of the sea where she belongs."

"What do you plan to do with me?"

She spoke as a seaman handed her a chart. "I am not a callous murderer. When I have finished, I will need someone who will tell my story. Let the world know I have served justice upon Nemo. You will stay upon the Nemesis until I am done."

"A prisoner?" Strock recoiled. "I've suffered once at the hands of a madman."

She glared at him. "Your alternative is death."

"If it's to be," said Strock bravely, "I won't go alone."

Strock reached underneath his sweater and pulled a round metal ball from a pocket. It was one of the Leyden balls, and before any crew member could stop him, he hurled it at the electrical control panel of the ship. In truth, Strock wasn't sure if it would have any effect, working on a mere assumption that the ball detonated with a forceful concussion. He needn't have been doubtful. Sparks and smoke erupted at the impact, followed by an explosion.

In the confusion, Strock heaved himself up to the topside deck. He was followed by one of the seamen brandishing a knife, and they grappled on top as smoke billowed from the open deck hatch.

The crewman was bigger than Strock and wielded a large knife, coming at him with an overhand thrust of the blade. Strock was not without the ability to defend himself, having studied self-defense with the renowned Edward Barton-Wright. The inspector interrupted the blow with his left forearm. He then stepped in quickly and ensnared his attacker's knife arm just above the elbow. The arm bent backwards with a satisfying crack of bone.

Ridding himself of his adversary, Strock rushed to escape in the small motorized skiff, but found it locked upside down into a protective watertight bay. Others would soon be chasing after him. Stripping his outer clothing and leaving only the rubberized suit, he found a paddle secured near the boat and dove into the water, miles from the dark Maryland shore. The rubber suit was going to save him for a second time, used for its intended purpose: it was made famous by the adventurous Captain Paul Boyton who had floated down rivers from the Mississippi to the Rhine equipped with this swimming costume.

Going feet foremost, he propelled himself towards the flickering evening lights of the distant shore. The rubber pants and shirt were tightly bound around the waist with a wide strap of leather. Strock fumbled for the long hoses and began inflating the air pockets inside his suit. Bobbing on his back in the water like a feeding sea otter, the air bag in the hood inflated to a comfortable pillow, leaving only his face exposed. The inspector used the paddle to direct himself towards land as he struggled against the wind and tides in the burgeoning darkness. No one followed, and eventually he lost sight of the submarine. It had either sunk or submerged on its own.

The strokes of the paddle became repetitive, and Strock pondered his escape. He had begun his investigation for a lunatic, and instead of resolving the riddle he had added another.

Robur had not returned, and perhaps he was gone forever. The woman had denounced the legacy of Captain Nemo, but she shared his consuming desire for vengeful retribution.

Most puzzling was the revelation about Nemo. Which version of the captain should he believe? Perhaps both. Such pioneers were unique, leaving a twisted legacy that might advance science for the betterment of mankind, or burrow a bloody path leading to a great world war of death and destruction.

In truth, he feared men such as Robur and Nemo. Such intellect constructs power greater than that of the natural world. The British politician Lord Acton had said power tends to corrupt, and absolute power corrupts absolutely. Great men are almost always bad men.

Strock could not argue with the sentiment. How could any man, especially one of genius, not succumb to his unconstrained hubris, driving him to the edge of sanity? Another quote came to Strock, as he meditated on his St. Augustine.

"Humilitas homines sanctis angelis similes facit, et superbia ex angelis demones facit."

It was pride that changed angels into devils, it is humility that makes men as angels.

Water Whispers

Gregory L. Norris

Joe walked the beach. His steps straddled the line where the spilled waves sank into damp sand. A fitting place for a land dweller who owed his origins to the ocean, he agreed. Sunlight warmed his skin. The Mediterranean, he thought at first, and that, too, was fitting. But two suns hung above the seascape, an orange dwarf and, farther away, a luminous blue variable star suspended in the sky like a massive chandelier. A curious pairing, he thought. Unique. He recognized this system, this ocean and its shore. Their precise identity eluded him the more he attempted to focus on the answer.

His gaze wandered out past the harbor and into the glittering turquoise expanse. An inland ocean, he was sure, one landlocked by arid wastelands to the distant east. For a shocking instant, he wasn't ambling along its western shore but looking down upon its figure-eight shape from high orbit aboard Nautilus. How many alien seas had he mapped and admired from that same lofty position?

How many hundreds of times had he relived visiting this planet's ocean?

As the truth neared close enough to grasp, the view around him shorted out, replaced by numbing darkness.

"Mister Bronson, do you hear me?" the voice asked. Male. Distant. It resonated through Joe's consciousness like a whisper in a dream. "Joe?"

It wasn't any more real than the thousand other dreams about a hundred different oceans, a common theme in the fugue of the past century.

"*Joe. If you hear me...*"

Joe could. He wasn't swimming with the gentle cephalopods in a warm tropical lagoon on Pacific Planet or surfing the Gray Atoll or maneuvering through a bathyscaphe on one of the watery worlds in the Bailey Vortiss Archipelago of Planets, no. He was deep at the bottom of a well. Deeper. So deep, the surrounding water blocked out the sun and was black and icy.

I hear you, he thought.

The dream cracked open; all illusions gone. There was only the cold, dark depths around him and that voice. Waiting for it to respond transformed seconds into long and miserable sums of time—what felt like minutes, hours.

A sigh of relief filtered through the darkness. "Joe?"

"I'm here. Who are you?"

"A friend," the male voice said, now closer, closer. Joe's soul warmed before again cooling. Friend? The only name that came to mind was the Nautilus, and, at last recollection, that intergalactic research vessel had been in a thousand or more pieces and falling like a comet toward unexplored ocean.

"*Mare Poseidonus,*" Joe gasped.

"Yes, Joe. Can I call you *Joe,* or would you prefer *Mister Bronson? Or Colonel?*"

He hadn't gone by *Colonel Bronson* since striking out on his own after his service in the Earth Exodus Militia. Cousteau had his Calypso, Darwin the Beagle. Joe Bronson had sailed aboard Nautilus and was still connected to whatever was left of her forward section following micro-meteor showers of unprecedented intensity at the inner orbit of System Jeg-311.

"Joe's fine. Yours?"

"Doctor Winslow Greene."

"*Winslow,*" Joe said and smiled. He liked it. There was poetry in that name. He imagined an ocean breeze, warm and flower-scented, whispering it.

"Joe, do you remember what happened? On the moon Mare Poseidonus?"

The sweet breeze died, sucked away by a dark maelstrom. Nautilus, her superstructure's spine shattered, main systems failing, the ship falling. Ironic that his intended destination now loomed before him, a shadowy ocean moon in orbit around a super gas giant. He'd separate the front fuselage from the damaged star drive engine block, forming a kind of life raft. Glide her down on the subluminal engines. Ride the waves on the biggest surfboard ever created. Wait for help to arrive, guided to his position by his SOS. Only—

A wave of coldness embraced him. "The emergency signal?"

"It was smothered by the gas giant's natural emissions, which we also believe were responsible for your initial problem. Those micro-meteors were whipped into a frenzy by gravitational eddies. I've been searching for your signal for a long time, Joe. And I'm so very happy to report that the team I assembled has finally found the Nautilus. We've found *you.*"

A measure of warmth returned, but its time was brief as Joe contemplated Winslow's words. "How long? How long have I been on Mare Poseidonus, Winslow?"

"A while, Joe."

"How long is a while?"

"Ninety-seven years, eight months, and change."

Winslow told him about finding the needle in the haystack— one stray piece of debris from the Nautilus' superluminal engine block that hadn't been vacuumed up by the greedy gas giant.

"Assumptions over the years were that you were headed toward Callix del Gest or Baden-Omega but never got there. After the Bailey Vortiss Archipelago, the trail vanished," Winslow said. "You know, the fate of Joseph Lee Bronson has become legendary, like the Flying Dutchman and the Marie Celeste. Like Captain Nemo and his Nautilus."

Winslow laughed, and how the sound was poetic, too, like his name. Almost enough to soothe Joe's anxiety.

"Winslow, where am I and why can't I see you?"

"I'm tapped into what's left of Nautilus' receivers but after almost a century in the brine, they've degraded, as you can imagine, so I'm only able to reach you on voice and not visual linkup. At this moment, I'm aboard a deep submergence vehicle dispatched from the Louganis, one of Earth Exodus Militia's newest research vessels. You, well…Joe, you're pretty deep. Marianas Trench deep. Your pressure hull's held up great, considering. Nautilus was a sturdy ship."

"Winslow?"

"I'm right outside, Joe. Almost close enough to touch."

Relief washed through him. "You'll stay with me, right?"

"Not going anywhere, I promise. Not after traveling so far to find you. Not after finding you alive."

Joe's mind began to drift back toward the abyss that ran to depths even deeper than the deepest trenches on Mare Poseidonus. Like Nemo trapped aboard his Nautilus, dying beneath Lincoln Island, Joe was alone, doomed. His consciousness threatened to dissolve.

"Joe, don't leave," Winslow said. Now, his voice sounded farther away, a whisper, the distance growing. "Hold on. You need to wake up and come out of stasis for what I have planned."

Joe willed himself to steady. The vibrating darkness stilled. "I'm here."

"Good. Now, it's imperative that I tell you the rest."

The darkness. He was still inside the Emergency Life Unit he'd gone into upon splashdown. The ELU functioned, but a century of constant use had drained most of the ship's remaining systems of power.

"I need you to run an energy supply inventory from within," Winslow said. "If there's enough to kick Nautilus' subluminal engines into starting up, we can navigate you back up to the surface and from there to the Louganis."

"And if not?"

A noticeable pause followed. "We'll have to come up with a Plan B, then, won't we?"

He liked this Winslow Greene—clearly an optimist, a man used to getting the job done even when the job looked impossible. Joe's insides thawed. He imagined himself smiling in the dark, mostly at the reassuring notion he wasn't alone. Funny, he agreed, given the loner's nature of his life following his Earth Exodus Militia service. That penchant had led him to wander and explore deep space without crew or companionship like a modern, real world Prince Dakkar, the tragic Captain Nemo who'd inspired his love of the sea at an early age.

In the frigid dark, he was beyond grateful for Winslow's presence.

"I'm making that inventory," Joe said. "Computing now."

The ELU had become the center of operations for what remained of the Nautilus' forward fuselage, all of its key systems and life support functions designed to protect that one key facet of the vessel and all linked to Joe's consciousness. Though his eyelids remained shut, Joe caught flashes of the lights beyond as they activated, drawing further upon the ship's power reserves. A necessary drain, he knew. Still, Joe's mind moved quickly, his eyes ticking as he mentally flipped switches and assessed the situation.

Winslow Greene. His new friend said the legend of Joe Bronson and the Nautilus had become a modern era version of the Flying Dutchman. He wondered if there was more. What could lead an exploratory team here, this far out, at such great expense aboard one of the E.E.M.'s shiny new deep space laboratories?

"Joe?"

Winslow's voice soothed him in ways that were as surprising as reassuring. For the next several seconds it was difficult to focus.

"I'm here," he replied. 'Finalizing power inventory."

The computer finished its calculations. Nautilus was down to a meager seventeen percent. Eleven was the bare minimum required to power up the engines. But they were already damaged, and there were kilometers of alien brine over his head. A sinking emotion attempted to crush him—until he remembered that Winslow was out there, close enough to touch. That strange, happy warmth again embraced him.

"Seventeen percent," Winslow said, as though reading his thoughts. "Actually, I'm reading the chatter between our two vessels."

"How—?"

"I'm tapped directly into your communications network on a neural interface, so your thoughts are being broadcast directly to me."

If so, that meant Winslow knew about his emotional responses, and also that biggest of questions—*why?*

Winslow drew in an audible breath. "I'll be honest with you, Joe. It goes back to my time in school and a lesson the teacher gave on the legendary Joe Bronson, who went missing aboard the research vessel Nautilus. I was intrigued. I've always loved the ocean—Earth's and other planets'. I grew up near the Atlantic, north of Grand Metropolis in Massachusetts and loved the Verne novel, too. But I'll admit I became hooked on ocean exploration and finding you when the teacher showed us that famous photograph—the one taken of you surfing the wild sea at Five Moon Bay on Aqua Nova."

Joe remembered the capture, which had graced various media forms for years before the crash at Mare Poseidonus. It depicted him riding his long board, clad only in a pair of navy boardshorts with white piping. The image showed off his physique, which was in amazing shape, he admitted, only to feel somewhat guilty and foolish at the hubris of such a claim. He was, after all, trapped in the wreckage of an intergalactic exploration vessel deep beneath an alien moon's sea.

But then Winslow absolved him.

"I'll confess, I fell in love with that photograph," the other man said. "And here I am."

Love? Suddenly the warmth Joe experienced in Winslow's company made a kind of crazy sense. It couldn't be the real thing, his inner critic tried to convince him. Fondness borne of attraction, perhaps. It was an old photographic capture showing him riding the wave, his flesh glowing in the resplendent light of Aqua Nova's twin suns, one an orange dwarf, the other a luminous blue variable. But that attraction had conquered untold leagues and light years, nearly a century, and the many fathoms separating Nautilus from the surface. Who was he to dismiss Winslow Greene's love for a legend?

"Thank you, Winslow," Joe said.

Silence. He sensed the other man, separated by pressure hull, crushing depth, and the alien ocean, smiling as his greatest dream was about to come true.

"We're not there yet, Joe," Winslow said. "First, we have to raise the Nautilus. And when we do, it will be my great honor to shake your hand."

"When we do," Joe said. "It'll be my great honor to meet *you*."

Winslow whispered something beneath his breath, what sounded to Joe's ear like, "*I love you.*"

"Powering up," Joe said.

Not lost on him as the dark vessel began to shake and its long-dormant systems reactivated was that he, too, was coming back to life after a long sleep. Though still in the life pod's slumber state, he imagined blood pumping and heart strengthening its beat, resuscitated by Winslow Greene's love. *Love.* Now he believed it.

After ninety-seven years, the subluminal engines struggled and steering rockets tipped Nautilus' prow toward the distant surface—one so far away that it didn't register on visual through the blackness.

"Are you there, Winslow?" Joe asked.

"Of course I am, Joe. Holding less than a kilometer off your starboard blade."

Nautilus wasn't fully intact, he knew. According to the inventory, her entire topside array had been shorn off on splashdown, along with the port blade. But Nautilus' main fuselage had kept its integrity. The engine would be shooting his ship to the surface like a missile. They didn't need Nautilus to remain there long—simply long enough for the Louganis' crew to extricate his life unit.

One of the steering rockets sputtered out. Nautilus slumped until the two remaining thrusters compensated.

Power had already dropped to fifteen percent.

"I'm sending her up," Joe said. "In five...four...three...two...*one!*"

He activated the subluminal engine. Energy flared into the rock ledge upon which the damaged spaceship rested, dislodging ancient boulders and kicking up towering plumes of nepheloid. The mud clouds formed a barrier between Nautilus and the nearby deep submergence vehicle, but soon the fallen spaceship was moving, *ascending*.

His mind traveled back to that last time Nautilus had been whole, aloft. The jarring jolts, the damage that tossed him against the bulkhead, the decision to ride it out in the safest place on the ship— safety being relative and also an illusion. The ship had suffered a near-catastrophic impact event. She jolted again almost a century later.

Nautilus' ascent was short and violent. Part of the ship's aft, grown brittle from its time beneath the ocean, crumpled from the stress. Deck cladding detached. Water streamed in. The subluminal engine shorted out far from reaching target.

"Winslow," Joe called. "*Winslow!*"

The wreckage of Nautilus glided another half a kilometer on thrust. And then she again started to sink.

Maybe Winslow Greene had been a hallucination, one more dream created by the dying remains of his consciousness, which had been entombed for too long deep at the bottom of the deepest well at the end of the universe.

It was possible, Joe realized, that activating the Nautilus' engines by neural interface was only a kind of sleepwalking, a dream playing out.

He sensed the ship filling up, its remaining systems shorting out, the cold, dark descent down into shadow and death. Power levels had flatlined. The ocean was soon to claim him fully, finishing off what it hadn't been able to do ninety-seven years earlier. Unlike Nemo and his Nautilus, there would be no second chance for him, no mysterious island. And while there was poetry in that thought, Joe also suffered regret for the figment of his dying mind that was embodied in the fantasy of Winslow Greene.

For so long and across so many distances, he'd been alone by choice, riding barrel waves at Five Moon Bay, mapping the oceans of a dozen different worlds, but always alone. He recalled the second novel, and how Captain Nemo was initially alone until choosing to anonymously help Lincoln Island's human castaways. Winslow Greene, as figments went, had been ideal, the kind of patient lover he should have welcomed during his life when he was still living it. Winslow…he matched a face with that warm, imaginary voice, making it up as time ran out and the hull of Nautilus buckled. In the real world, he could have believed in their love. He would have loved Winslow in return.

Nautilus again shook violently.

This is it, Joe thought. The impact with the sea floor. He only hoped—prayed—the end would be quick. That the water rushing in through shattered pressure hull plating and compartments would end the ship quickly, his misery brief.

Still, he lived on.

In the frigid dark, alone, he waited. The sensation of falling teased his senses, only drifting down felt more like up, and the flash from the expected implosion never came. Maddening minutes—or it could have been hours—later, light and sound streamed around him. The brutal chill renounced its grip.

The Emergency Life Unit lid activated and released. Briny air poured down, along with the strobing beams of handheld lights.

"Plan B. We got you—in the DSV's magnetic arms," said Winslow's familiar voice from one of the dark outlines visible among the strobes. "But we need to move you quickly, Joe. Not sure how long we'll be able to hold on to what's left of Nautilus!"

Crew in diving suits removed him from the pod and placed him on a stretcher. Then they were racing through the dark, salt-stinking corridors of the Nautilus.

"Winslow?" Joe asked, his voice barely there.

The man moving at his side took his hand. "Right here like I promised."

He caught his rescuer's face in the flashes of light. Winslow was even more beautiful in the real world than he'd imagined.

"Welcome back, Joe," Winslow said. "I look forward to getting to know you."

At Strange Depths

Jason J. McCuiston

*T*he *Nautilus was silent.*

Nemo opened his eyes to a red haze. Blood trickled from a gash on his forehead, pain throbbing in his temple. The hard deck against his back, he smelled the stale quality of the air. The captain struggled to his feet, leaning against the ship's control panels.

"The Maelstrom." He remembered the climactic struggle off the coast of Norway. Wiping blood from his eyes, he scanned the readouts, quickly assessing the damage to his vessel. Grabbing the speaking tube, he bellowed, "All stations, report in!"

Damage and casualty reports came in as other members of the crew regained their bearings. The Nautilus had survived the battle with the vortex, but not unscathed. There were breaches along the hull, a flooded compartment, and damage to the propeller.

The ship had come to rest on a shelf at a depth very near the limits of the hull's strength. Every moment the Nautilus lingered in this precarious position courted ultimate disaster.

Of more importance to Nemo was his crew—seven men had been badly injured. Two, including his first mate, suffered wounds that might prove fatal without proper medical care. Nemo would have cursed Aronnax for his desertion at this inopportune moment, but chose to waste no more thought on the man or his surface-dwelling companions. He had more than enough problems at the moment.

For one thing, the ship's instrument readings made no sense whatsoever. "Until we can affect repairs and surface, we have no idea where we are."

"What are your orders, Captain?" The short, mustachioed ensign with the prominent forehead looked familiar, but was not one of the original members of the crew.

"Ready a deep-pressure dive team, Ensign."

"Aye, sir."

"Six able-bodied men equipped with Ruhmkorff lighting rigs and metalworking tools. I'll lead. I need to make a full assessment of the damages, especially the propeller... Make certain the batteries are at full capacity and the engine is in working trim."

"Aye-aye, Captain."

Moments later, Nemo entered the dive chamber with six crewmen, all wearing diving suits and armed with electric guns. As seawater flooded the room, he felt a sudden sense of relief bordering on euphoria. In spite of the imminent threat to his ship and crew, the dangerous situation gave him focus—a renewed strength of purpose, something he had felt slipping away in recent days.

This reluctant softening of resolve was due in part, Nemo ruefully admitted, to the presence of his recent uninvited "guests." Even the simple-minded courage of the irksome sailor, Mr. Land, had inspired some rough admiration. And the brilliant Professor Aronnax and his loyal manservant, Conseil, had reminded him of the misplaced idealism of his youth, when he had once believed that a world characterized by civil discourse and international harmony might be possible.

In the days before the Maelstrom, Nemo had begun to think his thirst for revenge might one day be satisfied. That realization had thrown him into a pit of melancholy and despair. If the world could be righted by civilized men of science leading their barbaric brothers into a Utopia of peace and harmony, then what purpose did all the bloodshed and oppression truly serve? If it was that simple, why had he lost so much? Why had his countrymen and millions of other "less-civilized" peoples suffered such atrocities at the hands of the industrialized colonizers?

But those questions and doubts had been washed away by the whirlpool and rinsed in the blood of his crewmen. The wreck of his ship had awakened his hatred, reminding him that he was as human as those who ruled above the waves. So long as that hatred lived in his own heart, Nemo knew it would live and thrive in the hearts of all mankind.

His war against the surface world could know no end.

Exiting the damaged submarine, Nemo led his team into the murky depths and onto the rocky shelf. By the sweep of their lanterns, he saw the vast gulf yawning beneath them. He also saw a high rocky ridge topped with curious miniature volcanos spewing plumes of black smoke into the water. "What an odd formation. I've never seen the like."

With a wave, the ensign called Nemo's attention to a massive shape. A giant creature fled from their lights, diving into the darkness of the abyss.

Unless he was going mad, Nemo recognized the fish from a drawing in one of the obscure histories of Herodotus. It was an extinct coelacanth. "Clearly we are in warmer waters than those of the Norwegian Sea. A mystery to ponder at another time..."

He signaled his men to get to work. They had less than an hour before the extreme pressure did their bodies unforgivable harm.

The Nautilus was not too badly damaged, all things considered. The few breaches were a simple matter of riveting on new plating. The damaged propeller, however, was a different matter. Men would need to hammer and smooth out the battered blades. All this done with alacrity if they hoped to escape these ponderous depths before their time—and their air—ran out.

As Nemo studied the problem, a low creaking groan echoed from the ship. The noise was audible through the deep water and his helmet. Clearly time was of the essence.

Having repaired over half the breaches, Nemo led his crew back to the airlock. Rounding the side of the Nautilus, something struck him hard in the breastplate. The impact sent him skittering toward the abyss.

Staggered, Nemo dropped his rivet gun. The ensign caught his hand, arresting his momentum before he descended over the ledge. Nemo blinked at what appeared to be an obsidian-tipped spear lying at his feet.

Frantic motion drew his attention back to the crew.

The men's lights splashed across greenish gray scales and pale white bellies. Long-fingered claws glistened. Soulless black eyes shone like those of freshly-caught barracudas or moray eels.

Nemo stared in wonder, noting the sharp teeth, the long talons, and, impossible as it seemed, the bundles of barbed spears grasped in those prehensile appendages.

He raised his electric gun and fired. His men followed suit.

Another spear glanced across his helmet. The murky water turned to a boil of cloud and electric flashes. The confused confrontation was over in seconds. Both wounded creatures fled with prodigious speed.

The two monstrosities were the first unknown creatures he had seen in many years. His scientist's mind raced at the tool-making capabilities of these beings, indicating a rudimentary intelligence.

But one of their spears had nicked a crewman's breathing apparatus and it was leaking air. The dive team raced to get the stricken man back into the airlock before he suffocated. Nemo ascended the rocky ridge, staying clear of the smoking vent holes, to see whence the bizarre enemy had fled. Standing on the submerged promontory, he was stunned by what he saw.

In the middle distance a sunken city rested on a gentle rise. But the edifices, somehow illuminated by an eerie green glow as if by a million bioluminescent creatures, were never fashioned by the hand of man. The sight of the towering obelisks and cyclopean structures—each a monument of blasphemous defiance against Euclidian geometry—made Nemo want to tear off his helmet and scratch at his eyes until the sight of the metropolis made sense.

A bit of poetry came unbidden to mind:
Lo! Death has reared himself a throne
In a strange city lying alone…

A tug at his shoulder almost tore a scream from Nemo's throat. He turned to see the ensign motioning him back to the ship, reminding him of the danger to the crewman in the compromised apparatus.

Nemo hurried to the airlock without a second look at the hellish scene beyond the reef. But the image was already burned into his mind. He knew he would see that accursed city in his nightmares for the rest of his life.

The next several hours were a blur. Nemo dispatched an armed crew of twelve to continue the repairs and maintain a defensive perimeter. A trip to sickbay confirmed the seven men injured in the Maelstrom were stable. The groaning, threatening moans and creaks continued as the Nautilus struggled to resist the immense pressure casually pulverizing her.

Nemo sat in the salon, staring out the great oblong window. Staring into the abyss.

He tried to focus on the troubles at hand, but his mind wandered back to that accursed city and its deviant inhabitants. What kind of intelligence must reside in such beings? For, having erected such a citadel in this world of watery night, the things must be intelligent. They used weapons and they attacked without provocation, revealing an ideological kinship to the mammalian species now in control of the Earth's surface.

"Even here, in the paradise of the world's oceans, the tools of war and hatred are to be found. I had thought to discover an eternal peace and harmony with the vast reservoir of Nature beneath the waves. I see now that violence is the defining quality of all sentient beings."

"Excuse me, sir."

Nemo turned to see the mustachioed ensign standing in the door. "Yes, what is it, Ensign—?"

"Po, sir. I've come for your orders, sir."

Nemo motioned the man into the room and closed the cover to the viewport. "Well, Mr. Po, until the first mate has fully recovered, I shall need you to act in his stead. That is the first order of business."

The short man stood a bit taller. "Thank you, sir. I shall not let you down."

Nemo looked again at the diagram of the Nautilus and the red marks he had made to indicate the damage. He checked the bulkhead chronometer and consulted the equations scrawled in the margin. "I reckon we have considerably less than twenty-four hours before these depths kill us, Mr. Po. And that only if those … things from the sunken city do not decide to come upon us in full assault."

"They were barbarically armed, sir."

"True. As ever, our advanced technology is our one great advantage. We must rely upon it. However, until the breaches are sealed, the electrified plating is an imperfect defense. And while the men are outside, they are exposed. We were fortunate that the spears were not poisoned. I doubt such a capability is beyond the arsenal of our enemy."

"I shall check the stores of anti-toxins, sir."

"Good. And update me on the progress of the propeller blade repair. We need to finish that before it is too late."

The ship lurched as if struck by a cannonball.

Nemo clutched the table, turned to the viewport control. As the sliding cover panel opened, a gigantic saurian shape moved past his vision. A crewman surrounded by ribbons of blood flailed in its fanged maw. The monster vanished from sight, chased away by bursts of electric shot.

Nemo closed the viewport, saying a silent prayer for the lost crewman. His heart ached for that loss, but his mind puzzled over the impossibility of that living monster from some long-ago epoch. *A plesiosaur?*

He recalled a comment from his recent conversation with Professor Aronnax: "With its untold depths, couldn't the sea keep alive such huge specimens of life from another age, this sea that never changes while the land masses undergo almost continuous alteration?"

And yet another, far more improbable notion took form at the edge of thought. "But is it a notion without some evidence?"

"Sir?"

Turning to Po, Nemo mused aloud. "As Darwin has postulated, all life, including human life, originated in the seas and oceans… What if those creatures from that city are not some abominable offshoot, but are in fact, the true ancestors of all humanity?"

"I don't follow, sir."

Nemo paced the room, punching his palm. "The Maelstrom, Po! I have suspected since first stepping outside that the vortex pulled us in from the North Atlantic and spat us out in equatorial waters." He turned on the ensign. "But what if—and I know this will sound utterly mad—but what if the Maelstrom, combined with the power of our dynamos, somehow generated enough energy to not only displace us in space, but also in time?"

Po's expression remained blank.

Nemo ran a hand through his hair, narrowing his eyes. "There is no shortage of myths recounting such a thing. Why, the Irish *immrama* alone are rife with tales of adventurers who travelled to otherworldly islands where they tarried for but a few days, only to return home to find that all they had known had perished under the weight of centuries.

"What if these fables were somehow based on fact? What if, given the proper set of variables, these highly improbable time-shifts are not impossible?"

Po continued to stare at him, as if expecting more evidence than ancient folklore.

"The coelacanth, the aquatic humanoids, and now a plesiosaur! I am not saying that this is in fact the case, but, theoretically, is it not possible that we now find ourselves in the deep waters of the Mesozoic era?"

Po swallowed. "But if that *is* the case, sir, how should we proceed?"

Nemo took a deep breath. "We proceed as planned, Mr. Po. We repair the Nautilus, then we must find the Maelstrom again. If my hypothesis is correct, the vortex is most certainly our best chance of returning from whence we came."

"And if the Maelstrom no longer exists, what then, sir?"

Nemo smiled for the first time in seeming ages. "Then, Mr. Po, we set out to build a new world in our own image."

"Captain."

Nemo woke with a start. Something in Po's tone indicated danger. "Yes, what is it?"

"The repair crew, sir—"

Fully awake, Nemo brushed past Po. He hurried from the darkened cabin, coming face to face with three crewmen. Their expressions showed a mixture of surprise and worry. "How long? What happened?"

"Just now, sir," one of the men said. "I was observing the repair crew from the starboard window as per your orders. They had almost finished their shift and were preparing to come aboard when at least two score of those … those things came swimming out of the darkness. Before anyone could do anything, they had scooped up all twelve men in these big … I don't know, something like bubbles or nets, sir. And just as quickly, they were gone."

Nemo digested this. The enemy had not come with spears to kill but with nets to capture. This worried him all the more. He shuddered to think of his men hauled away to that accursed city in the sea. And for what nefarious or savage purpose?

Another bit from that poem floated through his thoughts:
"While from a proud tower in the town
Death looks gigantically down."

"Is the propeller finished?"

"Nearly, sir."

"Then Mr. Po and I will attempt a rescue. If we are not back aboard before the repairs are complete, then depart without us and may Fortune favor you all."

The three men looked at him and each other with confusion before hurrying to their duties.

Nemo turned to the ensign. "Come along, Mr. Po. It is high time we introduced the culmination of all man's scientific knowledge to this barbarous epoch."

Nemo and the repair crew soon filed into the diving chamber with their essential gear. With the injured, the dead, and the captured, only five men were left to affect the final repairs, leaving but three aboard to monitor the ship's systems. If he and Po failed, the crew of the Nautilus stood slim chance of survival even if they did escape these crushing depths.

Leaving the ship, Nemo waved his men to their task. He and Po loaded a heavy brass-lined, barrel-shaped device onto a specialized electrically-powered diving sled of Nemo's design. Setting off for the abominable city, Nemo worried what damage his new weapon might cause to the surrounding waters and the life therein. Harnessed within the fragile metallic canister was the fulfillment of all the known chemistry, physics, and electrical engineering of the modern world.

Nemo had theorized what the thing might do to a surface city, but he had never tested it. Primarily because he feared it as much as he feared anything. He feared it because he understood its potential for mass destruction, and that understanding revealed his own inner darkness.

Nemo feared the device because it embodied the very things he hated most about the destroyers on the surface, the very things he hated most about himself.

These recriminations were washed away by the sight of the abysmal fortress jutting out of the deep horizon. Crossing the smoking ridge of vents, Nemo realized the distance was not as great as he had first imagined. Or else the city's weird dimensions somehow mutated all sense of perspective. With the aid of the sled, he and Po made the outer walls rather quickly.

Nemo was surprised by the lack of sentries on the green-glowing bastions. Even more so at the lack of a barrier to prevent entrance to the fungoid-covered streets. His teeth were on edge from the moment his lead-soled boots touched those aeon-old paving stones. Seeing it up close, Nemo held no doubt that the architects of this place had never been born of woman. The freakish statuary adorning the black edifices and surmounting the pinnacles of obscene obelisks testified to this.

Most of these effigies represented a bulbous, squatting thing with the head of a monstrous cephalopod and a pair of great dorsal fins resembling the wings of a bat. For all this otherworldly horror, the thing that filled Nemo's belly with cold seawater was the presence of glyphs and sigils carved into the stone. Whoever or whatever had reared this city possessed a written language.

If Nemo's suppositions about the time-shift were true, then everything mankind believed about itself and the uniqueness of human intellect was a lie. Some learned sentience *out there* was ancient long before the first man took his first breath on the primordial shore.

This realization threatened to overwhelm him with a crushing sense of cosmic irrelevance and desolation. All his achievements, all the achievements of his race, his species, all the strife, the struggle, the successes and failures, were as nothing in the grand scheme of the eternal and ineffable universe.

Po patted his arm, stirring him from this gulf of despair. Looking through the faceplate at the man's somber eyes, Nemo recalled his purpose. He was the captain of the Nautilus, the lives of his crew were in danger, and they were his responsibility. He would do all within his power to save them, the uncaring Universe be damned.

The city was laid out in a spiral pattern, everything emanating outward from a central point. In spite of the chaotic twists and turns, Nemo realized they were being funneled to a hilltop pyramidal structure. He suspected he'd find his crew—and the entire populace of this inhuman civilization—there, in the center of the metropolis.

He cast a regretful glance at the device resting on the motorized sled. He would have no choice but to use it.

Nemo and Po guided the sled and its lethal cargo to the outskirts of the complex surrounding the dizzying pyramid. Illuminated by the sickly green glow, the apex was a titanic sarcophagus. On the lowest tier of this great temple stood a large specimen of the bestial breed, wearing an elaborate headgear of coral crests and a necklace of teeth and shells. Surrounding the base of the stepped structure danced a swarm of the aquatic race numbering in the hundreds, their barbed spears and obsidian-studded clubs raised in wild gesticulations.

Between this vast fishy horde and the apparent shaman of the barbaric tribe stood Nemo's crew. The twelve men wore their dive suits—thankfully—and were bound in a thick webbing that resembled seaweed. A globule of solid air seemed to hang about them like a net. Nemo could only hope this strange barrier kept the great pressure of the depths at bay. If not, the men were as good as dead, rescue or no.

Drawing his electric gun, he nodded to Po. They set the device onto the flagstones where Nemo activated it. They had twenty minutes to free the crew and be beyond the city walls before detonation.

Nemo and Po charged the rear rank of the creatures, a barrage of electric projectiles cutting a swathe before them. Nemo released a motorized grenade from the dive sled, its tiny propeller sending a larger version of the electric charge into the horde with devastating effect.

The onslaught was sudden and overwhelming. Nemo found himself facing his captured men in a matter of heartbeats as the primitive monsters scattered. He and Po breached the strange air bubble and began cutting bonds. They then distributed electric guns from the dive sled to the freed divers. Where the fish-men had faced two determined warriors of the nineteenth century armed with the best marvels of the age, they now confronted over a dozen.

Leading his men away from the awful temple, Nemo dared to hope he might not need to use his doomsday weapon. He thought to disarm and retrieve it on their way out of the city.

A shockwave knocked him and his fleeing men flat, destroying that hope.

Struggling to his feet, Nemo saw the force had originated at the temple's apex. The sarcophagus' lid moved.

A flood of nightmare images—visions unseen in the most demented and sadistic of diseased mortal brains—washed over Nemo, drowning all reason, all thought, all sanity. If his first glimpse at the accursed city had made him wish for the ignorance of blindness, the horrors now haunting him made Nemo crave the ultimate oblivion.

Something struck his shoulder.

Po shook him and pointed to his men. Nemo saw them thrashing and rolling on the ground in terror. He grabbed each of his crewmen, shaking them until they regained at least some of their wits. They, in turn, began helping their comrades. *Why are they suffering madness, too? What if this madness is not natural, but instead the result of some outside stimulus, such as occurs with the exposure to mercury or other contaminants in the bloodstream?*

Nemo turned a wary eye on the chaotic activity of the underwater tribe.

The creatures seemed similarly affected by the mysterious shockwave. The shaman hopped and gesticulated wildly as if giving orders. But most of the surviving fish-men appeared enraptured by activity at the top of the pyramid.

Nemo almost looked up. But some deep, primordial fear warned against it. Words from a recent conversation echoed in his head: *"No one has ever seen anything like it; but the sight may cost us dear ... things which God never intended man to see."*

For the first time in his life, Nemo chose to ignore his curiosity and listen to fear.

Order restored to his beleaguered crew, Nemo got them on the move. He cast one final glance at the brass barrel as they hurried out of the heart of the city.

Another shockwave, this one of terrible sound, battered their backs as they fled. Even through the stifling waves and the muffling of his helmet, Nemo discerned a hundred blasphemies in every language in that unearthly roar. With that demoniac utterance, more of the nightmare visions flooded his mind. Gnashing his teeth, he clung to his reason with every fiber of will, forcing himself to recount scientific data and minutiae.

One of his crewmen was not so disciplined. The diver paused a meter away, shook his head violently, then turned his electric gun upon himself. The ruptured helmet collapsed like a tin can beneath the wheel of a locomotive. The man's body stood limply, swaying in the current, weighed down by his suit's ballast.

The rest of the crew's reaction to this latest psychic assault was one of abject terror. The men moved even faster through the depths. Nemo struggled to keep up.

A barbed spear arced overhead, sinking to the paving stones. Nemo turned, his weapon at the ready. A ragged mob of the fish-men loped after them, weapons raised.

But what caught Nemo's eye—what nearly drove him into the madness eroding the edges of consciousness since first seeing this infernal metropolis—was the thing-that-should-not-be at the pyramid's summit.

The sarcophagus' lid had opened. A clawed hand that could have crushed an armored cruiser between two fingers emerged. Nemo recalled the misshapen effigies adorning the buildings and obelisks of the sunken city. It occurred to him that these did not represent some mythological or fictitious deity, but rather a real entity dwelling in the physical world, dwelling in this very place.

"Those words," Nemo muttered in the depths of his helmet. "How true those words are now: *The human mind delights in grand conceptions of supernatural beings. And the sea is precisely their best vehicle, the only medium through which these giants ... can be produced or developed.*"

Nemo might have stood there, gaping at the doom about to overtake him, had not a gloved hand roused him from his stupor. He turned to see Po at his elbow, urging him to rejoin the retreat. Shaking off his ennui, he did so amid a shower of hurled spears and war clubs.

Every step of the way, Nemo battled the urge to turn and take one final, maddening look at the monstrous being at the pyramid's apex.

The fleeing crew had reached the outer walls of the city. Titanic black shadows jutted out ahead of them. The white light at their backs was blinding. Another shockwave followed, this one of boiling water. It hurled the heavy-laden men like ragdolls even farther from the perimeter of the sunken city.

Nemo caught a glimpse of flashing white fire burning bright in the depths of black walls as he cartwheeled through murky waters. For that infinitesimal moment, the monumental import of the city and its blasphemous existence was seared into his mind forever. The final lines of the poem came to him then:

The waves have now a redder glow-
The hours are breathing faint and low-
And when, amid no earthly moans,
Down, down that town shall settle hence,
Hell, rising from a thousand thrones,
Shall do it reverence.

Nemo came to rest in total darkness, every inch of his body alive with pain. Raising his head, he saw his stunned men surrounding him.

He saw this by the floodlights of the Nautilus hovering above, running under her own power.

Nemo smiled in relief.

Hours later, after the Nautilus had put a dozen leagues between herself and the hellish city, Nemo stood in the chartroom poring over his maps. He tried to make an educated guess about where to find the Maelstrom's entrance in this part of the world. From the flora and fauna he had observed, he estimated they were now somewhere in the South Pacific. But he still believed that several million years separated the Nautilus from home. And the powerful vortex was their best chance to close that gap.

Nemo admitted to himself that this belief was as much founded in hope as in actual observations. His mind recoiled at the notion that the horrors he had beheld in those strange depths might still exist in the modern world he called his own. And yet, what if they did?

"Sir?"

Nemo turned to see the first mate, his head wrapped in a bandage and his left arm in a sling. "Glad to see you on your feet, Mr. Wilke. But are you able to resume your duties?"

"Yes, sir. The ship is in fine trim, all things considered, and the crew awaits your orders."

Nemo glanced again at the charts. He gave Mr. Wilke the heading based on his best guess as to the Maelstrom's location. Nemo added, "One other thing. Mr. Po performed exceptionally well in our recent crisis. He deserves a commendation. We shall have an award ceremony following the funeral service for the two lost men."

The mate looked at Nemo with some confusion. "Mr. Po, sir? I am unfamiliar with a Mr. Po on this crew, sir."

Nemo stiffened. "Never mind. Carry on, Mr. Wilke."

"Aye-aye, Captain."

Nemo hurried to the library. Stepping to the bookcase, he scanned the shelves. Removing the volume of *Modern American Poetry* from among the rows of books, he flipped to a dog-eared page. He had read the piece several times in the days leading up to the encounter with USS Abraham Lincoln, but had subsequently forgotten the American's dark and unsettling imagery.

At least consciously.

Nemo touched the cut on his forehead, smiling at the prophetic poem and the now-familiar portrait of the mustachioed author. "The City in the Sea, by Edgar Allan Poe. Published 1831."

The Maelstrom

Maya Chhabra

On the Nautilus every crew member is prepared to lay down his life for the others. There is real camaraderie amid the undersea isolation. But the captain stands alone. For him, the isolation is complete.

And so there is a chamber on the Nautilus into which no one but Captain Nemo enters. It is the gallery of his heroes—the American emancipators of slaves, the champions of oppressed nations in Europe. Like those of John Brown and Daniele Manin, his actions will one day be remembered as glorious, an inspiration to those who come after. He has, after all, given everything.

There is only one portrait in that room full of heroes before which he feels anything other than calm conviction.

Prince Dakkar had come back from Europe and did not recognize his wife-to-be. She was no longer the child-princess he had been betrothed to at nine. Then she had been all shy smiles, drowning in brocade too heavy for her small stature. She had grown up, and grown fiercer.

"Now that you are back," she said, "we must do something about the Company."

The East India Company, that strange mix of a trading corporation and a mercenary army, had only encroached further during his years away. But he had not expected the princess' first words to him to be about politics.

Neither, apparently, did his aged father, the rajah, who turned on her.

"What, do you think the British will underestimate you because you're a woman? They won't spare you for your sex. Remember what happened to Jind Kaur, the Sikh maharani? When the British won, they took her son from her, to be raised in England. Do you want that to happen to your children?"

Then he reached out to embrace his son.

"It's wonderful to have you back. Your homecoming, and your wedding, will be the event of the year, and you'll have thousands of well-wishers. But no one can wish you as well as your father, eh?"

"I don't," the princess said suddenly, "want the British to take my children."

"Then be careful," the stooped old rajah said firmly. "I want the Company put in their place as much as you do, but let's be sensible about it. The moment is not yet ripe."

Prince Dakkar had not seen his father since he was a boy of ten, and instinct told him to agree with him, to placate his parents. But his wife-to-be looked at him with burning eyes, and he thought, *I am not a child any longer, not only his son. This woman will be my wife, and will depend on me for protection in her new household.* Though judging from her outspoken ways, she did not seem particularly in need of protection.

"Father," he began. "The moment is not yet ripe, but surely we can do something to speed it. I have seen much in my travels. All across Europe, nations once counted for nothing are coming into their own, but not without a struggle. I see no reason why we will get what we desire without a fight, any more than the Russian Empire will suddenly grant the Poles their freedom. So yes, we will be careful, but we will not be docile and wait until they control every pocket of this vast land."

"This vast land can go hang," the rajah blasphemed. "I want their eyes off *our* territory. Some of our neighbors are fool enough to allow them a foothold, but we will never do so voluntarily, and they know it. So they watch us carefully, waiting for a misstep. Neither of you must give them any excuse. Wait for the moment."

His speech dissolved into coughing, and Prince Dakkar reached out to support him. The princess had done the same from the other side. Their eyes met.

"The moment will come," Prince Dakkar said, more to her than to his father. "I'll make sure of it."

After the birth of his second child, Prince Dakkar took up his travels again, this time in India, meeting everyone and anyone who might help him.

He met with the Mughals, shadows of their former selves. He met with disinherited princes, who lost everything when the British refused to recognize their adoption as legitimate and seized their lands. He met with the sepoys, frustrated Indian soldiers who knew they could never rise above their East India Company masters, and were beginning to see they have been used.

The uprising came unexpectedly, but Prince Dakkar was well-placed to help convert it from mutiny to true rebellion. The connections he'd spent years building were carefully spread oil to the sepoys' match. But he had no desire to remain in the background.

"You'll have to look after my father and keep the funds for the rebellion flowing," he said to his wife one day. "I'm going."

She did not ask where. She knew, and she smiled.

"I will give you a hero's welcome when you return," she said. Always so confident—*when*, not if.

For all that his heroes are democrats and liberators, Nemo is the undisputed master of his undersea kingdom. He has always had an autocratic streak, and is it any wonder? He has seen the wildfire of revolution rip across a land, and he has seen it swiftly and bloodily crushed. If he wants his vengeance, it must be disciplined, secret, deadly. And he will have it. It's a matter of when, not if.

A British warship obligingly fires on him.

Nemo has just been visiting the wreck of the Vengeur du Peuple with Professor Aronnax. He's missed educated company, and the chance to show the French scientist his country's famous warship is too much to pass up. Besides, the sight of that gallant wreck, whose sailors nailed their colors to the mast and sang the Marseillaise as they sank, fills him with the same pride and conviction as his portrait gallery.

Nemo will have to be careful not to mingle the corpses of perfidious Albion's sailors with those of the revolutionaries who preferred death to rescue by the English navy.

"How can you take lives indiscriminately?" Aronnax challenges him when he realizes Nemo's intention. "What have they done to you that could possibly be worth this slaughter?"

Nemo responds with ferocity, with a rage long held in check but never banked. "I am the law, and I am the judge. I am the oppressed, and there is the oppressor!"

Not done yet, he enumerates everything he has lost at the hands of that hated nation—his country, his wife, his children, his father, his mother. Is it any wonder he does not venerate the flimsy rules of civilization, when everything he ever held sacred is gone?

Aronnax flees before Nemo's wrath, joining Ned Land far from the captain. Seeing the scientist abandoning him, Nemo almost regrets his outburst, but then his firmness of mind returns. Let Aronnax think him mad if he will. He wonders if the Frenchman has ever spared a thought for Algeria, which his nation seized on a whim and has oppressed ever since. It's a pang to lose the sympathy of someone who could truly understand the scale of his vision, but then again— Aronnax has just proven he only ever understood part of it.

Not that Nemo is planning to change the world, for all the gold he gives to the Cretans and other revolutionaries. It's just a parting shot. The lands above can fend for themselves. The sea is his country now.

He watches through the windows of the salon as the British sailors struggle for breath, fail to swim. He watches without pity. He could take them onboard as he did Aronnax, Conseil, and Land, but he will not. He will watch them drown instead.

It does not help. It does not soothe the pain that grips him like a crocodile pulling its prey down to drown it. But he keeps watching, grim and impassive as ever he was under fire, and his men and his prisoner-guests watch him.

He withdraws from the salon before he cracks. In that chamber of the Nautilus which belongs to Nemo alone, he looks at a portrait quite different from the rest of his gallery. This is a young Indian woman, with two small children on her lap. He does not look at her portrait often. There is little inspiration to be found there, only the crushing pain of loss.

Here, alone, he need not fear giving way to sobs.

The seasoned fighters were not impressed by a young prince throwing money around and demanding to fight in the riskiest positions. Then they saw what he could do with artillery. The tiny improvements, the clever engineering, the way he could make machines do impossible things.

Science was still his passion. Perhaps one day, he would turn his researches toward peaceful purposes. But that day would not be while his country groaned in chains.

His fame spread day by day. The engineer-prince, with his grave manner and his coolness under fire was spoken of in the same breath as legends like his near neighbor, Lakshmibai, the warrior queen of Jhansi. No wonder the British had put a price on his head.

Prince Dakkar laughed when he found out.

"You may live the life of a king if you turn me in," he said to his men. "The life I abandoned to fight here with you. Is anyone tempted?"

"No, never!" came the reply, a chorus of defiance.

Even though it was clear even then they were losing. Prince Dakkar knew of the failures of 1848 in Europe, of the failure of the Polish revolutionary Kościuszko, his favorite hero, of the failure of Prince Dakkar's own uncle, killed in battle in his third war against the English.

He himself might be one more glorious failure. It was no reason to give up.

He exchanged letters with his wife; she had a plan, in case the British came for her. At first, that plan involved swords and gunfire, but Prince Dakkar insisted she live for the children, and help his elderly parents escape as well. There was a boat along the river, inconspicuous and plain. No one would ever believe royalty sailed in it.

He had not seen her for a long while. How tall were the children now? Were his parents still healthy?

One night a messenger came with all the answers.

"My prince…your wife…"

From his faltering tones, Prince Dakkar assumed the worst. "I told her to live for our children!" he burst out, anger safer than sorrow.

"She took them to the riverboat," the messenger went on, cringing. "With your parents. But they were betrayed. A British boat pursued them. My prince, they wanted her as a hostage to lure you. When she refused…" He stopped, unable to go on.

Prince Dakkar would not show weakness in front of his men, though he was not sure what strength he could summon.

"Out with it," he spat, determined to hear the worst.

"They fired on her boat and they all…they all drowned."

Prince Dakkar let the news break over him like the tall waves that came after earthquakes. He was stone, he was iron. He was a dead thing.

"Captain Nemo?" Only the Frenchman is fool enough to disturb Nemo after he's sunk a ship. None of the crew would do so.

Nemo almost snarls, "What?" but remembers he is the captain and must always be in control. So, he turns to Aronnax and says, in an urbane but dangerous voice, "Did you have something to tell me?"

Aronnax is a civilized man; he ignores whatever suppressed emotion lies behind that tone.

"I wanted to tell you something, yes." The professor shifts from side to side. Nemo knows what this is about. Ned Land is after him again for his freedom, and poor Aronnax is the go-between. The diplomacy is futile. Let Ned Land search for his freedom elsewhere. Nemo didn't ask those three to hunt him down in the first place, and in fact had saved them from death.

Ned Land, of course, would prefer freedom and a watery grave. Let him take it, then! Nemo isn't the one keeping him captive, only the one keeping him from shore, from spreading the news that would destroy Nemo's refuge and his weapon.

Of course, it isn't always that easy to die.

Aronnax, however, has not come about the Canadian and his longing for freedom. He has something else to say.

"It's about the Vengeur. I thought, as a man of science, you'd want to know the truth." Aronnax hasn't got the bright look, the uncomplicated happiness, that scientific discovery brings. He looks a bit like that messenger had. It had taken forever to get a word out of him.

But Aronnax is braver, or the news he carries of less import, because he comes right out with it. "The Vengeur du Peuple didn't go down with all hands, refusing rescue and shouting 'Long live the republic.' That was a myth. The English rescued most of the sailors, who were glad enough of it. The revolutionary Barère invented the whole story for a political speech. I didn't even know that myself until Ned Land told me to check the English accounts, and though I hate to say it, they're more believable. They're right there in your library."

"Why are you telling me this?" Nemo asks. Aronnax doesn't seem to take any pleasure in destroying one of Nemo's few remaining illusions, but the captain feels it as a cruelty nonetheless.

"I thought you should know the truth." Aronnax repeats.

"Yes. Of course. It's our duty, as men of science, to follow the facts wherever they lead us." The words echo hollow, and a sullen silence settles between them. Finally, Nemo breaks it. "You may go, Professor. What you have told me is food for thought."

Dark thoughts only. He had taken so much trouble not to let the British boat sink onto that hallowed wreck. Hallowed by propaganda and lies. Are there no heroes in the world? Is he alone in expecting better?

Perhaps even the fiercest revolutions partake too much of the civilized world. Yet more confirmation that he has done well to abandon it.

Prince Dakkar rigged together a diving suit, his own invention. No one had seen anything like it, and his men thought him mad. He went in search of the sunken riverboat, and the bodies of his loved ones.

He had thought to raise them up and cremate them properly. But underwater they seemed at peace, and he didn't want to bring them up, didn't want to go back. He could wait here until his air ran out—surely he would not be tempted to come up for more—and join them. The world above had nothing left to offer him, and he had nothing left to give it.

He had lost his country and his family, but despite his fearless attacks, he had not yet lost his life. More's the pity. Well, he would not wait for chance to take it. He would die here, with the wreck of everything he loved.

A shadow came between him and the filtered light, leaving him in the dark with the dead. A riverboat had passed over him, much like the one whose remains he stood beside. It looked so frail, so vulnerable, from below. Like an animal with a soft underbelly.

The Royal Navy planned to armor its great battleships, to build new ironclads to conquer the world with, but armor could be pierced. Especially from an angle no one expected.

That was the germ of the Nautilus. Filled with new purpose, he rose from the depths.

Captain Nemo barely navigates. He can't bring himself to. Destruction is no solace, and neither is the wonder of the sea. He watched the sailors drown, and all he saw was his wife, weighed down by her heavy clothes. What is the purpose of vengeance, when it aggravates his wounds rather than providing a temporary salve?

And yet he will not give up. It's not his way. Perhaps the Vengeur du Peuple had surrendered, but he'll destroy himself and everyone on board first.

Captain Nemo does not believe in karma or the Last Judgment. If there is to be any cosmic justice, he will mete it out himself. But he is still a believer. He has shaken off the vestiges of what is called civilization, that of his birth as well as that of his European travels, but he does not choose to discard this.

He is answerable to God alone for what he has done and what he is now doing. Only God will hear him despair. And so he voices, finally, the words he has been holding in since his family's murder: "Almighty God, enough! Enough!"

He thinks he hears someone behind him, but for once, lethargy has dulled his sharp instincts. Or mercy. He heads to the chamber with the portraits to await the maelstrom.

They look back at him: Abraham Lincoln, Daniel O'Connell, Markos Botzaris, his wife. The Nautilus is tossed and battered as if it were an ordinary ship in a storm, but these portraits remain serene. Their work is done, as his will shortly be.

The crew may be panicking beneath their external calm, but his is unforced. He wants to spend these last moments in the company of the dead. But they seem reproachful.

"What more do you want?" he snarls at them.

A rare event in his life as a scientist and fighter has occurred—he has miscalculated. These heroes are not explorers or scientists; they are fighters. And they do not accept his surrender. You can escape the world, escape humanity itself without dishonor, but you cannot escape the struggle.

The Vengeur may not have drowned heroically as he had believed, but nevertheless—he has checked the accounts Aronnax mentioned—she fought until she could no longer fight.

His wife's brown eyes are fierce in the bright electric light. It wasn't him she died for, or at least, not only him. It was to prevent him from laying down arms to save her.

I'll give you a hero's welcome. Someday, yes. But not like this. And the pride that had consigned the Nautilus to destruction is roused once more to save it.

No one dares knock at the captain's private cabin to tell him the prisoners have escaped and the submarine itself is trapped in a whirlpool. Not even the threat of destruction can overcome the mingled respect and fear they feel for the prince-engineer, the tyrannical hater of tyrants. The man has mastered and channeled the most intense of human passions as he did with electricity, and mastered the crew as well.

But the door opens nonetheless, and their hero emerges. Prince Dakkar has come to lead his men in battle with the maelstrom.

The Game of Hare and Hounds

Stephen R. Wilk

*S*hip!" *came the voice from the lookout.* "Ship ahoy!"

"Where away?" bellowed Captain Playfair, pulling on his jacket as he dashed from his cabin.

"Two points off the starboard bow!" came the reply.

"What colors?" asked the captain, taking his own telescope from under his arm and directing it towards the horizon.

The reply was slow in coming; the watchman was carefully scanning the ship himself.

"None showing yet that I can make out," bellowed the lookout.

"Tell me the moment you know!" called the captain. "Report her course when you can!"

"Aye, aye!" was the reply.

"Show me the chart," Captain Playfair commanded. Mathew, his first mate, unrolled the chart and pointed to their location. The Dolphin was at latitude 32° 15' North by 57° 43' West, about three-fifths of her way across the Atlantic on her route to Charleston. It was perhaps a little soon to expect to encounter a ship of the Yankee blockade, but it would be best to be careful. The Dolphin's 1500 tons was crammed with gunpowder, rifles, cannon, food, and clothing to supply both the Army of the American Confederacy and the Southern civilians. For this, Playfair would exchange all the cotton that could be fitted into the Dolphin, to feed the idle cloth mills of his native Glasgow.

It would net his family two million pounds, at least, for a single round trip. There was always a risk where great profit was concerned, but James Playfair was sure that the speed of his ship and his skill as a navigator and tactician would easily overcome any threat posed by the Union Navy.

"I can see her colors!" yelled the lookout. "She's a Union ship! Captain, I think it might be the Iroquois!"

"He's right, sir," affirmed Mathew, after having a look through his own glass. "We saw her in the Mersey. She was nosing around to see what ships were being readied there."

"What does she carry?" asked Playfair.

"Eight guns, sir," replied Mathew.

"How fast is she?"

"One of the fastest in the Federal Navy, sir."

"We'll see about that. Coal up, Mr. Mathew. See that the boilers are up to full steam." Playfair took the speaking trumpet from its rack and gave orders for setting the sails to best advantage, then regarded the approaching ship. Playfair called for the Dolphin's own colors to be broken out. They would see if the Iroquois had the gumption to fire on a ship of the United Kingdom that was making no threatening actions.

"Smoke, sir!" came the cry from the masthead. "She's fired on us!"

Playfair could see the drifting tendrils of smoke coming from the Federal ship, and a moment later the bang of the guns, softened by the distance, reached his ears. After that he was able to make out the sight of a splash in the water between the Iroquois and them. The range was hopelessly long, but there was no problem with their aim.

"They have a sixty-pound Parrott gun, sir," said Mathew, at his elbow, "and a hundred-pound one, both with rifled bores."

"They're accurate," said Playfair, "but short, all the same."

"Testing the range, perhaps. Or a warning shot, maybe, sir."

"And as close as they'll ever get," replied the captain. "Show these Yankees what real speed is, Mr. Mathew. Full speed ahead!"

"Aye, aye, sir!" replied the mate, and he relayed the orders.

The Dolphin had no armament. Her strength lay in her speed. Her high-pressure Lancefield engines were rated at 500 horsepower, and drove twin Millwall screws. She had been built with a careful eye to the balance between strength and speed, with armor plating sufficient to hold off all but heavy bombardment, yet allowing her to outrun any warship afloat. The Dolphin would not triumph by fighting with her clumsy dogging opponents, but would elude them with the speed and agility of the hare.

"Sail to Port!" came the voice of Scott, the lookout.

"Where away?" asked the captain.

"Two points off the port beam."

Playfair swept the sea with his glass and studied the sails, but he did not have the advantage of the lookout's height; the hull was not yet visible to him.

"What ship is she? What is she carrying?" he bellowed up to the masthead.

"United States flag, Captain! No guns that I can see."

"What do you say, Mr. Mathew?"

"I don't know her, sir. But many of the Blockade Fleet are place-keepers, with no guns to speak of, or just a bow-chaser."

"So she may be, but we'll make her fight for her chance to salute us, if she even can," said Playfair. "Alter course a point to starboard. We'll see if she can close with us. They mean to pinch us between their claws like a crab, but they'll clap together on open sea."

There was some exhilaration in this chase, running toward the Southern States as fast as they could between two enemy ships. Captain Playfair breathed in deeply as he surveyed his ship's path between the two adversaries, and nodded in satisfaction. It was soon clear that, run as they might, neither ship had any hope of coming within shot range of the Dolphin, let alone closing with her.

"Captain," said Mathew, I think I ken the ship to port. It's the Abraham Lincoln. She's got high pressure boilers. I hear she can do eighteen knots, and maybe better."

"Guns?"

"I don't know what she carries, sir."

At that moment a puff of smoke came from the ship, and a few seconds later a dim bang followed. There was no sign of the splash from the shot.

"She'll have to do better than that, and we'll not give her the chance. I intend to be out of her sight in an hour."

"Their pursuit is futile," said Mathew. "Why do they do it?"

"What else have they to do? They're hoping that we will have a mechanical breakdown, or some other accident. But they will continue to chase us until we are out of sight. Their pride will not let them do otherwise. Farewell, Iroquois and Lincoln. Perhaps you will have better hunting elsewhere."

Playfair and Mathew returned to their charts and re-plotted their course for the Sullivan Island channel, certain that they would not be overtaken.

Two hours later there came another hail from Scott atop the mainmast.

"Ahoy, sir! Something dead ahead!"

"Dead ahead? What is it?"

"Not a ship, captain. Flotsam, it might be."

Playfair trained his glass ahead and saw the dark blotch that Scott had drawn his attention to. Just what it was, he could not tell. It did not have the well-defined lines of a ship's hull, and there were no sails. Try as he might, he could make no sense of it. But reflections and imagination, he knew, could play strange tricks on the eyes. This might be some piece of marine debris, or a whale. It might even be some Union torpedo, blown out to sea from its offshore station. Whatever it was, it would be wise to avoid it, but that would easily be done by any small shift in course as they approached.

"Call it out when you can see it better, Mr. Scott!" he bellowed up.

"Aye, captain."

If it were a whale, they'd know soon enough. Scott's eyes were keen; he'd done six years aboard a Nantucket whaler.

"It might be an upturned derelict, sir" volunteered Mathew, studying it through his glass. "It has a squarish look unlike any whale I've seen."

"We'll know in a couple of shakes, Mr. Mathew. See that we don't hit her."

"Aye, aye, sir."

Playfair went aft to check the speed on the patent log himself. It was holding remarkably steady, with no griping from the ship, so he saw no need to slacken speed. When he returned, Mathews was still looking forward through his telescope.

"Well, Mr. Mathews?" he asked.

"No change, captain. It's still before us. I think a whale would have moved on by now. It's got a round light patch set against a black border, and I swear it looks eerie, like a cyclops' eye peering straight at us."

"I was once on watch when I first shipped with my father," volunteered Playfair. "I swore that I saw a bogey in the water that stared straight at us all the time we approached. I ran to tell my father we were being watched by some devil of the sea. 'Twas an old pork barrel with a dark blot on it. I was months living that down. This will probably be its brother." He shut up his glass with a snap and walked away.

Twenty minutes later the lookout hailed again.

"It's moving, captain—the black blot. It mooooved." He drew out the last word.

"Jehosaphat!" swore Mathews. "I would have bet a Spanish dollar that was just a wreck!"

Through the glass they could see that it had not only moved, but that it had turned. Only one *eye* seemed visible now, and the black blot was moving to starboard of the ship, as if giving it way to pass without collision.

"Mr. Scott! What whale is that?" bellowed Playfair.

"No whale that I know, sir!" came the reply. "'Tis no fish I know, neither!"

Playfair and Mathews looked at each other. As long as the black blot did not interfere with his ship, its identity bore no importance. But a captain wants to know all that goes on about him in the sea. Both the men had heard stories of unknown creatures glimpsed in the ocean, but no one wanted to be thought a believer in sea monsters.

As they drew closer the identity of the black thing remained as mysterious as ever. It kept its distance as the Dolphin passed by, but even the magnified view through the telescope did not help to identify it. All idle hands had gone to the starboard side to gape at the thing. Mathews wanted to clear them all away with a stern rebuke that this was no raree show, and they should get back to work, or he'd find things for them to do. But Playfair held him back. Perhaps one of them might recognize this mysterious visitor. But none of them volunteered any knowledge of it, even after the captain asked them directly.

And so, the black blot slipped away astern, having completed its viewing of the Dolphin as the Dolphin had viewed it. It was, Playfair decided, just another of those mysteries of the sea. It would make an interesting point in his log book, but now he could devote all his attention to the run to Charleston harbor.

Half an hour later he was hailed again from the mainmast.

"Captain, she's following us! The black blot is running behind us, and keeping station!"

Playfair looked backwards immediately.

"Are you certain?" he bellowed back.

"Aye, sir! I've been taking a rough bearing on it. It's not slipping away as it should."

Through his glass he saw the shape astern, its great eye—if eye it was—staring back at them. There was something not right about this.

"Have you ever heard of a whale chasing after a ship, Mr. Mathews?"

"Most of those fish are happy to swim away from a ship, sir. Especially ones with mechanical screws. They say the noise of the engines scares them, or hurts them."

"Well, this one has a bad case of curiosity, it seems."

Playfair wanted to ask Scott about other whales that followed ships, but he did not want to hear the answer he'd likely get. Whalers still spoke about the Essex, sunk in the south Pacific by a whale that came after her and stove in her side, almost half a century ago. And that American writer published a book about something similar a decade ago—*The Whale*, it was called. Better to not remind the crew. One thought nagged at him, however.

"Mr. Mathews, how fast can a whale swim?"

"I hear big whales can do ten knots for a long haul. For a short time. they can do sprints—maybe four times as fast, sir."

"So, there would be nothing unusual in this one keeping up with us. As far as speed went, that is."

"I don't think so, sir. But unless he took it into his mind to run at us, I wouldn't see him getting any closer."

"Well, let's see if he gets tired of this chase and drifts off. Maybe he hopes we'll toss our slops over the side."

The thing stayed behind the *Dolphin* for another half hour, keeping the same distance. Then, with no warning, it began to grow closer. This was immediately reported forward not only by Scott, but by the crew that was watching off the stern. The acceleration was obvious—the creature was rapidly appearing to be larger.

Even though they were at top cruising speed, Playfair called for an increase. He knew what the engines could take, and he did not intend for this creature to outrace him. The pressure in the boilers was increased, and the ship sped up, groaning a little under the strain. The Dolphin regained her lead over the creature, which kept the same distance.

"How long could your whales sprint, Mr. Mathews?" asked Playfair.

"Maybe ten minutes, sir. It tires them out. Sometimes the whalers wear down their fish in that way."

No sooner had he said this than the creature again started to draw closer, accelerating upon its already great gain in speed. Playfair ordered the ship to match the speed. Mathews made as if to protest, but stopped when he saw the determination in Playfair's face. But again, the sea beast overmatched their speed, and began to draw nearer.

Playfair issued rifles to the idlers at the stern. He might not have cannon at his command, but his ship was not wholly defenseless. He ordered the men to fire upon the thing, and offered a bounty to the first man to draw blood.

The thing drew closer still, and the shots fired were undoubtedly striking home, but the creature was not dissuaded, until suddenly it dove down into the water, its passage making a space into which the surface waters flooded, creating a great wave and spout when they met. The men let out a great cheer when the thing disappeared beneath the waves. There seemed to be a sound as of its passage communicated by the body of the ship. All felt a sense of relief at the end of this stern chase.

Five minutes later Scott roared from the masthead like the whaler he had been.

"BREEEACH! Breach Ahead!"

To the astonishment of all aboard, a long black shape burst forth from the water five hundred yards ahead of the Dolphin. In form it was much like a weaver's shuttle, tapering in the front to a long and sharp point, like the horn of a narwhal. On the creature's back—there was no other way to describe it—was a bulbous extension with what they had taken to be an enormous eye. Perhaps twenty-five yards of its length projected at an angle from the surface, with the Lord only knows how much more below.

The suspended portion of the beast crashed back into the water making a tremendous splash, then the creature turned back towards the Dolphin.

It could be argued that it was another of its kind, popping up directly ahead of the ship after the first one had tired of the chase. But it was on the same course the one chasing them had been on, and how likely was it that two such anomalies had crossed their path at the same time? None doubted that this was the same one that had chased them, and had now arrogantly passed under their keel with outlandish speed, to appear blocking their path.

Playfair's eyes were afire. The beast was taunting him, humiliating him, and he would have none of it.

"Mr. Mathews!" he bellowed, though the first mate was at hand, "Take the boilers to ten atmospheres! Ram that whale!"

"Sir! The boilers won't hold that pressure for long! And the damage to the ship—"

"Damn the damage!" roared Playfair. "We've two inches of steel plating, and more at the prow. That thing is only flesh and blood. We'll tear through him as if he were a paper reef."

There was no arguing with the captain. Mathews gave the orders, and the Dolphin surged forward to meet the arrogant creature and plough it under.

The thing acted as if it cared not. It, too, aimed straight at the Dolphin and came on, faster and faster.

"Brace yourselves!" Mathews called to the crew. There would be an impact, whatever the captain said, and he wanted his men ready for it.

The features of the creature became clearer as the collision approached. Now they could see the regular markings and the apparent scales on its back, its single huge and unblinking eye. And then—there was no collision, no impact. The creature had again dived below the ship, again producing noises that reverberated through the hull of the Dolphin.

For several minutes nothing happened. The creature did not surface behind the ship, nor appear anywhere else. Then the ship lurched abruptly to port, and there was the sound of a terrible crash from below. Men ran to the side of the ship to see what they could. But Mathews raced down the ladder, below deck. What he saw froze him. The sea was pouring in through a hole a yard wide in the side of the ship. The hole was in the shape of an isosceles triangle.

There was no hope of putting any sort of patch in place. Fortunately, the ship was divided through its entire height into water-tight sections, so that a hole anywhere in the ship would not sink it. But many of the men in that compartment were already dead, unable to escape the torrential influx.

Mathews reported what he had seen to Playfair, who took it with the proper stoicism of an officer upon whom the life of the ship depended. Already he was working out the results of this catastrophe, and their options. The ship would sit lower in the water, and its drag was greatly increased. The engines continued to run and the screws to turn, but they might not now be able to outrun any Federal Navy ships.

As they were recovering from this blow and coming to terms with the situation, the ship was struck again from the port side, closer to the bow. Men ran to help those below, and to man the pumps, but it was futile. A fire broke out. Some lowered the lifeboats, not waiting for orders. The ship listed significantly, and then suddenly the immense cargo of gunpowder was touched off, and the hull exploded. The force of it swept men from the deck and shattered the lifeboats. Within fifteen minutes, the greater part of the ship had sunk, leaving only random flotsam behind. There were no survivors.

The submarine surfaced again near what little remained of the Dolphin. A hatch opened aft of the wheelhouse whose windows had been taken for an eye. Three figures emerged onto the small platform at the top, two men and a woman.

"Sweet Jesus!" exclaimed Crockston, the younger man, shaking his head. The woman stared wide-eyed in horror and disbelief. The other man looked dispassionately at the floating remains, studying them carefully.

"Was this necessary?" asked Crockston.

"There is a great war proceeding on that continent to the west," said the submarine's captain, Nemo.

"You will find scenes of destruction as bad or worse along the path of the American Civil War," said the other man.

"You cannot prosecute a war without producing such destruction. If I could, I would magically stop the engines and spike the cannons of all warships at sea. I do not have such powers. To achieve our ends, there is no way except to produce as much damage as we can.

At least the deaths of these men were sudden and merciful, without pain. You cannot say the same for most of those fighting on land."

"Even so, I had no idea…" began Crockston.

"If you begin along this path, you must be prepared for the results that follow. Your imagination must be powerful enough to foresee these ends, and your will must be strong enough to deal with the consequences. Every man who died there corresponds to at least one hundred human souls held in bondage. The munitions this ship carried will not arrive at Charleston, and will not become part of the great Confederate engine of war. The end of that state has been brought slightly closer. Is this not what you wanted?"

"I am sorry, Captain," said the woman, speaking mechanically. "I see that this follows logically from our request, but to see it in reality is…daunting."

"You wish to see the Confederacy defeated, and the slaves freed, do you not Miss Halliburton?"

"Yes."

"Believe me, the men who lead the Confederacy will not willingly let go of their power, or release the dark people from their bondage. They must be forced, and when hands are forced, this is frequently the result. I have fought against oppression for many years, and this is always the way. Do you agree, Mr. Crockston?"

"Uhh…yes. Yes, of course," Crockston said.

"Do the two of you have the will and the fortitude to complete your mission? Will you be able to do what is necessary to free Miss Halliburton's father from the Charleston jail, even if it means hurting or even killing more people?"

"Yes," replied Jennie Halliburton. "If I do not, then the same fate will be visited upon him."

"So. We each fight against injustice in our own way. But you see that it is often a literal fight. One on which we must not lose hope. I will put you ashore tonight at the place we have decided on, before news of this is known. I am most grateful to both of you for bringing me word of this ship. If the Nautilus had not sunk her, she might have caused untold damage with her deliveries of weapons and supplies."

"When I learned of the Dolphin's construction and abilities, I knew that I had to do something," said Jennie Halliburton. I had heard rumors of your remarkable ship, but no one took them seriously, except for Mr. Crockston here. He is the one who learned how to contact you through the Greek diver."

"If you learn anything else that would be useful, you may contact me the same way. I rely upon your pledge to keep silent about me, else I could not continue my work."

"You speak as if you have fought against oppression elsewhere, before this American War, Captain Nemo. Can I ask where?"

"You can ask, but you will not receive an answer. My past is my own, and I do not wish to reveal it. English is not my native language."

"You have worked to expunge any accent. I do not perceive any. Nor can I tell your nationality," said Crockston. "When this war is ended, if I survive through it, may I join your crew on its next mission?"

"You may not, Mr. Crockston. If you truly understood our background, you would not ask. We are a brotherhood bound together by our own baptism of blood. We do not choose this life, but are driven to it. It is not something I would wish upon any other man or woman.

"You may look upon the Nautilus as a wonder and a vessel of discovery. Would that it were so! I find my only peace in studying the oceans and their mysteries, but that is all secondary to our mission. Perhaps someday I will be able to discuss this with a man sufficiently learned to understand what we have wrought, and to appreciate the craft. But for now, we must continue the fight against the oppressor, only taking the odd moment to appreciate the beauty that surrounds us. Come, we must be off before other ships approach."

With that, the mysterious Captain Nemo led them down into the interior of the Nautilus, and the submarine ship slipped quickly and silently beneath the waves.

Recruiter

Andrew Gudgel

*I*t was well after dark when he tied the ship's dinghy to the side of the wooden pier in Valparaiso and made his way up the ladder. No one met him at the foot of the dock. The old night watchman that wandered his way wandered back off when he waved his straw hat and said, "*Buenas noches.*"

He strode towards the warren of stone and wooden buildings that lined the streets that ran up from the port. However, he continued past the cheap bars and taverns until he found a quiet street and a darkened doorway. There he waited.

He heard footsteps and tensed. He'd never been followed before, but there was a first time for everything. The footsteps grow louder, and a man appeared, walking along on the other side of the street. But the other man either didn't see him or paid him no attention. In another moment, the man passed out of sight, footfalls growing fainter until they were gone.

When he was sure he was alone again, he unbuttoned the gray coverall he'd been wearing. The seaweed-fiber-and-fish-skin garment rustled as he took it off and folded it down into a square package as big as a dinner plate. Underneath he wore a dark-gray sack suit. He produced a matching gentleman's hat from inside the straw one. A piece of string from his jacket pocket tied up his two previous outer garments into a tidy package.

The man checked the bottom hem of his coat, feeling for the small gold coins that had been sewn inside. Then he checked for the pocketbook that contained his ready source of funds. He scanned the street again, looking for anyone watching. Satisfied he was still alone, he continued away from the port with his bundle tucked under his arm, like a gentleman strolling up from a visit to the docks.

He spotted a hotel across the Plaza de la Aduana. The man walked to the front door and saw that it was plain, but respectable. The doorman held the door open for him.

"A room please," he said to the clerk behind the desk.

"I'll be here a week. Business," he said in response to the clerk's question. A key appeared and was set on the counter. The man reached into his jacket and removed his pocketbook. The clerk's brow wrinkled at the sight of the gold coin that was placed on the counter.

"I've run out of pesos," the man told the clerk, "and of course, my letter of credit is useless until tomorrow when the *Banco* opens. It's an American twenty-dollar piece. If you won't take it in payment, hold onto it until morning when I can get more pesos."

After a moment's consideration, the clerk dropped the coin into the cash box, then turned the register around for the man to sign.

"Welcome, Mr. Secundus," the clerk said, reading the upside-down signature. "Do you have any luggage?"

The man smiled apologetically. "Still in Santiago. Should catch up to me in a day or two."

"Very good, sir."

He picked up the key and his bundle. "I'm just going to run this up. Is your dining room still open?"

"Indeed."

"Do you serve steak?" the man asked.

The clerk smiled. "The very best in town."

"Wonderful," he replied and turned towards the stairs.

The first bite—medium well—almost made him weep. He took his time, cutting a second small piece and spearing it on his fork, followed by a chunk of potato. Both were rubbed in the reddish-brown juices that covered the bottom of the plate. He stuck the bits in his mouth and began chewing.

The captain had severed all ties with land and extolled the propriety and health benefits of eating nothing but the fruits of the sea. He, on the other hand, had dreamed of this steak since the last time he was on land, almost four years ago. Yet even something this sensuous could never make him reconsider his choice to go with the captain. As a fellow victim of injustice, he'd been the first to throw in his lot with the man—even before they'd escaped prison. Together, they'd made their way to the remote island where the ship had been assembled by the captain's team. Five men had died in an accident with the electrical apparatus; the same number had declined to accompany the captain on his new adventure when they realized what he intended.

Those who'd stayed with the captain were barely enough to crew the ship. The captain himself had acted as pilot while he, an engineer by trade, had run the engines, shouting orders when needed. In the weeks that followed, the captain had repeatedly sent him ashore—the man himself steadfastly refused to set foot on any land inhabited by man—and found three more men of their nation who'd been wronged and were willing to go to sea for the rest of their lives. A clerk, a steelworker, and a student of languages who had been sent down from university for radical tendencies. Together, the eight of them had been the nucleus of the crew. Yet they were still always at the edge of being shorthanded.

During that initial period, the captain gave him letters to post and once, sent him to a certain address to pick up a bundle, which contained three letters in return. He'd so quickly fallen into the habit of thinking of the captain as "the captain" that it'd been a shock to see the man's true name written on the envelopes.

The increasing danger of discovery in the shallow coastal waters of their nation and the radical student's recitations of international injustice had convinced the captain to search farther afield for crew. Over the next year, the number who sailed away from their old lives grew to almost two dozen from fourteen different lands. The international nature of the crew led the radical student to devise a simple *lingua franca* in which to converse, and the captain enthusiastically adopted it as the language of the ship, severing his final tie with his homeland.

Five years on, they'd lost enough men to squids and accidents and illnesses that couldn't be treated that after much private discussion, he'd convinced the captain it was time to begin replenishing the crew. His instructions this time around were simple and based upon the plan the captain had established through the early spate of letters: put a certain chalk mark on the alley-side corner of a certain building in Valparaiso on a certain day, find a seat in the nearest cafe, and wait for whoever came to him. That certain day was tomorrow.

He took his time finishing his steak and potatoes, then ordered a small brandy, neat.

He sipped it slowly, watching the dining room entrance to see if the man he'd seen twice while he ate passed by the doorway yet again. Fortunately, the man didn't return. When he was done with his meal, he asked the desk clerk to have him awakened at dawn so that he could go for an early-morning walk, then went upstairs.

He scanned the room as he opened the door. Bed, dresser, his bundle of clothes—all appeared undisturbed. He double-checked the knot on the string around his bundle and it, too, seemed untouched. After locking the door, he undressed, hanging his clothes carefully to prevent wrinkles and crawled into bed. Despite knowing that it stood firmly on a wooden floor attached to a sturdy building resting on the bedrock of Valparaiso, he still felt the rocking of the surfaced ship as he drifted off to sleep.

It was only a gut feeling, nothing more, but something about this man didn't seem right. This morning he'd put the chalk mark on the building's corner; was now interviewing a prospective crewman. The most difficult part of the job of finding new crew, he'd expected, would be to separate those who'd truly suffered injustice from those merely criminal. Both had reason to flee their old lives; only one could be trusted. The candidate before him was definitely hiding something. But what?

They'd met at the cafe in the afternoon. The other man had known the password: Mobilis in mobili. A middle-aged man, a native of Santiago, and a fellow electrical engineer. After a few minutes of pleasant chit-chat, Secundus had suggested they retire to his room for further conversation. Now they sat together, sipping sherry from small glasses and talking about the state of electrical science.

"I'm surprised you haven't heard of Plante's and Leclanche's work on electrical cells," the candidate said.

Secundus shrugged. "I've been working on an isolated project for some time and haven't been able to keep abreast of the literature."

"What sort of project? Mining?" the candidate asked.

He shrugged again.

"And it is in connection to this mining project that you're looking for men? A gold mine? Hence the secrecy in looking for engineers?"

"Perhaps. But what if my—our—project required some considerable time at sea? Years, say? Would you be willing to commit to such a project?"

"A new oceanic telegraph cable? One for the Pacific?"

Secundus smiled but said nothing.

"How often would we return to port?" the candidate asked.

He frowned. The intermediary was supposed to only send candidates who had no ties. "You have family?"

"No, no. But a man's got to have wine and certain companionship at times. And, of course, you'll need supplies."

"Ah," Secundus said. "Actually, the necessary crew is small and the ship has enough in store to last almost indefinitely. Assume you'll never see land again."

The candidate snorted. "Impossible."

"And if it were? Would you be willing to do electrical work unlike any other—unique, in fact—in exchange for a life lived entirely at sea?"

The candidate leaned forward in his chair, then burst into laughter. "You're serious?" he said, after a moment. He wiped a tear from the corner of his eye. "By God, you're serious." The candidate motioned towards the bottle of sherry, then went ahead and poured himself another glass. After a sip, he looked towards the ceiling. "Unlike anything else?"

Secundus nodded.

"But never feel a woman's touch or take a drink again. Like a monk."

Secundus nodded again. He understood why a man might balk at living like a monk. Tonight's brandy and sherry would have to hold him until the next time the captain sent him ashore, whenever that was. And as for women, there had been only one for him, and she was now long dead. "I'll have to think about it," the candidate said.

"I leave tonight. You're being sought, yes? For what crime?"

"Crime?" the candidate said. His face reddened. "No crime. Merely loving my nation and not the men who rule it."

Secundus stared, impassive. That, too, had been his *crime*. And the captain's.

The two talked until the room grew dark and Secundus had to light the lamp by the window. The candidate's answers were all suitable, and the man seemed to be coming around towards accepting the rigors of a life lived permanently aboard the ship.

Yet there was still something that bothered him about the man, and he couldn't put his finger on why. Secundus' engineering training suggested to him then that one way to define a problem was to change one of the variables and see how the whole system changed.

Their conversation reached a natural pause. He picked up the bottle of sherry. "Would you like another drink?"

"Yes, please," the candidate replied and started to hold out his glass.

Secundus took a deep breath. By changing just that one variable, he had simultaneously defined his problem and answered it. He had made the offer of sherry in his native language. The reply had come in the same tongue.

The candidate looked stricken for a moment, then shrugged, smiled, left off speaking Spanish. "Enough of this charade. I *will* still have that drink, though."

Secundus nodded and filled the candidate's glass. "So what now?"

"We talk some more. But now it's *you* who have to make a decision."

"About?"

"Whether you wish to work with me to end this man's reign of piracy or if you'd rather I—and the gentlemen waiting for me down on the street—give you over to the local authorities. In which case, all of Valparaiso turns out to witness the hanging of a notorious pirate."

"One man's pirate is—"

"Spare me," the candidate said. "The Frenchman's book—oh yes, he wrote of his adventures after he escaped—allowed us to argue to the world that the ship and all on it were an international menace. There's not a navy on this globe that won't take every opportunity to sink you on sight and not a nation on earth that won't see justice done to any crew member that falls into their hands."

"I see," Secundus said. "I guess if I'm a dead man anyway, I might as well hear your offer."

"Simple, really. You take me on as a crew member. I assume I'd be allowed to bring a few items as mementos and such?"

Secundus nodded. He himself had none, having come directly from prison, but the captain had no prohibition against it.

"Good, that will make my job easier. Are you familiar with the work of Maxwell and the young man Hertz?"

Secundus shook his head.

"Electrical waves that move through the air and can affect a properly tuned coil with no connecting wires. Action at a distance. I have a device that produces the waves. Every ship of our navy now has a coil that can receive the clicks made by the producer. After you have taken me on board as a sailor, I begin producing clicks. When I order you to do so, you will disable the electromagnets that turn the screw. The ship will have to surface within a day or two for air, correct?"

Secundus nodded, saying nothing. If needed, the ship could stay underwater much longer than that but in general, the captain *did* surface every day.

"And when it does, our navy will have the ship surrounded."

"Your navy," Secundus said.

The candidate shook his head. "Our navy. In exchange for your help in capturing this pirate, you'll be given a full pardon. A small, but adequate pension. And be reunited with your family."

He sat silent for a long time. "I have no family. Not anymore."

The candidate shrugged. "I was told, 'be reunited with his family.' They didn't say more than that, though."

His mind raced with the hope that his wife and daughters might still be alive, yet Secundus forced himself to confront the situation before him. A question of variables, again. The first choice had been made for him. "Not wanting to be hung, it seems there's nothing I can do but agree," he said after a moment. Secundus tried to think ahead to the next step of the problem. Having acquiesced, at least on the surface, he now needed to turn the situation to his advantage and still be in the right place for his scheduled pick-up. He checked his pocket watch. "We don't have much time. The dining room closes soon."

The candidate looked confused.

"The captain asked me to bring him back a steak dinner when I returned to the ship, whether or not I was successful in finding a new crew member. He was quite emphatic about it." Secundus stood. "I assume you're coming with me."

The candidate smiled and nodded. "Of course."

"And I assume you need to get your special keepsake before we depart."

The other man shook his head and pointed towards the window. "I can have one of them bring what I need here." He went to the window, held up the lamp, and waved. "Done." He set the lamp down and turned back. "Now, shall we go get your captain his last meal?"

"I should have had you row," the candidate said, panting between each stroke of the oar. They'd been fortunate that the night sky was clear, allowing the moonlight to shine down on the waters of the bay.

"Some sailor you are," Secundus said, watching from the back of the dinghy. Between them sat the cloth-wrapped bundle that was ostensibly the new crew member's belongings and a small wicker basket that contained a full meal—steak, potatoes, rolls. "It's not even a league to the end of the point."

"I'm no sailor. I'm an agent of the government."

"You'll get used to it."

"I don't plan on getting used to it," the other man replied. "I have better things to do back in the capital."

Secundus cocked his head, listening for the sound of the surf off to their left. "Stay a little farther out to sea."

Three-quarters of the way there, the candidate stopped, oars still in the water. "I need to rest."

"We won't make it to the ship on time if you do. They'll only wait so long."

"You row, then."

In the moonlight, Secundus shook his head. "I'm the second lieutenant of the Nautilus; you're a recruit sailor. It would look strange."

The candidate cursed, but soon began rowing again. "You're doing this on purpose," he said between strokes.

Secundus smiled. "Normally petty revenge is beneath me. But in this case—"

The candidate had rowed on in silence for some time until Secundus told him to stop. Then he stood, inserted his fingers into his mouth and gave three short whistles. He paused, listening. "On we go," Secundus said, sitting back down.

The whistles were repeated once they got to the end of the point. The fourth time around, Secundus heard an answering set of whistles: one long, one short. He looked in the direction from which they had come. "Row a little to the right," he told the candidate. "Not far now."

A few minutes later, the moonlight revealed a low shape in the water. Secundus pointed. "That way."

As they got closer to the ship, Secundus saw two men standing on the platform outside the hatch. He held up the basket. "Tell the captain to come up!" he shouted in his native tongue. "I've brought him dinner!"

By the time they pulled alongside the ship, the captain had joined the two sailors on the platform. Secundus had the candidate throw the bow line to one of the sailors, while he handed the stern line to the other.

Once they were tied off to the side of the ship, he stepped out ahead of the candidate, holding the basket in front of him. "Sir, I've brought you the steak you asked for."

The captain looked confused for a moment. He reached out, took the basket. Then he nodded at the two sailors.

Secundus heard a short scuffle behind him. Then a thud as something heavy dropped to the deck.

"What now?" He asked the captain in the language of the ship, then looked over his shoulder at the man crumpled on the deck. "It's one thing when they attack us. This doesn't seem the same."

The captain stared at him for a long time. Then he sighed. "No, I suppose it's not. Though it will be a shame to lose yet another dinghy." He gave instructions to the sailors.

"Keep the man's possessions," Secundus added. When he looked over his shoulder a second time, the candidate's bundle lay on the deck. The man himself lay across the seats of the small boat. One of the sailors pushed the dinghy free of the ship, where it slowly drifted back toward land on the incoming tide.

Secundus went to the bundle, untied it, and held up a wooden box roughly the size of a man's head. On the side was a crank. Two metal balls on posts that curved towards each other adorned the top.

The captain looked at him.

"Some sort of signaling device so he could tell them of our location." He made to pitch it over the side.

"Wait," said the captain. "Keep it."

"Why?"

"It may yet be useful. Think of the angler-fish. It waves a lure to draw in its prey. Maybe now we have a lure, too."

Secundus stood.

The captain came over to him, took the device. He held out the basket. "This is yours, my friend. You know I have no taste for this sort of food."

"I was hoping you'd say that," said Secundus, and smiled.

Nemo's World

James J. C. Kelly

The rewriting of Earth's history began with a sharp knock on Dr. Michael Chen's Caltech office door. He'd been poring over his expedition's planned course to the North Pole when the sound jolted him from his focus.

After a breath, he said, "Come in."

The door swung open and a brown-skinned woman with a short-cut afro stepped inside, beaming as she pulled a large, rolling suitcase. It had been months, but the effect on him returned at full strength. Seeing her, his world fell away to only her light brown eyes and full lipped smile.

"Livvy." He sprang from his seat, bounding around the desk to wrap her in his arms.

Dr. Olivia Johnson was an anthropologist and archeologist. He hadn't heard from her in months, and he was too blinded by emotion to realize when trouble walked into his office.

"Wow, CHO." She laughed and squeezed him back. "Missed you too."

He told himself to relax before she became aware of his true feelings for her. "I can't believe you're here, and you cut your dreads, rocking a mini afro. I can see your neck. I love it." He pulled her away only to be met by her shocked, knowing gaze. His careless mouth had betrayed him.

"Oh my God, I never realized," she mouthed.

His face warmed. He pretended to busy himself with paper on his desk. "Last time we saw each other we were back in Harvard. Over the years I've gotten use to talking over texts, Facebook, satellite phones, and emails. Then, you go incommunicado for months. Today, you just show up. I hope things won't get weird."

"Um, I mean, why would they?" She glanced back at the door. "Uh, we're here to see you."

"We?"

Into his office stepped Professor Bernadetta Johnson, graciously ignoring the awkwardness. Her brilliant smile spared no teeth as she hugged him like a proud mother seeing her son after years apart. "Michael."

"Professor," he said, his smile born anew.

"Oh, I'm going to strangle you. I've told you, call me Berna."

"Uh oh, both of you together. So, what's going on? Why are you two here? I'm worried."

Berna laughed. "Smart man. Well, Liv here will do the talking. I'm just here to support my daughter."

He was suddenly aware of their appearance. Their smiles looked forced and their eyes drooped from exhaustion. "Uh, sure. Sit. So, what's up?"

Livvy laid the bag flat and after a long, smooth zip pulled out a relic of a book. Already intrigued, CHO leaned in. When Livvy eased open the cover, the pages weren't typical paper, and they emanated a stale, salty odor.

His eyes darted between the women. "What is it?"

Berna nodded to a framed poster partially concealed behind a bookcase. "It's time to believe. Unless you're still denying it."

It was the X-Files poster she'd bought him after grad school. "I Want to Believe," it read, one of a framed pair, its mate in her Harvard office. He wanted to be taken seriously as a scientist. Despite what he saw as a kid, he couldn't admit to his belief in UFOs. She was well established in her field and could afford ridicule. He was proud to claim her as his mentor when it came to her traditional career, but had distanced himself from her eccentric theories.

CHO looked away without answering, but not before seeing her smirk with disappointment.

She turned to her daughter. "Well Liv, don't keep him waiting."

"Uh, okay, so this is going to sound crazy. Hear me out." She sounded distracted.

He slumped back in his chair, cursing himself. She was avoiding his eyes. He made her uncomfortable.

"As you know I was in East Africa on that dig. Well, the guide and I got to talking. He tells me his great grandmother had this capsule she found as a kid, on the beach. They could never get it open. Well, hell, that type of thing is right up my alley so I told him to bring it by."

She pulled a photograph from her bag. "The capsule had these markings here. To sweeten the mystery, get this—the metal it's made of, an unknown alloy, is stronger than anything we know about."

Berna interjected, "The team at Harvard identified three new elements, called it the discovery of the century. I call it the tip of the iceberg."

"Really? I haven't heard anything," he said.

Livvy nodded. "No one has, yet. So, on a hunch, I had a friend in the math department look at the symbols. It turns out they aren't words. They're a pattern, so complex he needed a super computer to assist him. There were buttons with the symbols. When I pressed them in the right order to complete the pattern, the capsule opened."

"What was inside?"

"Captain Nemo's autobiography."

A laugh escaped him, contemptuous. Immediately, he wanted it back. He cleared his throat. Livvy and her mom were shooting the same narrow-eyed glare. He swallowed. "I'm sorry. It's just, for more than a century, everyone's been looking for proof of Nemo. He's a legend right up there with Bigfoot."

Livvy pulled a folder from the bag, handing it to him. "Alright, you need more. Well, look at the results of tests we had done on the capsule and this book. As we said, the capsule is made of some futuristic alloy and the book's pages are marine eelgrass, which Dr. Aronnax said Nemo used for paper."

CHO couldn't help but smile at Livvy's passion.

She continued, "It gets better. It was uncertain if the Nautilus had wrecked the night Dr. Aronnax and party escaped, or was sunk at Lincoln Island before the volcano there erupted. Neither of those happened. Truth was, Nemo made it to the North Pole."

CHO leaned back in his chair and groaned in understanding. "You want to come with me." Combing his hair back with his fingers, he continued, "Why me? Harvard should be funding you."

Livvy's brows furled and she opened her mouth to respond but her mother raised a hand to stop her. "I'm funding this one, my entire retirement savings. I just don't have enough for transportation."

Michael was floored. "You're crazy."

Livvy rested her head in her hand, her voice weary. "CHO, look, we don't need to go all the way north with you. We have our own equipment. Give us four days. If this doesn't pan out, drop us off whenever you resupply and we're out of your hair."

The Professor leaned towards him, her eyes a tired, weathered version of her daughter's, her voice desperate. "Michael, I didn't want to come here, but Liv reminded me to get over myself. So, here I am, hat in hand, asking you to throw your old professor a bone. What do you say? Isn't there room on that ship for two stowaways and their equipment?"

His eyes fell to the X-Files poster. She believed in him when no one else had, used her connections to get him his professorship at Caltech. He didn't have the audacity to make her beg. He allowed his head to drop back with a deep sigh. "So, let me guess, you got the book, now we're all chasing after the Nautilus?"

Berna smiled and Livvy pumped a fist.

He took a long breath. "I can say we're extending the expedition a few days to study currents or temperatures or something—"

"No," Livvy snapped. "No calls, no mentioning this to anyone, okay, CHO?"

"Why not?"

The professor smirked, "It's simple. If we're right, you'll have what you've wanted from the first day I met you, a prestigious career and your name in history." She nodded at the X-Files poster, "But, if we're wrong, do you really want it known you were looking for Bigfoot?"

Three days later Livvy and her mother arrived at the port wearing the same clothes they wore to his office, odd for the ever-fashionable pair. He didn't care, excited at the idea of being together with Livvy for what he hoped would be a lengthy period.

That evening, after getting underway, Livvy stood alone by the bow's railing, and Michael seized the opportunity.

"Dr. *Mona Thomson*, you're finally alone," he said as he approached.

Livvy turned and smiled. The bags beneath her eyes had deepened further. "Hey, CHO, Try blowing anyone's cover lately?"

"Okay, then perhaps you shouldn't be calling me CHO."

She smirked. "Nah, you'll forever be CHO."

He spoke in a hushed tone, leaning on the rail close to her. "We keep secrets now? You're using an alias. And I had to find that out when Captain Doyle gave me a copy of the crew manifest. Livvy, what's really going on? We've never lied to each other."

Her light brown eyes caught his. He couldn't say how much time passed. When she finally spoke, it wasn't to answer his question. "Really bad timing, CHO. Why didn't you ever say you had feelings for me?"

He groaned, gazing out at a lightning storm illuminating the distant horizon ahead. His cheeks burned. "You were the professor's daughter. The first time you met me, I was doing a keg stand."

She laughed, nodding. "You were freaking beet red drunk. You remember anything from that night?"

He smiled wryly. "Not really, but I remember the next day you kept calling me CHO."

"The night before, you couldn't remember your name, so I called you CHO, as in C_2H_6O."

"Ethanol," they said together.

"I remembered waking to you standing over me with that smirk of yours, thick dreadlocks, and those beautiful eyes. Later, I found out you were Johnson's daughter. I thought, black girl, professor's daughter, not a chance in hell."

"Black girl?"

"I know. Hey, I grew up in a predominately Asian community. You were, *sassy black girl and Hip-Hop.*"

"Wow," she laughed.

"But I've grown. We've grown. Now we're friends, and you're so much more than thick dreads and Hip-Hop."

"And you're more than keg stands and almond eyes."

"I'm glad we got to know each other. I'd like to believe I've earned your trust and proven myself a friend. So, *Dr. Mona*, what's really going on here? Why are you off grid?"

She turned her gaze to the wake churning off the side of the ship. She closed her eyes and breathed. "Look, some of this is pretty out there."

"Listening."

"I got the capsule open and found the book. It had several pages of Cuneiform written in the back so I took it home to translate. Before that, I brought the capsule to the mass spectrometer at the university—a mistake. Next day, my university office was ransacked."

"What?"

"It was obvious *they* were looking for it. I found out the techs running the mass spectrometer sent the numbers out to a national lab, accessing a bigger pool of data. I think, and this is going to sound more like something my mother would say, but I think it was the government."

She wasn't joking, he could tell by her furled eyebrows and the way she bit her plump bottom lip—she was serious. And scared.

"I told Mom, reluctantly. She made me stay in a hotel. A day later, when she went to my place to get me some clothes, it was all in shambles too."

"Holy shit."

She nodded. "Well that was it. If *they* wanted it so bad, I'd stumbled onto something big. Being my mother's daughter, I immediately went into conspiracy mode, pulled out all my cash, ditched my cell, went totally off grid, until we came to you."

"Something doesn't make sense. Why would the government be coming for you if all you found was Nemo's ship? And, I'm sorry about how this sounds, but the evidence you do have isn't rock solid."

"You're wrong. The stuff in the back of the book proves a lot of my mom's theories."

He raised an eyebrow. "Stuff like, UFOs?"

She nodded. "Dr. Aronnax quoted Nemo, 'The earth does not need new continents, but new men.' Well, Nemo found both. How familiar are you with the Hollow Earth Theory?"

His cheeks wanted to pull into a smile. The implication of the question was insane. He managed to subdue it with a simple clearing of his throat. "Basically, it claims the center of the earth is hollow, but Charles Hutton's Schiehallion experiment disproves it. That's first year geology. Are you about to tell me that's wrong? Because, UFOs, okay, but I can't accept the world is hollow."

"I'm saying if what Nemo wrote in his book is true, when we find his sub, first year geology is going to be rewritten."

"Doctors Thomson, Chen, calm waters this evening, beautiful night," Captain Doyle said approaching, carrying a tablet. He was a pepper-haired man with grey eyes.

"Good evening, Captain," Livvy replied.

"We should be at your coordinates by dawn." Doyle's eyes went to the distant lightning flashing along the horizon. "Supposed to miss us. We're keeping an eye on it, but I'm not too confident in the forecasts. Here's the projected track." He handed the tablet to Michael. "My apologies, Dr. Thomson, I know you're anxious to get down there. Hey, there's always the next day, right?"

She lowered her eyes and nodded, "Right."

Doyle placed his hands behind his back. "You know, I'm a bit of a fan of Dr. Johnson. Curious, what is it you're looking for, exactly?

Dr. Johnson is often on those shows that talk about aliens." He leaned in conspiratorially, "Thirty-eight years I've been out here. I've seen things. Did something crash?"

Michael laughed, handing back the tablet. "We're not out here hunting aliens. The professor might have eccentric theories, but she's still a geologist and her day job pays the bills. Harvard is doing a study on global warming's effect on ice algae."

Livvy must have realized her angry demeanor, turning her frown into a warm smile. "See, the amount of algae in an ice core can tell us the extent of sea ice, giving us historical data on climate change over centuries."

"I see. So, no UFOs then?" Doyle asked.

Livvy shrugged. "Sorry."

Doyle nodded and waggled the tablet. "Dr. Chen, we should discuss contingencies. I'll be on the bridge."

"Be right up." Once Doyle was out of earshot, Michael turned to Livvy. "That reminds me of college, how we would get into and talk ourselves out of trouble."

Livvy looked to the sky and cursed. "Come on Mama Nature, you're supposed to be my girl. Don't do this." She took a calming breath with a hand to her temple. "You should get up there, find out what's up," she urged.

He sighed. Doyle had killed his moment. "Right, so what are you going to do?"

"Well, if the weather holds out, I need my sleep to dive. I'm going to knock out."

After an awkward moment of silence, Michael nodded and began to walk away. Livvy grabbed his hand.

"CHO… You're right. We are a great pair." She looked deep into his eyes. "Outside of, you know, all of this, sunken ships and hollow earths, we have a lot to talk about. And I'm looking forward to it, long overdue. Good night, CHO."

Next morning, he went topside to be met by a sky that was a miserable twist of greys soaking the deck with a fine mist.

The professor was chatting with a ship's officer. Michael waved. She glowered back.

He rolled his eyes and sighed. "Already?"

He started over but she was already striding towards him, growling before he could speak.

"Just what the hell were you two thinking last night, speaking to the captain?" She demanded in a whisper.

"What are you talking about?"

"He had it in him that we're out here hunting for a downed UFO, saw right through your idiotic ice algae story. It's all over social media. Now, the Coast Guard ordered him to hold position and wait to be boarded."

Michael cursed. "Seriously? How'd he know?"

"Come on Michael. You and I are geologists, Liv, aka Mona, is an archeologist. Algae research without a marine biologist?"

He winced.

She shook her head, exasperated. "I told him what we're really out here looking for. It's better he's on board with it, anyway. We're in a bad place. Doyle says the Coast Guard is two hours out."

"This is all your fault. You know she's only out here for you, and you just let her ruin her career."

With that, her eyes narrowed.

He didn't mean to say it. Through the silence, he could feel the bonds between them severing further. "Look, I'm sorry. I—"

I'm glad you finally found the balls to say it," she snapped. "But she's an adult. You want a prestigious career? It's served with a side of risk. Eat up. Liv understands that. Unlike you, she's not *scared* to admit what she believes."

"I'm not scared—"

"Aren't you?" She raised her voice to be heard by everyone in the area. "Did you see a UFO, as a child, visiting your grandmother in China?"

Several of his grad students turned to look at them.

Michael glowered at her and responded matching her volume, "Yes."

She smirked. "Attaboy. Now, we're at the coordinates. Nemo's ship is somewhere below. If we're going to help Liv, we need to get going. The Coast Guard is coming to shut us down. You love Liv? Give her your support. Light a fire beneath those grad students of yours and let's get her in the water."

Thirty minutes later, a palpable buzz of excitement filled the air as the mixed crew of sailors and scientists hustled about the deck to start the dive. They had an hour before the Coast Guard arrived.

Michael still simmered over the professor's words as he made his way to Livvy, donning her diving gear. He had to establish himself in his field before doing anything to jeopardize it. He wasn't scared, he was calculated. Why didn't she understand that?

When he reached Livvy, she was shrugging on her breathing rig, only her face visible through the hood of her bulky dry suit. She acknowledged him without looking, fastening her rig's buckles.

"I spoke to Mom." She glared at him. "No big deal, we'll make a believer out of you, too." There was hurt in her voice, slight, but there.

"In a single stroke, it seems I pissed off the only two women I love." CHO reached for her hand.

She knocked it away, her eyes warning him not to try it again, then began testing her regulators.

He whispered, "Come on Livvy. I'm not allowed to have doubts? How many people looked for that ship, and now you're dropping this Hollow Earth thing on me? I mean, it's a lot to take in."

He combed his hair back with his fingers. "Look, I don't want you mad at me, not you. Okay, I can honestly say I want to believe the Nautilus is down there. But, come on, you really believe the earth is hollow, or are you risking your credibility to prove Berna's theories?"

She snapped, "You think I'm doing this for— So, I can't think for myself?"

"That's not—"

She cut him short, placing a hand to his cheek, tapping her chest with the other. "I feel it in here. I'm right on this." She pulled him into a kiss that left him breathless. When she released, she stared into his eyes. "Tell me, should I stop listening to my heart?"

His words were breathy. "Livvy, that's not fair."

"Yes, it's hard to believe, but I'm more certain now than ever. I stayed up last night completing the translation of Nemo's journal."

"And?"

"And, I know exactly what I need to do." She patted a bag she wore at her hip. "When I'm done, the world will be changed forever."

Her eyes went to the distant storm firing snaps of lightening. She cursed. "It's not going to miss us, maybe thirty minutes. I'm racing Mama Nature and the Coast Guard. We can talk later. I got to get down there. I won't have a second chance."

Less than five minutes later, she was in the water. She and a companion diver, his grad student, Henry, disappeared beneath the waves.

She was right. A moment after she was under, Doyle reported the storm's change in direction, cutting the dive short by half, from ninety minutes to forty-five.

Twenty-three minutes later, despite the threatening storm and the shortened dive window, the ship erupted into cheers when Livvy reported, "It's here! We found it! It's just where Nemo said it would be! We found the Nautilus!"

Michael and Berna rocked each other in a glee-filled embrace among the cheers and hoots. Berna's eyes burst with tears of pride. Doyle blew the ship's horn. History was made. Everyone aboard would have their name memorialized.

Twenty-eight minutes later, a defiant Livvy was still searching the wreck, sixteen minutes beyond their cutoff.

"Dr. Thomson, I'm not asking. Start your ascent, now," a crewman demanded over the underwater telephone. A growing group including Michael, Berna, and a red-faced Doyle were gathered around the small submersible command center set up near the ship's stern.

Doyle's brows were furled, his tolerance of Livvy's defiance nearing its end.

"I told you, five minutes," Livvy persisted.

Michael stood with his arms crossed. He turned and whispered to Berna. "She's making it worse on herself. Doyle is never going to let her dive after this. Sometimes she's so…bull-headed."

Cracking a wry smile, Berna whispered back. "Well, you know, I hear it's not entirely her fault. She gets it honest from that damn mother of hers. Good thing you're not in love with her or anything."

The crewman cursed.

Doyle placed a hand on the crewman's shoulder and took the microphone. His voice was level, yet commanding. "Dr. Thomson, Captain Doyle. I'll allow you five. But, one second longer and there's a cozy spot in my brig waiting just for you. Understood, Doctor?"

After a short silence, Livvy responded, "Thank you Captain, I—" She screamed, "Oh my God, what is—"

Everyone jumped at the electrical snap of the phone going dead. At the same moment, something beneath the ocean pulsed a brilliant electric blue. The deck lights went dark. Radars and antennas whirling above crept to a halt and engine vibrations faded. The sounds of a living ship gave way to the distant rumble of thunder and waves crashing.

"Livvy," Michael gasped, his panicked eyes meeting Berna's.

Doyle scanned the state of his ship, his face stoic. "Everyone, stay calm. General Quarters! Command Staff to the bridge." He turned and growled at the phone operators. "Get those divers up here, if you got to cast a damn net." He stepped out.

Michael gripped the deck railing, fixated on the swells slamming the powerless ship. His watch useless, he estimated it'd been approximately thirty minutes since anyone heard from the divers. The storm was threatening, almost atop the research vessel. The helpless crew were in a frenzy to restore power, still having no clue what killed all shipboard electronics.

Michael turned to the professor to see how she was faring. Livvy and she had found the Nautilus, but at what cost?

The professor sat on a small folding stool, leaning forward on her knees, gazing into the storm bearing down. A proud woman, her true feelings were guarded behind a confident smile. Her eyes betrayed her. In trying times, they'd cry her true emotions in encrypted whispers Michael learned to decode after years under her mentorship.

She was human after all, and nervous.

A cheer from the phone operators pulled his attention. They were monitoring the guideline dropped in the water, now their only way of communicating with the divers. A series of tugs from the divers communicated their status. They counted five tugs.

"Divers in distress," a crewman called, translating the tugs. "They're at their last safety stop. Get medical ready."

"What type of distress? Which diver?" Michael asked trying to hide his panic.

The crewman's response was grim, "You know what I know."

"There they are!"

The cry sent Michael and Berna bolting to the starboard railing.

Livvy struggled to stay atop twenty-foot swells, clutching an unconscious Henry in one arm, waving frantically with the other. They'd surfaced right as the storm began to intensify, ship and divers at the mercy of gale force wind and waves. Adding to the danger, lightning struck the water about a mile out.

"Two ships to port!"

The announcement whipped Michael around and he saw two large cutters, clearly labeled US Coast Guard.

Once the divers were on board, Henry was rushed away. Michael and Berna were immediately at Livvy's side.

Livvy was all teeth, a flashing blue light emanating from her bag.

Doyle ran over, demanding, "What happened down there? We're dead in the water."

"I found the homing beacon! It works!" Livvy exclaimed.

"My God, you found it," the professor gasped. "What happened? Are you all right?"

"I'm fine," Livvy assured him.

"Tech on Nemo's ship did this?" Doyle asked.

Livvy shook her head slow. "Not Nemo's ship."

"What about the Coast Guard?" Michael asked.

Livvy's smile dropped as she gaped at the giant ships sitting only a mile out. "Um, shit. Okay, uh, we need to buy some time. I need a satellite phone with a camera."

"Phone," Michael barked to one of his students who darted off.

"That phone isn't going to work," Doyle said. "And, what's coming? Are we in danger?"

"No." She reached in her bag and snatched out the homing beacon, a black, metallic rod with a silver tip. It flashed blue, light emanating from the metal itself. "It must be doing it, disrupting everything."

"Beacon? Who the hell is it calling?" Doyle insisted.

"Whoever Nemo found inside the Earth. It's letting them know we're ready," the professor explained.

Michael's impatience was bubbling. "What's happening? Someone fill me in."

Livvy pointed to a line where two halves of the rod came together, a faded black half that had spent many years beneath water, and a glossy onyx half.

"This shiny half was in the capsule. Nemo wrote the two halves would connect automatically. I didn't know how. When I pulled it from the bag, this half shot up from the wreck and smacked Henry. Shattered his arm. The halves joined and the phone went dead."

They gaped at it, light coming right out of metal. Michael's doubts began to falter.

The sky opened in a blinding downpour.

"Here's the phone," the student said running up.

Livvy took the phone and began punching buttons.

Berna glanced back at the ships and grabbed Livvy's hand. "Liv, we should get in the water with the phone. The Coast Guard may not look for us there."

Michael was bemused, "Wait, what?"

A wave slammed against the side of the ship, sending everyone stumbling. Doyle cursed. "I need control of my ship. Turn that damn thing off first."

Livvy stared at it for a moment, grabbed it with both hands, and tried pulling it apart. It wouldn't budge. She tried twisting, nothing. Her eyes went to the shiny piece at the tip. She pressed it. The halves split.

The ship's deck lighting came on. A crewman yelled, "Captain! Everything is coming up! Coast Guard wants us to hold position and prepare for boarding!"

"Do what they say," Doyle commanded. "If you two are going, now's the time."

Another flash of lightening streaked the sky with a boom of thunder casting chills down Michael's spine.

Livvy and her mother locked eyes as if to ready themselves.

Michael cursed, realizing what was about to happen.

The two women bolted aft and hurdled over the railing.

Michael darted after, went up and over the rail to splash near them.

Both women looked surprised. Livvy beamed. "CHO."

He threw his hands up. "I might be crazy, but not scared. And, you disappeared from me once. Not again."

"Welcome to the fold, Michael. You're all in now," Berna said.

He nodded. "Now what?"

Bolts of lightning lit the sky. Livvy lifted the satellite phone, pressing buttons. "We go live. Hope the beacon was on long enough."

"Who you calling?" Michael asked.

"Anyone willing to listen. I'm broadcasting on Facebook," Livvy replied.

Berna said, "Give me the phone. I'll hold, you talk, baby."

"Okay, Mom. Get in here, Michael, you're part of this now, too."

The professor nodded.

Livvy began, "I am Dr. Olivia Johnson, with Doctors Bernadetta Johnson and Michael Chen. I may not have much time, so I'll get to it. After discovering Captain Nemo's lost journal, we found his Nautilus. There's more. Nemo found an inner world via an underwater tunnel while trying to reach the North Pole. The inner earth is home to another race of Earthlings, responsible for UFO sightings throughout history."

A giant wave sent them tumbling, only to yank them back in the opposite direction, choking.

The rain stopped.

Michael rubbed frantically at his burning eyes, distantly aware of Livvy and Berna staring upward. His vision cleared to find the research vessel and distant ships veiled behind a heavy wall of rain.

"What the…" Rain fell all around, but not on them. Something blocked it from above. He turned his gaze skyward.

A triangular craft, pitch black and larger than any aircraft he'd ever seen, hung silently above them. Blinding white lights ran along its outer edges.

"My God, just what I remembered," Michael gasped, "

Berna handed the phone to Livvy. "Say something, baby."

Livvy swallowed, finding her words. "Nemo left us a beacon to call them. No more secrets. No more cover ups. The aliens we've searched for were here all along beneath our feet. Not extra-terrestrials, but fellow earthlings. We are not alone."

The Silent Agenda

Mike Adamson

*T*he journey to 188 Fleet Street was a familiar one for the distinguished Reverend Lewis Page Mercier. The fifty-one-year old Oxonian scholar, chaplain and headmaster recalled making numerous prior visits to the premises of Sampson Low, Publishers, in connection with his religious texts. Now, in the blustery September of 1871, Mercier felt honored to accept an invitation from the firm in connection with a new work they wished to propose.

A doorman opened the carriage for him to alight upon the busy footpath, and escorted him into the foyer with all deference due a man of his stature. An aide then whisked him to the first-floor offices and into a very august presence indeed, for, important writer though he may be, rarely was he graced with the company of the venerable Mr. Sampson Low Senior himself.

A crackling hearth added light and heat to the sumptuous office. Now seventy-four years of age, the portly Low rose stiffly from an overstuffed armchair with the help of a walking stick, to shake hands. The Oxonian, relieved of hat and coat, sank into a companion chair as the aide served brandy. When they were alone, the again-seated elderly publisher folded his hands on the curve of his stick and eyed the academic.

"Delighted you could come, Lewis. I think it'll be to your benefit."

Mercier could have read many things into that statement. Despite his discretion, word had leaked that he owed money, having borrowed 250 pounds six years earlier, a sum secured by his friend and associate, Lord Leigh of Stoneleigh. His declining health prevented him from settling the debt, forcing him to supplement his income on the side. He had raised much-needed capital by translating a number of books for the Lows, from both French and German, but always under some pseudonymised rearrangement of his name, preserving his actual moniker for his serious, religious work.

"Your telegram mentioned a major translation project," Mercier began, his smile in no way suggesting he was desperate for the income. He was happy for his financial circumstances to remain unmentioned between social equals.

"Indeed. Would you be available to take on some book-length projects?" At Mercier's smile, the elderly Low nodded. "Excellent, excellent! Tell me, have you heard of the Frenchman, Verne?"

Mercier gave the faintest shake of the head.

"No? His novels have been causing something of a sensation on the continent over the last several years. Grand adventure stories but with a strong theme of educating the reader as to the whys and wherefores of natural history, geology, engineering, and all such matters scientific."

Mercier spread his hands and shrugged. "I am a cleric by both inclination and training, sir, a man of God. I know precious little of these modern sciences. Indeed, they are a source of veritable antipathy to me, since even before that Huxley fellow so shamed the great Owen over the whole unsavory Darwin business." His manner was cool, and for a moment his propriety almost overcame his need. "In view of this, I'm uncertain if I would be the best man for such a task."

"Nonsense, old man. You're made for it! Just hear me out..." Low frowned and sipped his brandy, taking his time reaching his words. "I've been in this business a long, long time, Lewis. I've seen the nature of the world ebb and change, and it cannot be denied that science has been of great benefit to mankind. Where would we be without the steam engine, the electric telegraph and so forth? At this very moment, railway trains are passing beneath the streets of London, carrying tens of thousands of passengers each day. The venerable Mr. Charles Babbage has long promoted the notion that machines may some day routinely perform complex mathematical operations. Why, there are visionaries who say there will even be flying contraptions that go where they will, with the command and alacrity of ships upon the sea, that make the balloons of today seem as far back as the Ark." His straggly eyebrows rose over eyes that glinted with firelight. "And, mark me well, Lewis, all such notions are the grist for our Monsieur Verne's particular mill. Since 1864 he has been under a twenty-year contract with the publisher Pierre-Jules Hetzel, delivering three volumes a year, first for serialization in Hetzel's magazine, thence into book form. Those delivered to date have met with enormous public approval. They have been translated into German, Russian and many other languages." He paused with a frank smile, as if he spoke of the most elemental practicalities of business. "Naturally, we feel it's time for an English edition, and are delighted to have secured those rights."

"And you're offering me the task?" Mercier smiled affably, less stiff now. "An honor, sir."

"If the success of these titles throughout the English-speaking world turns out anything like that of its Francophone original, it will be an enormous success for the company, and your translations will doubtless be read internationally for many years to come."

"I shall do my best, sir." Mercier sipped his brandy, regarding the firelight through the golden fluid. "You mentioned *books*, plural."

Low reached to an occasional table at his side where three massive, leather-bound hardbacks rested. "We're hoping to release three titles into the British market in time for Christmas, 1872. That gives you a little over a year. Can you count on at least some assistance?"

"I'm sure I can secure the services of Miss King for the duration. She has worked with me on previous projects." He was eyeing the volumes with slight apprehension at their size. "All three in a year?"

"If at all possible." Low hefted the first volume, green leather stamped with gold foil. "This is Verne's latest best-seller, published by Hetzel last year. *Twenty Thousand Leagues Under the Sea*. It's a rather fanciful tale of a ship which travels not upon the sea but beneath it, allowing explorers and naturalists to examine a whole new world revealed below." He passed the volume over and took up the next two. "These are about adventurers making a voyage to the Moon and back!" Mercier laughed with a scoffing inflection and a shake of his greying head. "Indeed, indeed. Well, everyone is agreed. Monsieur Verne's imagination is second to none. He has captured the public's enthusiasm in no small way, and the fact of the matter is that the Anglophone population is eager to enjoy these works too. Britain, the United States, the Canadian and Australian colonies, why the market is enormous, and we foresee subletting the English rights to partnering publishers elsewhere." Now he sobered somewhat. "But first comes the task of producing a palatable English text."

"Palatable?" Mercier raised an eyebrow. "Meaning what, precisely?" He set the volume down in his lap, having barely glanced at the contents. "Do you have a guideline to which you wish me to work?"

Sampson Low took his time finding his reply, and Mercier's brow furrowed as the seconds passed. At last the aged publisher sipped the fiery spirit again and began with a tight, somewhat sour expression. "Propriety admonishes us to tread with care in this, Lewis. We are dealing with a special writer, and seeking a potential fortune, yet our own interests are also very much in focus."

Mercier frowned in puzzlement.

"Allow me explain," Low went on. "Verne is being acknowledged a giant, whose works are expected to flow like water for many years to come. He's only forty-three years of age, and absolutely has the bit in his teeth. The man is being hailed a prophet, a visionary, though he remains personally quite modest on such matters, I'm told. In 1870, they made him a Knight of the Legion of Honor—yes, they think that highly of him. But that same year English literature lost Charles Dickens, a blow from which some felt it would be a long time recovering. Now, Verne is popularizing science, inspiring a new generation of scholars to seek practical means to make his sort of imaginings reality." A grizzled brow was raised at the cleric. "And the continentals are taking him *seriously*, both as a writer of proper literature and a foreteller of the future." His expression was less than amused, despite the obvious fields of profit which seemed to beckon any publisher able to secure a selection of works, and Mercier's eyes narrowed in anticipation of his next words. "His work is of unquestioned value, but—" here, Low paused "—different national characters and attitudes view certain aspects in differing ways."

Mercier sat forward and handled the book as if it were uncomfortably warm to the touch. "How exactly do you wish me to proceed?"

"Oh, preserve the adventure. The adventure comes first. Our own best brains see a rich market among the young, indeed for many in this country, and others. But we anticipate little interest among adults for Verne's work. Despite the age of very real wonders in which we live, they are unlikely to be credible enough to entertain notions such as *he* puts forth, nor follow his scientific passages. And children, who are sure to love the adventures, will also be lost by the latter. So..." Low lowered his voice and spoke candidly. "We feel it would be best if the scientific material were to be trimmed well back. There's no call to agonise over the precision, if you follow me. One may take it as read that the submarine boat *works*, in the way one accepts that dragons in fantasy fly. They just *do*, no need to belabor the explanations as to how. They slow down the show and serve only to puzzle most." Low took the volume back and browsed through the heavy-stock pages, pausing at the plate illustrations. "The same with his interminable catalogues of marine life encountered, and his digressions into historical events." He turned a page, tapped a passage. "Just a few pages in, he's telling us the horsepower and tonnage of Cunard's fleet. I ask you, do we really need such details? And so forth, throughout the text... You can comfortably delete a fair part of that. No one will ever notice it's gone, and it'll improve the flow for the average reader. Then there are other matters..."

"Such as?" Mercier asked, his brows down.

"Well, if we are styling the work to be best aimed at children, there are lengthy characterization passages which would bore young readers or simply be over their heads. It's actually an uncomfortably long book to ask a child to concentrate upon. You could easily lose, oh, a fifth of its length."

Mercier squinted for a long moment, "You're asking me to substantially edit and abridge the volume, not simply transpose French to English?"

"Just so."

Now Mercier shook his head faintly and raised a hand. "I must interrupt you, sir. The role of the translator is to faithfully transliterate a work from one language to another, making neither deletion nor addition, but providing the best, most accurate and, where the idiosyncrasies of language come into play, the most sensitive approximation of the material. He must in the process preserve both fact, spirit and the native beauty of expression, if his work is to be deemed other than a failure. This is the art of the translator, and the time-honored ethic thereof. As a man of God, I may be antithetical to science's invasion of our lives and thoughts, but that does not mean I would betray the tenets of my trade, nor undermine the integrity of a fellow writer."

Low eyed him silently for long moments from beneath his bushy brows and sipped brandy before nodding slowly. "You are a man of integrity, Lewis, and I would have been disappointed had you not made such protest. I appreciate your finer sentiments here, I truly do, though I must question whether a gentleman who has found himself in unfortunate pecuniary circumstances can in fact afford ethics so elevated."

Mercier blinked and stiffened in his chair. "I am aware that beggars have not the luxury of choice, sir, but, though my situation is not as I would wish it, I have yet to be reduced to the status of beggary."

"Of course, of course." Low spread his hands and smiled. "Not insinuating anything, old man. But the fact remains we have developed a policy as to how we wish these works to be brought into our language, and the changes we propose are by no means petty or without carefully considered reason. There is purpose in this, I assure you. Will you at least hear what remains to be said?"

After a long moment Mercier, perhaps recognizing his all-too real circumstances, ameliorated his air and nodded. "Very well. Do go on, sir."

Low smiled now and explained in a fatherly way, "The matters I mentioned before simply require a tailoring of literary style toward an intended audience, the approach we feel best suits the majority audience in the English-speaking world. This tailoring accommodates the differences in national character and temperament across that narrow channel of water that have driven the tensions between our nations for so very long. We're roast beef, they're frog's legs, and that's the long and short of it. We're asking you to serve up roast beef."

Mercier had not failed to notice that, at his objection, the singular had become the plural, implying that the full editorial board of the company was united in its decision that Verne should be interpreted for this new audience. He breathed a long sigh and considered what he was being asked to do. "Science, characterisation, facts and figures, digressions…" The truth was, he *did* need the money. "Well, if I am to perform an editor's job, then I shall require an editor's pay, in addition to that of a translator."

"Certainly, old man, that would be entirely appropriate." Low eyed him shrewdly for a long moment. "I sense you're still not convinced that the task is ethically sound."

"I have reservations, sir, it's true. Is there anything else you wish to draw to my attention? Anything which may help clarify the firm's intentions toward this work?"

The fire's crackle punctuated a long silence, then Low tapped the green leather cover. "There is one other point. An important one, bearing strongly upon the need for a firm editorial hand. Those better versed in the language than I, have told me there is a strong political theme in this book. Monsieur Verne is a liberal, he believes in revolutionaries, socialists, abolitionists, all such radicals. Though he is careful, introducing the matters delicately and quite late in the proceedings, it is also quite unambiguous.

"At one point he informs us the mysterious captain of this vessel has a rogues' gallery of such figures framed and hung in his quarters. It is revealed he funds seditionists, and uses this strange vessel as a weapon of war to further such aims." Now Low shook his head firmly. *"No, sir.* The vessel as a weapon is part of the exciting adventure, certainly, and, couched in mystery, speaks merely to the madness of the captain, a masterly foil for our heroes. But the radical underpinning of his political convictions is nothing to which we would wish young readers in the English-speaking world exposed. Those are ideas we have no desire to promote as they encourage the destabilization of existing social order. We feel a judicious trim is indicated."

Mercier finished his brandy and breathed deeply. Low had perhaps found the fulcrum upon which he might be moved, and he acknowledged both a flash of sympathy to the sentiment and an abrupt sense of distancing from the work. Maybe his ethics were for sale after all. It did not feel right or comfortable, but as excuses went it appealed to both piety and nationalism. "Well, sir, as a man of the church I have no real issue with thinning out the ramblings of science." As he spoke, he wondered if Low had offered him the job for precisely that reason. "Politically, I am of conservative bent, and would similarly have no wish for French radicalism to be supported in this country any further, no matter the public sympathy for the sufferings of their peasantry. As we have read in our newspapers, just a matter of months ago France lost its defensive war with Germany. It has settled as a socialist state, even suffering a brief civil war in the process that cost twenty thousand casualties, so there's little wonder *intelligentsia* across the channel see Verne's leanings as topical and apt. But…" He forced the words out, wondering how far he would go to make good his debts. "I must concur, they are an uncomfortable sentiment to the British sensibility—an unrequired element, certainly a distraction, if adventure is to be the theme." The words sounded like justifications in his own ears, and his hands trembled in his lap.

"We're agreed, then," Low returned with a smile, smoothing over the difficulty with the skill of long practice. "Let's concentrate on the exotic aspects, the spectacle, the wonders of the world below, all sorts of watery myth and legend, and leave aside real-world overtones and the pedantry of mathematicians and physicists, alike." He smiled tightly, eyes in a maze of wrinkles lit strangely by the fire's glow. "I mean, it's uninteresting, unnecessary, not what we would wish the work be, to entertain the Englishman in his home, as distinct from the Frenchman in his. And for those of us who fought the French long ago, or are concerned by the ongoing naval arms race the French launched upon us in '59, do we really need a French writer to be hailed in our world as highly as in his own?" He shrugged. "The decision falls to us, at this point in time, to protect Britain, her territories and dominions, from even the shadow of such influences." He was whispering now. "Many would see it as a *duty.*"

Mercier saw he no longer had a choice, other than financial purgatory, and he accepted what part of him realized was a devil's bargain. He no longer outwardly allowed conflict to register. His expression had solidified, a solemn look that acknowledged the gravity of Low's words. He did not speak; he did not have to, his eyes gave all the agreement, all the assent, Low needed.

The publisher went on. "Let Monsieur Verne be a children's writer among us, and let that be enough. After all, few Englishmen will ever speak good enough French to know the difference, and even fewer Frenchmen would deign to open an edition in any other language. The odds of our ever being criticized for censorship are acceptably remote."

Mercier smiled with a polite chuckle, disappointed with himself but resigned to playing the part in which necessity had cast him. "And this applies more or less to all three books?"

"Certainly. I shall leave the minutia of the editorial process to your own good sense. I trust your intuitions and the certainties from which you proceed."

"Leave it to me, sir," Mercier said softly, his manner adding silently, *don't worry, I'll put this upstart frog celebrity in his place. And take all this science down a peg or two in the process. Just so long as I'm paid what I need.*

Low rang a silver bell and the aide appeared moments later. The publisher gave orders for the three volumes to be placed in a valise for the translator, then rose with the aid of his stick to shake hands once more. "Thank you, Lewis. We would like the volumes ready as soon as possible, typesetting runs away with time, as you know. Let's say, November next year as the proposed date of issue for our French fabulist's watery romp?" They shook again and the aide accompanied Mercier from the office, carrying the valise.

Soon they were in Fleet Street and a hansom was hailed, the bag placed aboard, and Mercier gave directions to the driver. But as the horse clopped away into the traffic of the city, he ran a hand over the bag, felt the solid weight of the volumes, and for a moment regretted the impasse to which he had been forced. But that was the doing of powers greater than the mortal, and he set it aside with some effort of will, to glance into the valise. He knew what a task lay before him. Speed was key, it seemed, and he had been given a liberal hand to excise, so he foresaw some generous deletions.

Best to get started. He opened the bag and drew out *Twenty Thousand Leagues Under the Sea*, opened it to the first page and translated in his head.

Chapter 1: A Shifting Reef
The year 1866 was signalized by a remarkable incident...

His eyes raced over the text, the gears of his mind meshed upon the instructions he had received, and by the fourth paragraph he found reference to four great French scientists by name.

Yes, he thought, *parochial, difficult to pronounce, uninteresting to an Englishman. That passage can go for a start...*

Fools Rush In

Allison Tebo

Quirt **Jenkins took tight hold of a line and tried not to** think about how much air was floating beneath his dusty boots. He glanced at the others.

He reckoned they were the first people in the world to ever try to land a hot air balloon on top of a submarine.

"I think I'm going to be sick," Lopez announced. He stared dolefully over the side at the waves below. "I also think we're going to die."

Casper Archibald Ludenmeyer III, conman, gambler, snake oil sales man, and liar extraordinaire, hooked his fingers into the lapels of his fancy suit. "You can trust the plan, Señor! The treasure of the Nautilus shall be ours for the plucking!"

"And we'll be famous!" Juliette Dupont put in, fiddling with the gas burner of her balloon.

"And rich," Quirt pointed out. That was the important part and he didn't want anyone to forget it.

Everyone looked at Lee Chin for his inspirational input but he just twirled his knife and examined the whiny Lopez as if imagining how he would look without hair.

"You tricked me into being here," Lopez complained to Casper. "I was drunk and didn't realize I was agreeing to an early death!"

"Have faith!" Casper urged him. "I have no doubt in my mind that we will succeed. Between Mr. Lee's ingenious devices, Miss

Dupont's piloting skills, Señor Lopez's inside information, Quirt's uh, brawn, and *my* unparalleled mental superiority—how could we possibly lose?"

"I can think of about one hundred ways," Lopez mumbled. "Most of them end painfully."

"Tut, tut, Señor. You're demoralizing the team!"

Quirt, Lee, and Juliette exchanged looks. None of them looked demoralized.

"You simply have to believe," Casper insisted.

"I do," Lopez retorted. "I believe that this won't work."

Casper didn't respond, merely pointed to the sea beneath them. "There it is!"

Quirt took a look over the side as they sped across the sky and Juliette began their descent.

"Looks like a floating cigar," he remarked.

"More like a whale," Lee offered.

"*Magnifique!*" Juliette breathed, leaning over the basket for a better look.

Quirt grabbed her by the back of her dress. He didn't fancy the idea of her pitching out into the sea and leaving four helpless lunkheads alone in a hot air balloon.

"Unhand me!" Juliette snapped.

"I was just trying to keep you from killing yourself."

They glared at one another. Quirt had long since stopped trying to get on her good side. Juliette wasn't impressed by anything that couldn't fly.

Juliette Dupont was a Frenchwoman from Louisiana who had used to work with her pappy, a crazy aeronaut attempting to become a famous balloonist. He died before he could. Juliette had managed to transport her hot air balloon, Le Papillon, out West, thinking she might have more success making a living as a balloonist here than back East. No one had taken her seriously except Casper.

"All those critics," Juliette was muttering under her breath. "All those reporters who refused to interview me. All those stupid, simpleminded *men*."

"Hey," Quirt protested.

Juliette ignored him. "I will be the first woman to land a balloon on a seagoing vessel!"

Quirt rolled his eyes. "Pretty safe to say that you'll be the only one."

Casper, however, was bowing to Juliette. "You will go down in history, madam. I assure you."

"I'd better," Juliette growled.

"Just as long as she doesn't go down in the *water*, that's all I care about," Lopez groaned. Quirt rolled his eyes.

Not long ago, Lopez had been a rebel fighter with Benito Juarez. The captain of the Nautilus had been providing Juarez with weapons, and Lopez had met the man during a rendezvous in this very bay, just off the coast of Mexico.

At some point after that, Lopez had gotten in trouble with his own people and left Juarez's outfit. Sitting in a saloon south of Tijuana, he had started rambling about the incredible floating monster named the Nautilus with a cargo hold full of gold.

And Casper had overheard, bought him another drink, and hatched this whole crazy plan that very night.

And now they had to drag the whiner along because he had been aboard the Nautilus for precisely fifteen minutes and knew its interior layout, particularly the way to the hold. He had also given Casper the piece of information that had sparked the whole plan. The Nautilus had to surface to replenish its supply of air every twenty-four hours. It was their way in.

"There's someone on deck," Lee spoke up, pointing and he reached into his knapsack and coolly removed a stick of dynamite. "Should I use this?"

"Get that away from the burner!" Juliette screeched.

Casper's eyes bulged. "Mr. Chin, please control yourself."

Lee sighed, but did as Juliette instructed and stowed the dynamite away.

No one was quite sure why Lee was there. Casper called him a scientist determined to test his devices. Quirt suspected that Lee was there more out of sheer curiosity than anything else. He seemed to view the rest of them as some kind of bizarre sideshow that he had joined out of boredom.

As for Quirt, he was there because he liked fighting. That, and he needed the money.

They were dropping steadily now. Quirt could see the man on the deck of the Nautilus clearly.

"Must be a lookout." He drew his pistol and began taking potshots at the man.

"Ha, look at him, dance," Quirt laughed as the man scuttled for cover. "He's going below and he's shut the hatch behind him. The deck's clear."

Juliette turned down the burner and they began dropping even more rapidly.

Lee passed out gas masks and Lopez, Quirt and Casper tucked them into their belts. Lee began passing out the ropes anchored by large magnets that would allow them to catch a hold of the submarine's steel deck as they passed over it.

"Now!" Juliette shouted.

The men leaned over the side and let loose their lines. They reached for the Nautilus like tentacles, the magnets adhering to the deck with a series of thuds. The lines snapped taut and, for a brief moment, Le Papillon was floating directly over the Nautilus, no more than twenty feet from its deck.

Quirt dropped another line over the side. His boots hit the deck a second later and he hurried to secure the magnetic anchor Lee dropped down to him. He waved his hat at the others to signal the all clear when he had finished.

Lee was the first one down the rope and began wiring the hatch with sticks of dynamite, carefully connecting the fuses. Quirt watched as Lee shuffling backwards, releasing a stream of gunpowder from a canister that he had pulled out of his knapsack.

"You've got all kinds of fun things in that pack, haven't you?" Quirt joked.

Lee just grunted and kept duck-walking backwards.

Lopez had finally floundered his way to the deck and ended up on his knees, obviously dizzy. Casper followed, tried to make a grand leap to the deck, but ended up clinging to Quirt to steady himself.

Lee capped his canister and looked at Casper.

Casper took in a gust of air and looked ready to give another grand speech but Quirt cut him off. "Save it, Casper." He nodded to Lee. "Light it up."

Lee struck a match and touched it to the trail of gunpowder.

The four men ducked down, taking what cover they could. Lopez covered his eyes. The stream of fire raced across the deck, its hiss indiscernible in the wind.

The explosion wasn't as bad as Quirt thought it would be, but it was effective. The round metal hatch went flying into the air and over the side with a splash.

Lee removed a small grenade full of sleeping gas from his pack, flicked his thumb across its surface, and tossed it down the open hatch.

"Now we wait," Casper said, straightening with dignity. "And have your guns at the ready, Mr. Quirt, in case any of the crew try to come topside."

Quirt drew his pistols, itching for action.

They waited for what felt like an eternity to Quirt, but no one appeared.

"They must all be unconscious!" Casper said triumphantly. He doffed his cap to Juliette, who was peering cautiously over the edge of Le Papillon's basket. "We will return!" Casper turned to Lee. "We'll secure the ship and locate the treasure. Get the ship's boat ready and start assembling the sledge. Once we have carried the gold to the deck, we'll load it onto the sledge and slide it across the deck and offload it onto the dinghy. When we've loaded as much as it can hold, Señor Lopez—being the one most familiar with this part of the coast—will take the gold ashore. And Quirt will go with him to row."

Quirt scuffed the deck. It was no secret that he hadn't been recruited for his brains but Casper didn't need to go on and make it quite so obvious.

"Mr. Chin, Miss Dupont and I will take the balloon and whatever gems we can carry in the Papillon and rendezvous at our designated meeting place."

"I *know* the plan," said Lee, testiness coloring the edges of his inscrutable calm. He didn't look like a man standing on top of one of the greatest treasure troves in the world. He looked as if he were about to take a nap.

"Very well, then." Casper turned to Lopez and Quirt and gestured to the blown hatch. "Down we go, gentlemen."

Juliette began lowering the supplies for the sledge over the side of the Papillon to the waiting Lee.

Quirt, Casper, and Lopez hurried across the deck, slipping on their gas masks as they ran, but they all stopped and hesitated at the hatch. When it came right down to it, none of them were anxious to go down into this steel beast where who knew what might be waiting for them. Throwing the others a disgusted look, Quirt finally took the lead.

He clambered down a ladder and dropped down into the Nautilus, drawing both guns.

The gas from Lee's bombs was still lying thickly about the place, obscuring details. Quirt had a brief glimpse of metal riveted bulkheads, panels of levers and gears, and gleaming brass rails. It was something like a ship, but like no ship he had ever been on. It was like being in the belly of some monster.

He didn't much care for it.

There were a few bodies lying near the hatch: the Nautilus crew. All of them were unconscious.

Lopez and Casper joined him and Lopez gestured for them to head toward a circular staircase that led to a lower deck.

They descended, and as they made their way through the Nautilus, Lee stopped outside each doorway before they passed through it and tossed another sleeping gas bomb ahead of them to ensure that their forced entry went unchallenged. They met no one, and if they passed more unconscious bodies it was impossible to tell through the gas that enveloped each new chamber. Quirt had to admit that he was a little disappointed. He had been brought along because of his fighting skills, and he had rather been hoping he could knock a few heads together. If this all played out as peacefully and easily as Casper had planned, he wouldn't have a single dadblame thing to contribute.

"Well done, gentlemen!" Casper declared. "The ship is ours!" He gestured to Lopez. "Señor—lead us to the treasure vault."

Quirt raised his eyebrows. "Shouldn't we search the ship and see if the whole complement is accounted for? Maybe lock these sailors into their cabins?"

Casper nodded. "An excellent suggestion, Quirt. Why don't you begin doing that, while I just make sure that Lopez knows the way to the, er, ballast."

Quirt stiffened. "Not a chance, Casper. If you're going to start divvying the gold up now, I ain't letting you out of my sight."

"Tsk, tsk," Casper reproved. "Such mistrust is unseemly amongst a company such as ours."

"Yeah, yeah," Quirt snorted. He jerked a thumb at Lopez. "Go to it, amigo."

Lopez led them through the vessel. The passageways were lit by electric globes hanging from the overhead that cast a dull radiance over the dark chambers they passed through.

They hurried down yet another circular staircase, and stopped at the bottom in a small, round room full of various doors and cabinets.

Lopez pointed toward the one set of double doors and whispered. "The hold."

Quirt cranked the door open and it swung wide...revealing a treasure trove inside.

There were *piles* of gold. Coins mostly, but amongst the golden mountains was the glint of rubies, emeralds, and sapphires. There were crowns, scepters, statuettes, even swords—all of them glittering and encrusted with gems.

As they stared at it all, a ripple of coins suddenly slithered down one of the piles with a seductive clink of gold.

"My friends," Casper said in a hushed voice. "I give you the treasure of Atlantis. The loot of a thousand civilizations. The undisclosed mysteries of the ocean floor. The gold of kings and the gems of empresses. All I can say in this moment is—"

"Get outta my way!" Quirt bellowed, elbowing his way to the front. Lopez was right on his heels.

Casper abandoned all attempts at dignity and ran after them like a kid running toward birthday cake.

"I'm gonna buy me America!" Quirt whooped, scooping treasure into his pockets.

"With money like this, I can go somewhere safe!" Lopez crowed. "Like...San Francisco!"

Casper was polishing a ring on his vest, his expression dreamy. "The world is our oyster, gentlemen!"

Quirt began to respond, but stopped. Hidden beneath the sound of his own voice and the exclamations of the others, Quirt's ear caught at a soft metallic thud from behind.

He whipped around, and his blood curdled.

Standing in the anteroom and looking into the treasure room were four monsters. They were shaped like men, but covered in some strange rubbery skin. In place of heads, hideous, bulbous helmets with thick glass obscured their faces. If they had faces.

"G-glory be," Quirt stammered.

Lopez and Casper turned around to look.

There was a brief moment of silence broken by nothing but the sound of treasure dropping from frozen hands.

Quirt noticed that the four men each carried a weapon that looked like a cross between a gun and a harpoon. His suspicions were confirmed when one of them raised his weapon and fired a lance that would have impaled Quirt if he hadn't jerked to one side.

The seamen began to advance. Their voices were hollow, but they seemed to be shouting in some foreign language.

Scared out of his wits, and acting on instinct, Quirt slapped leather and brought both Colts up, muzzles blazing.

"Don't—!" Casper began, "It will richoche—heeeey!" He broke off struggling with one of the seamen as one of Quirt's bullets whizzed by his head and bounced off the bulkhead, sending all of them scattering for cover.

The crew of the Nautilus retreated into the atrium while Quirt, Casper, and Lopez took cover behind the doors of the treasure room. Quirt thought of slamming them shut, but the doors only locked from the outside. It would be the same as locking themselves in jail.

But the predominate thought in his mind was not how to escape.

"What in tarnation are these fellas wearing?" Quirt hollered, a little more shook up than he cared to admit.

"Diving suits!" Lopez called back from across the room.

He didn't sound as rattled as Quirt and that made him mad. "What in the name of all that's unholy is a diving suit?"

"It's a suit that allows them to breath underwater!"

"Son of a gun," Quirt murmured, his head whirling with this piece of indigestible information. He should have stuck to robbing trains and stagecoaches. They were things he could understand.

He leaned around the door and fired off another round. The bullet pinged off the man's helmet and didn't penetrate, but it still struck him with enough force to send him staggering back. The effect was probably like having a soup pot on your head and then having someone hit it with a ladle. The thought made Quirt laugh, but he stopped laughing when his own bullet came flying past his head after ricocheting off the man's helmet.

He dove for the ground and the bullet burrowed into a pile of gold, sending coins scattering. If he kept firing he would more than likely kill himself. He didn't so much mind about Casper taking a bullet—preferably to the jaw—but he needed Lopez in one piece to lead him out of this mechanical contraption if things went any further south.

Quirt holstered his pistols, snatched up a crown from a nearby pile of treasure, and sent it flying. It caught the seamen in the side of the helmet and he staggered backwards. Quirt spotted a jewel-encrusted sword in the pile of treasure beside him and snatched it up.

Aside from swinging around his daddy's cavalry sword when he was a tot, he hadn't ever handled a sword in his life but, as far as he could tell, there was nothing to it. He just started swinging.

Lopez had also holstered his gun in favor of his fists. For all of his previous whining, he was fighting like a devil, but praying like a saint—mostly in Spanish, for in his excitement, he seemed to have forgotten every scrap of English he possessed.

Casper, it seemed, was more of an ideas man than a fighter. His pearl handled pistol and nice manners might have served him well in a duel, but for a tooth-knocking, bone-cracking brawl he was sadly unsuited. He had tried to hit one of the seamen with the butt of his pistol but the gun had bounced off the man's helmet and snapped back to hit Casper in the forehead.

Casper fell to his knees, but he gamely tried to trip a seaman by clinging to his legs. The seamen brought an end to that by picking Casper up and tossing him into a pile of gold. Casper's head clunked against a scepter and he lay there, stunned.

Quirt managed to disarm the seamen he was fighting, more by sheer brutality than skill, but his sword went flying out of his hands when it bounced off the seamen's suit. Quirt planted a foot on the fallen man to hold him down, and his blurred gaze snagged on the one Nautilus crewman who had not charged the treasure room but was standing placidly by the staircase in the anteroom. He was the biggest man of the bunch and was clearly the one giving orders. Quirt took an instant dislike to the man that had come between him and his treasure and put his head down and charged with a roar.

The man calmly turned his harpoon toward Quirt's head and fired.

Quirt jinked to one side, but the harpoon bolt still skimmed the side of his head hard enough to send him stumbling backwards.

And then it was over. They were surrounded by the seamen.

The seamen that Quirt had attacked reached up and removed his helmet, revealing an aristocratic, bearded face and a pair of remote dark eyes.

Lopez had described him enough for Quirt to take an educated guess who this man was. This was the captain.

This was Nemo.

The man put his helmet under his arm with an elegant gesture, as if he were sheathing a sword, and surveyed them silently.

Nemo's gaze settled on Lopez with a dark look of recognition, and Lopez went pale.

"I've seen a great many things in my lifetime," Nemo remarked. "But you five are undoubtedly the most unusual." He thought for a moment and added. "And ridiculous."

Casper bristled. "I beg your pardon!"

"Your attempt to board my vessel and to rob me of my ship's ballast was bold, but doomed to failure. You walked directly into my trap."

There was a brief stunned silence.

"Trap?" Casper quavered.

"In a sense. I knew you would try to land aboard my ship and had one of my men observe you as you came down to ascertain your number and weapons. The gas you released into our ship might have overcome us, had I and my officers not had time to don our diving suits. All we had to do was wait for you. You would have been wiser to lock the rest of my crew in the hold and search the ship for others before you blundered so boldly to the lower decks."

"I told you," Quirt mumbled to Casper.

"It would seem that your days of piracy are over," said Nemo.

The crew emptied their bulging pockets and ripped jewelry from various appendages before marching the would-be thieves ignominiously through the Nautilus. Crewmen were beginning to stir in the passageways, coughing weakly, and leaning against the bulkheads as if they were ill. Nemo exchanged a few words with them as he passed, but Quirt was too distracted by all the dirty looks to pay attention to what he was saying. They'd be lucky if they weren't roasted alive in Nemo's galley.

Several seamen led the way up to the main hatch and Quirt, Casper, and Lopez were shoved after them. Quirt had a split-second glimpse of Lee and Juliette's surprised expressions. Lee took one look at the armed seamen and dove for the balloon's anchor.

Good old reliable and loyal, Lee, Quirt thought sourly.

"Come back here, you coward!" Lopez shrieked.

Lee hesitated, half-way up the rope. Juliette gaped down at them all. A bevy of spear guns swung in their direction.

"I suggest you surrender," Nemo remarked, stepping onto the deck. He looked up at Juliette. "I would advise you to come down immediately."

Lee slithered down to the deck and Juliette followed him awkwardly a few minutes later, obviously reluctant to be separated from her beloved balloon. Lee had to pry her hand away from the anchor line.

The wind had picked up in the last few minutes, sending storm clouds from the horizon scudding overhead, covering the bay in an ominous shadow and sending the waves slapping the sides of the ship with renewed vigor, like a wet mouth smacking its lips and looking to swallow the Nautilus.

They all stood there silently, looking at Nemo, waiting.

Casper coughed. "I don't suppose you would let us get into our balloon and fly away, would you?"

Nemo gave him a look that made Casper shrivel visibly and didn't deign to answer. Nemo returned his attention to Le Papillon, examining the balloon with the expression of a man who had found a bug on his shoe.

"Remove it," he told his crew.

Some of the seamen surged forward and swarmed over the basket, wrenching the magnetized anchor and cutting the other lines free of the Nautilus.

The balloon began to float upwards, leaving its magnetic anchor behind.

Juliette let out a scream and stretched her hands as if beseeching her balloon, as it tootled merrily away up into the clouds.

"Murderers!" Juliette shrieked. "My child is defenseless!"

Nemo watched it sail away with a disinterested expression then turned briskly toward them. "And now…over the side."

Casper balked. "You're going to drown us?"

At a nod from Nemo, one of the seamen went below, returned with a large life ring, and tossed it into the water.

Lee shrugged philosophically, as if he had planned on getting in the water all along, and jumped overboard.

Quirt stared glumly at the waves. "Dang," he said between gritted teeth before plunging over the side. Cool, dark water covered him and he floundered to the surface, clutching at his hat before it could float away.

Casper was still dithering on the deck, but spear guns jabbed at his midsection spurred him to action. He stepped over the side like a man walking the plank, looking utterly demoralized.

Lopez, who had no dignity to lose in the first place, clung to the deck with his nails, insisting that he couldn't swim. He was flung overboard like a piece of garbage.

Nemo gestured to Juliette. "You too, Mademoiselle."

Juliette backed away. She didn't look quite so uppity now.

"I won't!" she quavered.

Nemo twitched his forefinger at his chief and the man stumped forward and seized Juliette by the waist.

Juliette shrieked like a branded calf as she was thrown unceremoniously over the side. She splashed to the surface a moment later, cursing in French.

Quirt couldn't resist saying, "I guess men got the better of you after all, hey Juliette?"

"Oh, shut up," she spluttered.

Nemo stood on the deck a second longer. Quirt supposed he was getting one last eyeful of the five clowns clinging to a solitary life ring and spitting out water, because his dark expression lifted for a moment under the flash of an amused smile and then he said abruptly, "Don't ever board my ship again," and strode below decks.

The five would-be thieves treaded water, watching silently as crewmen began repairing the damaged hatch. A few minutes later, the

Nautilus was underway. The crewmen on deck calmly continued their work as the vessel headed away towards the horizon, leaving Quirt and the others bobbing in its wake like so much flotsam.

Quirt spit out a stream of water. "Now what, genius?" He asked Casper, sourly.

"That uncivilized boor!" Casper spluttered, his eyes snapping like fireworks. "He might have at least allowed us the dignity of being deposited on shore."

"He could have let us drown," Lee pointed out, philosophical as ever.

"Better to drown than to be humiliated in such a fashion!" Casper said feelingly.

"Oh, shut up, Casper!" Quirt muttered.

Casper looked abashed.

As soon as Lopez stopped gagging up water, he gave Casper a dirty look and spluttered. "I told you so."

This looked like the final blow to Casper's deflated ego. He went stiff as a post.

"My balloon," Juliette mourned.

Quirt, feeling a bit of sympathy at last, gave her hand a comforting and wet pat. "Sorry, honey."

She swatted his hand away. So much for sympathy.

"Perhaps the balloon wasn't the best idea," Lopez suggested dolefully.

"It was a superb idea!" Juliette protested savagely.

"What was so superb about it?" Lopez challenged with unusual fire. "We didn't get anything out of this except a wetting!"

"No!" Casper said. "We have not been totally defeated. We have gathered new and vital information that we can implement into our next attempt."

The others stared at him. Casper was visibly gathering his dignity about himself like a cloak, and his expression had changed from outrage to sheer determination.

Quirt had to hand it to Casper: he knew how to come out of his corner swinging.

"We shall make another attempt to claim the Nautilus!" Casper declared. "This is nothing more than a momentary setback!"

"Setback?" Lopez squawked. "We failed. We were beaten like children in a schoolyard brawl."

"I wouldn't say we did that badly in the fight," Quirt interjected, smarting the most over his failure to shoot anybody or anything.

"And it was my balloon, not yours," Juliette put in, sulking.

"I did my part," Lee said, unperturbed.

"Oh shut up!" The other four shouted, even Casper.

Lee shrugged, but still looked superior.

"So…what's the plan?" Quirt asked.

"First, we search for my balloon," Juliette interjected. "If I have a map, I can calculate where it might come down."

"I'm afraid *might* isn't good enough," Casper interjected, dispensing with charm. "We cannot allow the Nautilus to escape us while we search for a balloon. We must move quickly."

"And do what?" Quirt said, still sarcastic.

Casper exploded. "I haven't worked out every detail exactly! I don't do my best thinking in the water!" He took a look at their doubting faces and flew into a tirade. "You brood of doubting minions! Are you actually considering walking away? What will you do? Quirt is still a snaggle-toothed reprobate without a job—"

"Hey, I'm not snaggle-toothed," Quirt protested. He looked at Juliette. "Am I?"

"—Lee still has a price on his head!"

"You do?" Quirt asked Lee. He was kind of jealous.

Casper was still ranting. "Dupont still won't be taken seriously as a balloonist. Lopez is still on the run from his own people."

"—and you're a washed-up gambler with a head full of acorns." Quirt finished rudely.

Casper paused a moment, as if considering whether or not to hit Quirt in his snaggle-toothed mouth, then let the insult slide. "What other avenues lie open before us? What other opportunities? We have all come to the same crossroad, my friends. It's time for either death or glory."

"Please," Lopez cringed. "Can't you say either *failure* or glory? I can live with failure."

"Well, I can't!" Casper snapped. "Nemo tricked us. Humiliated us. Handed us our hats and put a boot to our britches. If we walk away from this now, we'll never be able to hold our heads high again. We stood on the very cusp of victory only to have our noses rubbed in the dirt by a bully, a bully I say! Are we really going to let that lie? Well? Are we?"

When he put it that way, Quirt was starting to get his blood up.

"Danged if I am," he said.

"I also will join you," Juliette declared. "Fame is no longer enough, I live for *vengeance* now."

Lee spoke up. "There was nothing wrong with my devices. The plan failed because of the people using them." They all glared at him, but he kept on talking, unbothered. "So, I would like a chance to prove my devices are successful. I'm with you."

They all looked at Lopez inquiringly.

"Never!" Lopez spluttered. "You're all fools! Crazy! Insane! Loco!"

There was a brief silence.

"So, are you coming or not?" Quirt asked.

Lopez dropped his head onto his arm and sighed. "Si," he mumbled. Honest as ever, he added. "I need the money."

Some of Casper's old vim was returning to him and he raised a dripping finger.

"It's unanimous. Forward to glory, my friends! Forward!" He pointed grandly to the distant shore.

They started swimming.

"Come, my brave comrades!" Casper spluttered, his eyes bright. "We have a submarine to rob!"

An Evening at the World's Edge

Alfred D. Byrd

*F*rom the verandah of a posh hotel perched on a seaside *cliff,* Professor Pierre Aronnax gazed at a moonlit sea. The sight of it brought him no peace. Somewhere to the south of Nova Scotia, a major storm, perhaps even a hurricane, was lashing the Atlantic Ocean. Heavy waves broke in foam and in ceaseless roar onto shingle far below him. The storm-torn shore reminded him of the forlorn Norwegian strand onto which he and his companions, Conseil and Ned Land, had escaped from the Nautilus on a night of inestimable peril. He had escaped from the vessel in body, but not in thought. *The world,* he thought grimly, *goes on in storm, though what might save the world may be lost.*

In the months and years since the professor's escape from the marvelous submersible, its fate had tantalized him. Did the vessel, driven by its obsessive captain's will, still glide silently on below the surface of world-girdling ocean? Since Aronnax had returned to what most called civilization and published his memoirs of a momentous voyage to scant acceptance from the public and to greater skepticism from academics, he had been looking into reports of mysterious sightings at sea. One such report had brought him to the hotel on the windward coast northeast of Halifax—brought him to more of the disappointment that he had met ever since his escape into the Maelstrom.

It was as if the Nautilus had vanished from the earth. Could a report of its master's death and of the craft's destruction that he had just read be true? He doubted the report, which seemed to him a rousing tale of adventure rather than a sober recitation of facts, but had to admit to himself that not even Captain Nemo was immortal, nor was the Nautilus indestructible. The loss both of man and of vessel was a possibility only too real to one who had shared the dangers to them.

Aronnax sipped a red Bordeaux that the hotel had provided for him—a vintage better than he had foreseen in the British part of Canada, but far inferior to what he would have enjoyed in France—and looked to the sea, an inscrutable oracle, for answers.

Beside him, someone cleared his throat softly. "Excuse me, *monsieur le professeur*," a bellboy said, "a guest newly arrived at the hotel wishes to speak with you. Shall I show him to you?"

Aronnax considered the bellboy's question. Any guest of the hotel's would almost surely be respectable; civilized discourse might dispel the fey mood that had enveloped the professor. "*S'il vous plait.*"

The bellboy retreated to the verandah's far end, where a man loitered in shadow. As he returned with the bellboy, Aronnax caught glimpses of the "newly arrived guest" in pools of light cast by the verandah's gaslights. The professor tried to classify the guest as Conseil would one of his beloved marine creatures. The guest was tall and gangly, walking with a stooped gait that somehow still projected confidence. With a carefree air, he carried under his left arm a wooden box, long, but narrow, of the size of a desk portrait. He projected both humility and arrogance with a childlike air of ignorance of either.

Aronnax smiled to himself. The classification had been child's play. *An American. Well, the discourse would be only half-civilized, then.*

The bellboy knew enough of courtesy to give the professor a slight bow. "Professor Aronnax, may I present to you Mr. Cyrus Smith?"

Aronnax stiffened, eyes widening in recognition of the name, unwelcome to him. Still, the bellboy could not have known of the contretemps that he had caused with his introduction of an outrageous account's author. Giving the bellboy his due gratuity, Aronnax said, "*Merci, garcon*," and waved for him to leave.

Alone with the guest, Aronnax spoke coldly. "Mr. Smith, I have read your manuscript, which my publisher forwarded to me."

Before the professor could express his opinion of it, Smith's eyes widened, and he grinned. "You've read my scribblings? I hadn't expected such luck. I—"

Aronnax held up a hand. "I would not speak of luck were I you, sir. Do you expect me to believe such a fantastical account as yours is? A mysterious island? A balloon ride halfway around the world? Not to mention an orangutan—an orangutan, of all things! It's all a joke, no?"

Cyrus Smith chuckled, clearly taking no offense at the professor's outburst. "I'd hardly call my account more fantastic than yours."

Aronnax sniffed. "My account has the virtue of being true."

"I can say the same of mine. Still, I understand your skepticism, professor. I'd doubt your account if I hadn't seen proof of it with my own eyes. I hadn't expected you to have read my manuscript already, but, by good fortune, I've brought along something that'll substantiate my story. I left mention of it out of my account from respect for the prince's privacy, but, from your own account, I know you'll recognize the item at once. He wanted me to take it as a memorial of him, and I can hardly bear to be parted from it. I'd meant to show it to you anyway, as I knew you'd treasure it as much as I. Take a look, professor."

Cyrus Smith thrust towards the professor the long, narrow box. Opened, it revealed to him a portrait of a young woman and a pair of children, all of them North Indian in appearance—

The professor's eyes watered, blurring their images. "His wife and children, murdered by those on whom he wreaked his terrible vengeance. *Mon Dieu!* I watched Captain Nemo—no, I must now call him Prince Dakkar—weep before this very portrait just before—before that terrible night." Aronnax turned a bleak gaze onto Smith. "Then, is it true, *monsieur*? The prince dead, the *Nautilus* destroyed?"

Cyrus Smith's look was as bleak as the professor's. "I'm afraid so, sir. As I wrote, I left him entombed aboard his vessel, which couldn't have survived the volcano's eruption. Nothing could. I wish I had better news for you. Still, didn't you know my news already? Why else would you have summoned me here?"

Aronnax blinked in confusion. "I did not summon you here, *monsieur.*"

Cyrus Smith, his eyes narrowed, shook his head. "That's passing strange, sir. On my honor, I swear to you I got a letter, unsigned, on his stationery—a letter telling me to come here on this very night. You must be familiar with his stationery." When Aronnax nodded, Smith went on. "When I saw your name in the guest register, I felt I knew what was going on. Your name made perfect sense to me. If you didn't summon me, how do you happen to be here?"

Aronnax smiled thinly. "I came here to look into a report of a mysterious craft offshore. I had hopes of its being a vessel that both you and I know well. Certainly, details of the report were promising—ah, but the promise failed me, as promises so often fail in this tormented world. Would you believe that the *mysterious craft* turned out to be a giant narwhal? *Quelle ironie!* My colleagues back in France will have such a laugh at my expense."

Cyrus Smith grinned. "Men of no imagination. I must say, sir, I'm astonished you're here without Conseil. From your book, I'd assumed that you and he were inseparable."

"Indeed, it is a burden to be parted from him, but circumstances demanded that we go in different directions just now. He is currently on Cape Hatteras on your country's eastern seaboard. When two reported sightings of the Nautilus came in at once, I sent him to look into the less likely of the two. Selfish of me, perhaps, but then he will welcome a chance to classify the marine life there."

The American nodded. "Then, who could've sent me the letter? Who besides you might've had access to the prince's stationery?"

"Ah, yes. It seems to me, *monsieur,* that your mysteries did not end with your island."

There fell a silence in which the professor contemplated those mysteries. When the creator and commander of the Nautilus was involved, what else could there be? When Aronnax turned his gaze to the sea, Cyrus Smith followed the gaze. Softly, the professor said, "It would not astonish me even now to see the Nautilus rising from the waves or him striding across the shingle towards us. If anyone could cheat death by means beyond ordinary men's, it would be he."

"I know what you mean. If ever a man could project his will beyond the grave, Prince Dakkar could. Still, it can't be a coincidence, your being here on the night I was summoned here. Could an agent of his have sent me the letter and arranged the reported sighting that lured you here?"

"You may be right. In fact, I can think of no other solution to the letter's mystery. Perhaps, we can expect the agent's appearance—and explanation of his summons—now that we are united. Still, just now, if you will permit me to say so, could you and I repair indoors—perhaps to the bar? The night is growing chilly, and I require a brandy to warm me."

"Certainly, sir. I could do with a shot of whiskey myself."

The professor thought of an amusing detail from the American's account. "An orangutan, really?"

Cyrus Smith nodded somberly. "I still miss Jup. He was better than many men I've met—hello, what's this?"

Aronnax rose, following Cyrus Smith's gaze along the verandah. The professor froze and stiffened at a moving shape that he could not at first recognize—a hulking shape both of flesh and of metal. After a moment, Aronnax nodded. Coming towards him was a man propelling himself in a wheelchair, a leather map case across his lap. He wore what seemed to Aronnax a uniform—his eyes widened—one he had once seen daily. Its appearance out of place and out of time at a hotel in Nova Scotia struck the professor as hardly less than a miracle.

"I know you, *monsieur!*" Aronnax called out in a voice louder than was strictly polite. "You were one of the crewmen wounded in the battle with the krakens."

The crewman smiled and spoke in a cultured voice in an accent that the professor judged to be Polish. "More than just wounded, *monsieur le professeur*—crippled for life. I shall bear the kraken's marks with me to the tomb. Still, Captain Nemo did well by me after my injury. I wish to do well by him."

The professor shook his head. "I fail to understand you, *monsieur.*"

"Also," Cyrus Smith said, "it'd be nice to have a name for you. It'd be hardly polite to call you 'stranger.'"

The crewman gave the American a smile shadowed with pain. "A name. I understand your request, Mr. Smith. Each of us must use a name, even if not the one with which he was christened. You may call me Tadeusz. It is the name by which the captain knew me—an alias I used in my native land's intrigues before I joined the captain's cause."

Cyrus Smith nodded, a light of recognition in his eyes. "Thaddeus? Is that after Thaddeus Kosciuszko, who served America nobly in the Revolutionary War?"

"You are correct, sir. He is also a hero to beleaguered Poland. He was, like the captain, one who felt that freedom should have no bounds."

Aronnax raised a forefinger. "Tadeusz, I remember a portrait of your namesake aboard the Nautilus—a portrait amid a gallery of heroes of conscience. Captain Nemo took inspiration from them."

"You remember well. I myself gave that portrait to the captain, a man worthy to stand at his side—a man at whose side it was an honor for me to stand. Where will any of us meet his like again? As for my wish to do well by him, he has left to me a bequest, a legacy"—he glanced at the map case— "a mission that goes on beyond his death. It is a mission that I believe both of you gentlemen will wish to join."

When Tadeusz, clearly trying to gather his thoughts, fell silent for a moment, the professor grasped that he had forgotten the evening's chill in his eagerness to hear more of the revolutionary's proposal to him. Smiling at Tadeusz, Aronnax said, "I am, as the Americans say, *all ears.*"

When both the American and the Pole had made polite-sounding chuckles at the professor's idiom, Tadeusz went on. "I have read your account of your travels aboard the Nautilus, Professor Aronnax, and I have learned at least the substance of your account of the captain's death, Mr. Smith, so I know that both of you have heard visionary discourses that the captain could deliver when the mood was on him. Still, *monsieur le professeur,* I have traveled with the captain for far more than the *vingt mille lieues* that you described. As one of his earliest and most faithful colleagues, I received from him confidences that he would never have shared with outsiders, however welcome their company might be.

"You know, of course, of his struggle against the empire that oppressed his homeland and cost him his family. Both of you were aboard the magnificent submersible, both a vessel of exploration and a weapon of war, that sprang from his vision. You, at least, *monsieur le professeur,* know of his fear that that vision would fall into warlike hands with devastating consequences to the world. He was willing to go to great lengths to avoid the catastrophe that he feared."

The professor nodded solemnly. "In the end, he did avoid it at the cost of his greatest vision."

"At the cost of a vision, though not his greatest, as you will learn. As for the catastrophe that I mentioned, he did avoid it for a time, but only for a time. He understood that, what a visionary could create in a matter of days, lesser minds could create over the course of years, especially if the lesser minds knew of the visionary's work, as they now do know. Still, a submersible like the Nautilus is but one of the means of destruction that lesser minds can create."

Tadeusz turned to Cyrus Smith. "You, sir, saw something of what I mean in your nation's civil war. Over four years of ceaseless slaughter, the engineers of the Union and of the Confederacy invented repeating rifles, rotating multi-barreled rifles that can fire hundreds of rounds a minute, cannons mounted on railroad cars, explosives buried under the earth, submarines rudimentary beside the Nautilus, yet still deadly—"

Cyrus Smith nodded. "Not to mention the observation balloon my comrades and I fled from prison in. Yes, I gather that Prince Dakkar feared that weapons of war would grow ever worse. Who can say he was wrong? All of the evidence supports him."

Tadeusz nodded. "The captain foresaw dirigibles and heavier-than-air craft that can bombard cities from the air, explosives that can destroy a city in a single blast, poisonous gases that can kill regiments in their tracks, humanly disseminated plagues—"

Professor Aronnax sighed. "Yes, it was clear to me that fear of civilization's fall preyed on the captain's mind. It was against that fall that he was fighting."

"He fought as well as he could with the weapon that he had, *monsieur le professeur*, but he knew the Nautilus alone could not prevail in his struggle. The submersible could not remove the seeds of war from the human heart or reverse the trend of human history."

"Are you referring to the predictions of Thomas Malthus?"

"In part. The captain foresaw that ever-growing numbers of our kind, using ever more of our world's resources, would irreversibly alter the world's climate. Fertile lands would become deserts, seas would rise, and civilized nations would fall into a new dark age."

The professor's brows rose. "Is that the mission to which Captain Nemo—Prince Dakkar—called you, to prevent a new dark age?"

Tadeusz shook his head. "In the captain's judgment, the dark age is inevitable because it lies in the human heart. What the captain has called me to do—the work in which I hope you two gentlemen will join me—is to restore civilization to the world after the dark age. The captain has left resources for this renaissance. They must be preserved and grown to yield the harvest of the world's rebirth. See for yourself what he has set in motion."

Tadeusz thrust the map case into Aronnax's hands. The professor thrilled, recognizing it as one Nemo had often consulted. As Aronnax withdrew with trembling hands the topmost map from the case, he did not mind that Cyrus Smith looked over his shoulder and let out a low whistle. The map was indeed worthy of admiration. From Spitsbergen to the South Sandwich Islands, the map recorded remote refuges from which fallen civilization might be restored.

Other maps detailed the refuges' layouts and held lists of supplies in place and supplies needed. The maps and lists were in Nemo's unmistakable hand.

While Aronnax and Smith viewed the maps, Tadeusz spoke on. "The two of you and I, recruiting likeminded individuals to our labor, will manage redoubts where fauna and flora that may become extinct in nature, and technologies that may be lost in the outside world, will be preserved against a new dawn for humanity—where treasures of literature, both ancient and modern, Eastern and Western, will be safe from moth and from flame—"

Cyrus Smith was wide-eyed. "Are you talking of a new Noah's Ark, sir?" After a moment's reflection, the American snapped his fingers. "No, more like a set of Noah's caves."

Aronnax smiled thinly at Smith's imagery. "You might more usefully think of what our friend Tadeusz is proposing as a new form of Freemasonry—"

"A secret society?" As the professor began to explain his analogy, Cyrus Smith held up a hand. "No, I understand, sir. Whatever we do must be done in secret. If not, the forces the captain was fighting against would seize his resources for their own, shortsighted ends. Eating the seed corn, his enemies would leave nothing to others for a new crop. The three of us must preserve that seed until it can yield new life to a ruined earth."

Tadeusz raised his brows. "You understand the captain's concerns well. Can I then count on your support, Mr. Smith?"

"Yes, sir, I'm your man to the very end!"

"And you, *monsieur le professeur?*"

Slowly, Aronnax nodded. "*Oui, mon ami.* To what better work could one devote one's remaining days but to ensure hope to humanity beyond one's days? May the effort that the three of us set in motion be enough to fulfill Captain Nemo's dream!"

Professor Aronnax looked up at the moon. Already, fingers of cloud were reaching across its face. Soon, the coming storm would hide the moon's light, and a tempest would break on a peaceful landscape.

In that tempest, how much that was precious would perish? Survival might well depend on chance, a doubtful hope at best.

Still, when the tempest ended, the foresighted could rebuild, perhaps better than ever. The land's trial would not be everlasting. When the storm had passed, the moon would shine again undimmed.

A Concurrent Process

Corrie Garrett

Part 1

It took Perrine three years to perfect the predictive neural network that allowed her to find the UFO, and three minutes to realize how wrong her peer-reviewed paper on the UFO's probable origins had been.

She twisted sideways in the tiny four-seater Cessna to get a better view of the unknown ship through the open window. She could almost touch it, as it had appeared nearly at their feet. Ed, her videographer, was buckled in next to her, pivoting his stabilized camera to take it in. The air tore wisps of hair loose from her tight braid and sudden turbulence shook their small aircraft.

The unknown ship was in the midst of a phase shift of some sort that left parts of it transparent and parts opaque. It was a whale to their minnow. The edges seemed to fluoresce softly. A beautiful pink dusk backlit the whole.

"This is amazing. Connie, go a hundred yards and circle back for a wider shot," Perrine instructed over her helmet mike. She sniffed, getting a distinct whiff of ozone and something like chlorine in the air that buffeted her. Some off-gassing from its engines, perhaps?

Her research into the airborne behemoth, which had begun disrupting flight patterns around Chicago about three years ago and caused four emergency landings, had concluded that there was a 45% chance that it was alien, and 55% chance that it was a prototype deployed by an undetermined government (but probably the U.S. or Saudi Arabia). Her model was based on many factors, but mainly the strange spatial pattern of the twelve data points the UFO had provided, the ramp up of carbon fiber production in various countries, and the few video recordings made by eye witnesses, which had been uniformly awful.

Perrine clutched her restraints as she narrated for the record. "It's got a blimp-shaped hull with a dark matte surface. I can confirm the glow previously described and the intermittent transparency." What none of those witnesses had captured, however, was its general vibe, which Perrine could only describe as...steampunk?

She groaned with impatience as the ship slipped away behind her while Connie circled around, but then the whole was in view.

"Instead of a fuselage below," Perrine continued, "it seems to have a living space above. I see two rows of windows, round like portholes. Some portions of the ship continue to be all but transparent. A—a simple rotator blade is visible at the aft end, but the ship appears to be hovering in place. Portions of the upper hull have a scrollwork pattern in gold over a dark blue background." She paused. "Any alien possibility seems remote."

The popular furor over her paper had all focused on the alien angle, though Perrine, when interviewed for the Chronicle, had insisted it was still the less likely eventuality. Worse, now it appeared that the rest of her paper was wrong as well. This didn't look like a top-secret drone or cutting-edge weapon. This looked like the whim of an eccentric.

"The scrollwork looks to be a word, but I'll have a better angle in a moment."

If it said Elon Musk, she was going to throw herself from the plane. Visions of shameful retractions danced before her eyes.

"Connie, closer but higher, please. I really want this shot."

Ed used his open window to get a downward angle. "It says..."

But then something happened. A silent pulse in the air, like the moment of silence after a firework but before the boom. Perrine's heartbeat pulsed in her ears.

The roar of the engine died. The plane soared silently over the unknown ship; even the wind felt muted. It was a fraught silence, like someone who choked on a bite mid-laugh. Connie began to move furiously, flipping switches back and forth, adjusting the yoke, and tapping at the onboard computer. Her lips were moving, probably muttering threats.

Perrine tapped her helmet. "We can't hear you."

Connie looked back at them. "Electrical systems failed. Engine's out, too. I've got manual control, but it's a glider at this point—a poor one."

Ed's eyes were huge. His bushy, hipster beard blew wildly in the wind. "Was that an EMP?" The camera LED had gone out and he lowered it to his lap to examine. It was dead, though possibly the previous footage could be retrieved later.

Odd, Perrine thought. The UFO had never attacked with an EMP before.

The Cessna had started to descend, but Connie was struggling with the yoke. "Getting too much wind turbulence. I can't land it like this. We'll have to bail."

Perrine's hands shook as she gripped her seat. They had known this could go badly, which was why they all wore thin parachute rigs, the best that Skydive Chicago could provide.

Connie undid her own restraints and used the handholds to get back to Perrine and Ed. "The auto activation on your chute will probably be dead," she explained, "so pull the cord yourself as soon as you're clear of our plane."

They were almost past the ship, maybe a hundred feet above it now. Wind tossed the plane and Perrine felt horrendously sick. She reminded herself that many people had been saved by these chutes. Plus, she had an A-license; she knew how to jump on her own, as did Ed and Connie.

Connie pointed with her gloved hand. "We're clear of the ship. Go."

Perrine jumped.

Free fall was always disorienting, but at least she'd mentally planned for it on previous jumps. Perrine's scream was lost to the air while she arched her back and spread her limbs to find a neutral position. Instead, she continued to tumble wildly, not flattening out at all. The eddy around the strange ship must be throwing her off. Ideally the diver was steady before chute released, but Perrine still cartwheeled. Sky, ship, land, flash of red—was that Ed's chute?—sky, ship, land. Perrine's breath came in gulps. How many seconds had she been falling?

She pulled the chute.

The bone-shaking jerk was no worse than normal, but something got tangled around her left ankle.

Completely disoriented as she was spun and yanked upward, Perrine didn't immediately realize when she hit a hard surface. It was the feel of warm rubber under her hands, textured and gritty like her dog's favorite ball, that grounded her. She ached, but nothing felt broken. Her red chute was twisted and limp behind her.

She'd been blown onto some sort of observation deck, complete with handrailing. The wind had calmed. The silence was intense. She was on the ship, which seemed to hang motionless in a peaceful bubble.

Perrine did the work to untangle herself and limped gingerly to the edge. She couldn't see directly down past the convex bulk of the ship, but to her right the smoggy outline of Chicago and Lake Michigan helped her reorient. She saw no red chute but hoped Connie and Ed were merely hidden from sight. "Please, God, let them be alright."

A man's accented voice made her heart clench in surprise again. "Do you mean it when you speak to God?"

Part 2

Perrine spun around. He was tall, with black hair going gray. Pakistani or Indian perhaps, based on his accent, she wasn't sure.

She instinctively offered a brief bow rather than a handshake, introducing herself as if they were at an academic conference and not on his… top-secret floating yacht?

He observed her silently while gathering up the corner of her chute and rubbing it curiously in his fingers.

"You were here to record me," he said. "How did you know where the ship would appear?"

"I'm a programmer." Perrine spread her hands. "I made a predictive model based on former sightings."

"But how could that help you when I myself did not decide my destination until this morning?"

"I don't know. If you're willing to tell me why you chose this spot, perhaps I can reverse analyze it." In instinctive self-preservation, Perrine added, "Unless it was just luck. It was probably luck. I also predicted that you were most likely CIA or alien, and…obviously there were flaws."

He smiled slightly, bunching more of the red chute in his hand. "Not so flawed, based on your success. Tell me, did your model also predict how a confrontation would go?"

"No."

"What a brave woman to attempt it, then."

Perrine noted the gender bias and condescension, but it was somehow expected.

"If you were a man," he continued, "I might have disunified and let you fall to your death. I cannot afford to be identified, and I made a rule never to take another permanent passenger."

"I can't identify you. I've a terrible head for faces."

He'd collected enough of the chute that when he dropped it over the railing, it fell, billowing fitfully. The trailing straps slithered like snakes over the deck and followed. "Your program or algorithm worries me. With what you have now seen, I fear you could uncover it all. My EMP has taken care of any devices you may have had with you, but if I let you go now, I may as well go on one of your talk shows."

Perrine watched the falling parachute, plummeting very similarly to her heart, but it seemed to stop in midair, settling gently into a pile as if on a gym floor.

"What's holding the chute? Magnetic field? Plasma window?" Perrine asked, curious despite her fear.

"No."

The chute began to sink slowly, as if being sucked into the ocean after resting on top of the waves. Perrine edged away from the railing, unnerved.

"You needn't worry; I won't push you over. History does have a way of forcing one to repeat mistakes." He held out his hand, "Welcome to the Nautilus III. I am Captain Nemo."

As Perrine shook his hand, she wished very much that she were an expert in human neuroses, rather than artificial intelligence. She didn't immediately get terrorist or murderer vibes from him, but how could one judge an eccentric genius(?) and billionaire(?) who thought himself a literary character...

"Nautilus, huh? I haven't read the book since high school," she admitted. "But this seems like a bang-up job. I can't tell you how impressed I am."

The Captain glared into the middle distance. "I had a regrettable run-in with that Verne fellow, and he took considerable literary license." He recalled himself and gestured to a hatch. "Would you care for a tour? I'm afraid we must get off the platform if we do not wish to die a most unnatural death."

Perrine swallowed. Was this the equivalent of going to the second location? Cops always warned people not to go with an attacker or gunman to a second location, better odds to try and escape at once, even if you got shot...But what else could she do?

"You could jump," he said. "But it seems a waste."

"I can't deny I *would* love a tour." Her hand slipped into the pocket of her flight pants and she caressed her phone. It was dead, but the shape of it was comforting.

The ladder led down into a large room with a mishmash of modern and antique furnishings. There had been an attempt at sumptuous European decor with chintz lounges, teak tables, and showy Persian rugs. But sitting on the beautiful tables were boxy desktop computers, floppy drives, and punch cards. A lovely early American bookcase held a pile of pagers, flip phones, and tablets.

"Nice collection," Perrine said. The thick porthole windows could have been right out of Moby Dick. A bundle of wires thicker around than she was passed from the floor to the ceiling.

Perrine ran her hand over the wall, which gave slightly. Definitely not carbon fiber. But how was this thing not falling out of the sky? The silence weighed on her.

"This way is our piloting room." He made a courtly gesture. "Being yourself a lady of science, I think you will enjoy it."

Perrine barely hesitated this time. There were myriad books in the piloting room, but no screens, which felt odd. Two wide, rectangular windows were set above a panel of gauges, dials, and burnished copper switches. A heavy book was open on a podium, and it showed a flowing topographical map of Illinois. He'd penciled in a scattering of numbers.

A large tube with an eyepiece extended from the wall. A periscope?

He adjusted it and turned slightly left. "Your friends are just now dropping past the north flank of the ship."

"What? No…they would be nearly touching down by now."

He gestured in an old-fashioned, gentlemanly way. "Please."

Perrine looked. The periscope showed her friends, as still as a photograph. Connie's chute was half open, her mouth as well. Ed was twenty yards beyond, arms splayed out…

"They're—they're frozen."

"They will be fine," the Captain answered. "*We* are frozen, inhabiting a split second for as long as the quantum wave takes to ripple us all the way back to the starting point."

"Starting point?"

He tapped one of the round gauges. "We are inhabiting the fourth second of 6:23pm, October 3 of this year. When the wave retreats, the entanglement will collapse into the past, as will we."

Perrine looked again at her friends and confirmed they were dropping, but so slowly it was almost imperceptible.

She cleared her dry throat. "Many physicists say time travel is impossible, but others have begun to crack quantum entanglement."

He pointed to another dial, which was labeled in microscopic orders of magnitude, and was now approaching zero. "And...Now."

A peaceful chime sounded. The ship began to ripple.

"But..." Perrine knew only the basics of quantum entanglement— she'd dated a physicist and watched "The Big Bang Theory," of course— but this made no sense.

"Even if you somehow exploded the entanglement in such a way as to engulf a ship..." She began to feel sick again. "I couldn't be part of your equation! Or did you decide to murder me after all?"

"No, no, I am quite sure you will not die. I have had birds breach the quantum net, and they lived."

Perrine held out her hands. They felt solid, but she could see between the metacarpals and knuckles; her wrist bones glowed in the evening light.

"Shades of Novikov," she breathed. "What did you do?"

A cat came around the doorframe into the piloting room, looking supremely undisturbed by its own phosphorescing appearance. It meowed at the Captain.

Perrine laughed, a little hysterically. "Schrödinger's damn cat."

She met the Captain's eyes and watched as the phenomenon died down and his skull solidified. At that moment it didn't matter to her if he was a psychopath or terrorist, she was experiencing a fundamental shift in the fabric of reality and it had to be shared with someone.

When it was done, she jerked. She spun to the periscope; her friends were not visible.

"They should be fine, in their time."

Perrine had never shinnied up a ladder so fast. She twisted the wheel to unlock the hatch and scrambled into the open air. Already it was different. The air was colder, the clouds were gone, and a steady hiss vibrated through the ship.

If this was an elaborate hoax...but no. She looked toward Lake Michigan and pressed a shaking hand to her mouth.

Chicago was there alright, but smaller, shorter, the downtown skyline evaporated. The highways and towns that dotted this part of Illinois were all but gone. A train, frozen in place, snaked its way toward the city, billowing steam.

"When?" she asked Nemo.

"1872."

Part 3

"It was Ingenhousz who started me on the path," Nemo explained, below. At Perrine's blank look, he laughed in spite of himself. "How soon the geniuses of yesterday are forgotten. A valuable reminder. Ingenhousz was the Dutchman who discovered photosynthesis. The gas exchange he sufficiently explicated, but on the actual movement of light particles, I felt he had only scratched the surface." Nemo gave her a glass of wine, "Drink, please. A particularly good Madeira."

Perrine realized her hands were still shaking and took a sip.

"I found, with the help of a dear friend, that among the actual organelles of the photosynthetic cell and the atoms within, there was a hole in my understanding. A hole wherein the light was several things at once, several places at once, each position precluding the others and yet each potential situation affecting the others in perfect balance. Quantum superpositions, I believe you call it. When I unbalanced them, I was able to enlarge the hole, so to speak, and enter it."

Perrine took another sip. "That's as if to say you made friends with electrons and asked them to sit down in rows so that you might make a computer."

"I'm simplifying. There was mathematics."

"I'm great at math. Please don't stop there."

He pulled several thick ledgers from the bookshelf. They were bound in leather and looked like they ought to be under glass at a museum.

Perrine opened the first, glancing through to get a feel for his notation. She absently petted the cat, which had curled up beside her.

"I cannot believe you did this without a computer. Did you even have a calculator?"

"Not as such, no. In fact, I understood computing technology so little at first, that I indulged in something of a research jaunt to study the science from its inception." He nodded to the odd assortment of devices. "My forte is in the study of nature and physics. Solid state technology was opaque to me."

"What about engineering?" Perrine tossed off the rest of her wine, ignoring his pained look. "You built this airship. Forgetting quantum theory, how does it even fly?"

"One cannot forget quantum theory in a time machine." A reluctant smile glimmered. "Although we rest in 1872, we are still within the quantum entanglement, which I have adjusted to proceed at one-eighteenth, to the power of ten, normal time. No lift propulsion is currently necessary."

Perrine lifted her eyes from his journal. "Do you mean to say that we are falling?"

"Quite."

"What is the lift propulsion when you reach the bottom?"

"Compressed air. The Naut is, in essential nature, rather like a balloon which a child may blow up and release as many times as the balloon's integrity will allow."

"But that would create only a hover vehicle, wouldn't it? Compressed air wouldn't get this beast far off the ground."

"It would if I increased the time lapse during release, controlling velocity and making the Naut nearly weightless."

"Weightless." Perrine shook her head and looked out the porthole nearby, her brain already turning to further problems. "Are we visible? Shouldn't we have seen...I don't know, daguerreotypes of your ship show up in my time?"

He stroked his trim beard. "Apparently not. Depending on the speed of the wave, the ship is not easy to see with the naked eye, and certainly not with film exposure. It is most visible when the quantum wave crests, so to speak, which does not last long."

Perrine got to her feet, too full of adrenaline to sit longer. She paced the length of his sitting room, a thousand thoughts warring in her head. Time travel, paradoxes, quantum waves, her dean's dubious face, twelve pieces of data that led her here...

"How did you know where my ship would appear?" Nemo asked. "You are the first to predict it. And as I have been further in the future, I can confidently say you are the *only* one to predict it."

Perrine picked up one of the flip-phones and pressed its rubber keys. "Do you know anything about neural networks? AI?"

He crossed one leg over the other. "A little."

The phone was dead. She cast it back on the shelf. "In short, I combined all the data I could for these appearances: atmospheric, geographic, city planning calendar, cell tower data at times of event... anything I could get my hands on. Then I used a type of reinforcement learning to teach a neural network to predict the next sighting."

"Ah. Pattern matching, you would say."

"Not just that," Perrine bristled. "Any computer system can pick out a pattern. I used what's called Temporal Value Transport. I nicknamed it Trevor. It can experience a possible action, say showing up outside Chicago on a certain evening, through the possible consequences of that decision, and then send the information back to itself. A lesson from the future, in a sense. TVT has only been used in a gaming environment so far, but I expanded and implemented it with this problem and...here we are."

Nemo frowned, disappointed. "Then you do not know how it works, how it found me. You merely utilized a machine more intelligent than a man."

Perrine scoffed incredulously, "I didn't *merely utilize* anything. I implemented a reinforcing, predictive neural network that has never been achieved before. I programmed the environment, the constraints, the reward and feedback loops, the coding of past and future "memories." In the last three years, I pioneered a new branch of behavioral neural programming." What really burned her though, was the edge of truth to what he said.

Nemo raised a hand, tiredly. "I did not mean to demean your achievement. I understand women are still unequal as scientists in your day. But with as little data as you had, I still cannot see—"

"Unequal?"

But another pulse interrupted Perrine. It was just like the one she'd felt on the Cessna, and she instinctively grabbed Nemo's chair to brace herself, although it caused no actual sound or reverberation.

He sprang lithely from the chair and made for the engine room. "My EMP fires automatically on proximity, but generally there is minimal air traffic."

"You really can't use EMPs with abandon the way you do," Perrine protested. "You're going to kill people."

They both froze before the windows.

Another Nautilus airship, all but identical, hovered fifty yards in front of them.

Nemo exhaled, as if he'd been holding his breath for a very long time. "Why would I retrace my path? I have eschewed the notion of changing my former life based on this machine. It is impossible to change the past."

"But is it you?" Perrine asked as a person became visible on the upper deck of the other ship, waving a hand. "I can't tell from this distance."

Perrine followed Nemo up the ladder this time.

The person, it did seem to be a man, swung something round and round over his head.

"If you weren't so trigger happy with EMPs, you could talk on a phone," Perrine muttered. "Can we get closer?"

"If we approached, the two quantum nets would, I believe, repel each other like misaligned magnets."

The man released his slingshot. Nemo and Perrine tracked the object with their eyes until it landed, bouncing on the India rubber hull. Perrine was closer and pounced on it before it could roll away.

She passed it reluctantly to Nemo, who tore away the twine and pulled away several crumpled sheets, closely written. He dropped the rock at his feet and turned away from her to read.

The other man raised a hand in farewell and disappeared into his ship.

"It's fluorescing," Perrine said. "He's going."

Nemo did not look up. "I've seen it."

Perrine was wild with curiosity, but the first man in the history of time to receive a letter from his future self probably deserved a moment.

The Illinois countryside was meanwhile locked in its own eternal moment. The fields were laid out in checkerboard fashion, long before center-pivot irrigation systems would scatter farmland with semi-circles.

"Do you have a dog?" Nemo asked abruptly.

Perrine licked dry lips. "Yes. A pointer mutt named Obi."

"We are recommended to fetch him."

Part 4

If floating above Reconstruction Era Chicago had felt surreal, it was nothing to entering her own university with Captain Nemo at her heels.

What's more, it was five days *before* she would encounter the Nautilus in the air. It was Saturday, so Perrine only saw a few colleagues in their offices as she took Nemo to hers. The building was alive with students, but it was the week of midterms, so an air of lassitude and gloom pervaded the campus as surely as the gray clouds above and the leaves piling into drifts in the nippy fall wind.

"I'm still struggling to wrap my brain around this." Perrine booted up her work computer. "And that is saying something. You truly never brought the Naut to Illinois before?"

"No."

"Three years of research and twelve sightings say you did."

"Please focus. We only need a list of the exact time and locations."

"Yeah, I have the data here. I practically have it memorized. I don't even need to turn on Trevor." She jerked her head at the two racks of hard drives against one wall of her rather decent lab and office. "Can't believe I thought two windows might be the high point of my career."

Nemo studied the configuration while she printed out two copies of the list they needed.

She gave one to Nemo, who folded it neatly and put it into an inner pocket of his formal winter coat.

Perrine hesitated before shutting down her computer. At this very moment, her other self was putting away groceries from Whole Foods and holding the phone to her ear while confirming the details of the flight with Connie. Then she would take Obi to a friend who was going to keep him this week. In case something happened, which as it turned out…

Perrine furrowed her brow and grabbed a pen and notepad, laughing with shock and a little horror.

"What are you doing?" Nemo demanded. "I believe we ought not improvise."

"I'm not. This is the opposite of improvisation."

Things to remember, she jotted down.

Don't forget Julie Ng's birthday. Make sure to restock Obi's treats. Insist on parachutes for Connie and Ed. Take out the lounge trash, it has chicken scraps in it.

Perrine left the notepad on her keyboard. "I'll find the list on Monday, and I won't remember writing it, but that's nothing new for me."

One of Perrine's students passed them in the parking lot. "Ms. A, if you catch those aliens, you gonna cancel midterms?"

"Not aliens, and not a chance."

Armed with the data, Perrine and Nemo would take the Nautilus and visit Chicago in each of the instances where it had been seen. With the EMP off, Perrine insisted.

But before they left to (re?)create history, Perrine went to get Obi.

"I just have a weird feeling," Perrine told her dog-sitter, rubbing Obi's ears. "I'm going to keep him close after all. Sorry to switch last minute."

"Okay. But get some sleep, Perrine, you've been living and breathing that project."

Obi hopped in the backseat of the rental car, which was very silent as Perrine drove.

"I do not understand the time machine." Nemo eyed the homely neighborhood in the shadow of the downtown skyscrapers. He sounded as if he were admitting a great sin. "I should not have insulted your use of the computer, for I am no better. I built the Naut III and that is a great accomplishment, but I do not know *how* I ought to use it. Years ago, my goal was to be free of human society, to wreak vengeance when I could." He shook his head. "But whether I do right or wrong, I change nothing here. Just as you changed nothing with that note. Everything we can or should do is done."

Perrine turned the heater to high, feeling chilled from within. "I'm no philosopher—their conferences are weird—but I don't think we can look at life that way, can we? In programming we build concurrent systems, modules of a greater whole that can be completed independently, concurrently, to speed up the process. You and I have just discovered that our existence is more of a concurrent process than we thought...but we aren't the program itself, don't you think?" her voice was a little more pleading than she'd realized. "We're the programmers," she reiterated. "We still get to write those subroutines."

"Perhaps," he conceded. "To what purpose?"

"I guess that's the ultimate question."

He sighed. "I resolved to give up vengeance, but I knew I could not remain in my own time and keep my vow. Therefore, when I transcended time, I chose to submerge myself in peaceful and sublime exploration. But my future self seems to have other plans."

"We don't know that. That's a subroutine yet to be written, but when it is, it'll be written by *you*."

Aboard the Nautilus, Nemo regained his vigor. "This, at least, I know." He marked the locations on his map, in neat red pencil, and began the trip. "We cannot do them all on one wave," he explained. "Each superposition has a start and end point where the quantum field rests. The Naut is only visible when it is at rest."

By the time they'd visited each of the twelve locations, spread over the last three years, it had been many hours.

"It almost feels like a shape formed in four dimensions." Perrine traced her fingers over the map. "I've often thought so. Twelve vertices, adjusted for the Earth's rotation…"

They had come to a halt in 1872, Nemo's "present." It was just before dawn. Nemo pointed the ship toward the gray east that they might watch the sunrise.

The brightness grew quickly; rather too quickly. Nemo's knuckles grew white where he gripped the wheel. The light resolved into a series of dots just in front of their ship, hanging like floating plankton in the atmosphere.

Nemo pressed a hand to the glass. "Twelve."

Perrine choked. "Is it aliens after all?"

The dots shifted until Nemo and Perrine were looking at an unmistakable corridor.

Nemo's hands twitched toward the steering, but he looked at her. "I can't decide for you."

Perrine stroked Obi's head. "I haven't tracked this for three years to back out now."

Nemo edged the Nautilus forward. "To sublime exploration, then."

Homework Help From No One

Demetri Capetanopoulos

*T*ake me with you to the beach today."
Daniel reluctantly peered over the top of his book at his younger sister, Valeria.

"Next time," he said. "Diego and I are going to the far side."

That meant a long, hot bike ride and the last thing he wanted was to be slowed down by an eight-year-old.

"You said that last time, so now *is* next time." Valeria planted her hands on her hips to emphasize the point.

Again, Daniel dragged his eyes from the page, but now his mind was scrambling. He had been planning today's adventure all winter and if he wasn't careful it would be undone if his sister appealed to their mom.

"Tomorrow we'll fly kites at Francesca Beach," he said.

Her frown indicated he needed to offer more.

"I'll let you fly my kite."

At this, Valeria's eyes grew wide and she broke into a grin. The kite Daniel had gotten at Christmas was steerable, with multiple lines. They were supposed to share it, which up until now had meant she watched while Daniel flew.

"Deal!" she said and marched from the room with her head held high.

Now Daniel became aware of the time. Frustrated at not being able to finish the chapter, he nonetheless got up, tossing the book on the bed. *Five Weeks in a Balloon* was proving to be a good read. He had gotten hooked on Jules Verne last summer after selecting *Twenty Thousand Leagues Under the Sea* from his school reading list. It was still his favorite, but each of Verne's amazing adventures was a welcome escape from the bounds of life on their little island.

Grabbing his backpack, he dashed for the door to limit the opportunity for his mom to remind him again about his Easter break writing assignment. It's not that he didn't like writing, it's just that this assignment had to be non-fiction, and he simply had nothing to say.

"Write about surfing or diving with Diego," his mom called after him.

Without breaking his stride, he tossed back, "Mom, we live in La Graciosa, everybody will write about that. I need something different."

And with that, Daniel was on his bike and kicking up sand.

It took only minutes to weave between the whitewashed walls of the island's only town and reach the road that stretched toward the interior. Here, Daniel was supposed to meet his friend, but he kept pedaling up the rising road of hard-packed sand. Diego had gotten a new bike with gears for Christmas and he knew his friend would overtake him. The two were competitive, and the unfair advantaged irked him. Sure enough, before long he heard a faint repetitive clink that signaled Diego was in pursuit. The noise came from a folding army shovel that his friend kept strapped behind the seat of his bike. Diego's summer reading selection had been *Treasure Island,* and when one of their teachers had told the class that historical events around La Graciosa may have inspired the book, it had lit a fire in Diego. Everywhere they went now, Diego brought his shovel and was forever scouting for possible treasure trove locations. It had been fun during winter when it was too cool for swimming, but on this first warm day in April, Daniel wanted to dive!

Laughing, Diego finally passed him just before their self-declared finish line. Here, the road crested the shallow saddle between two of the many volcanos that made up the island. Diego paused to let

Daniel catch up. The two boys took in the view and enjoyed the sea breeze that now reached them from the opposite coast.

"Even with a head-start you can't beat me." Diego said good-naturedly.

"You have gears," Daniel pointed out for the hundredth time.

Now Diego posed. "Naw, it's all muscle. I beat you before I had gears, too."

Daniel had to admit—though never out loud—that Diego had put on some muscle this year while he remained as skinny as ever. Still, there was one skill in which he had the edge.

"Doesn't matter, we're diving today and one of us has yet to do a twelve-count."

Daniel saw Diego wince at the reminder. Though a strong surfer, diving had never been Diego's thing and besides, no one in their class could match Daniel's ability to hold his breath underwater.

The heat of the day was becoming apparent as the boys rounded the large central volcano and headed toward another, farther along the coast. They passed only wiry shrubs, since there were no trees on the entire island. Thirty minutes after leaving town, their destination came into sight.

Before them lay an immense beach of golden sand. As usual, it was deserted. At the far end it terminated in a rugged tumble of rock that had once flowed down the flank of one of the lesser volcanos before being quenched by the sea. It created a coast of jagged overhangs around which the sea frothed and foamed in countless crevices and tidepools.

Daniel wasted no time. He made straight for the rocks, searching for a particular cove. When he found it, he noted Diego was lagging and toting his shovel. To preclude any proposals that they hunt treasure, he quickly zipped up his rash guard and stepped off the ledge.

A long second later, he plunged cleanly into the water. Moving quickly to ward off the chill, he executed a smooth jackknife and dove down a dozen feet. The cove was protected from the break of big waves and the walls were nearly vertical—at least as far as they had been able to explore on their last visit. Now as Daniel peered into the depths, it seemed bottomless. Inverting, he gave a few powerful kicks, and broke the surface in time to hear Diego shout, "Cannonball!" followed by a tremendous splash and tall fountain of spray.

Daniel pulled himself out and went in search of a boulder he could lift. This he carried to the ledge where Diego was now sitting. As expected, his friend served up a friendly challenge.

"C'mon, is that as big a rock as you could carry?"

Daniel was too focused to take the bait. He replied flatly, "I'm only going down for a ten-count on this first dive."

"Okay, I suppose I can wait that long," Diego replied. Though his tone was flip, he stared blankly at the water. Daniel sensed Diego's concern but refrained from ribbing him for it.

Daniel spent a few minutes breathing deeply, then without much ceremony, hefted the rock and strode toward the edge. "See you in a while," he said cheekily and then he was gone.

"Be careful!" Diego called after him.

Daniel opened his eyes underwater when the mad fizz of the surface had retreated. He began to count slowly, *one, two, three*. The wall of the cove slid steadily upward and he noted many creatures to inspect on the way up. *Four, five, six*. Here, the water glowed a diffuse blue, while the distant surface was a bright shimmer, *seven, eight, nine*. He guessed he was approaching thirty feet—an easy dive—and thought about stretching it to a twelve-count. *Ten, eleven...* Noticing how much closer the wall of the cove had become, Daniel gave a few swift strokes to pull away, but instead found himself swept closer still. His stomach tightened, and it broke his count. Glancing down he was pleased to see no sight of a bottom, which meant his next dive could be deeper, but the current— *Time to drop the rock*, he thought.

He shot up with the sudden change in buoyancy and to his surprise, his back struck rock. Instinctively he tucked his head and gripped his mouth to avoid expelling air. He thrust against the rock to gain clearance, but the current tumbled him, and he found himself once again bumping against rock that now seemed to be above him. Had he gotten caught under a ledge, or perhaps in a lava tube for which these islands were famous? There was no time to consider the matter because now the water was darkening. The current had driven him deeper into the opening and his buoyancy was causing him to bang along the overhead. He needed space to swim!

Reaching up and shoving off, he took three powerful strokes before realizing he could no longer see the opening. Had he gone the wrong way, or been carried deeper into the cave by the current? He couldn't be sure. Panicking for the first time, he swam furiously for a dozen strokes before it registered that he no longer fought against the current, but swam with it. He had gone the wrong way!

Paralyzed with fear, he felt the painful ache in his lungs and the narrowing of vision that experience told him was the limit of what he could endure. No longer swimming, he rose again. The back of his head struck the rock above. He grimaced and a few precious air bubbles escaped from his mouth. *Follow-the-bubbles* was part of his self-taught diving mantra, but this wisdom was of no help here. He gave a desperate push, then a few stokes that were little more than a panicked flail, and he again floated upward. He braced for impact.

Feeling strangely detached from what was happening, it barely registered that he could no longer see. Water crept into his mouth, and he failed to muster energy for surprise. Only as he began to choke did he realize he was drowning. And then his head broke the surface into air.

Either his vision had not yet recovered, or he was in total darkness. But it didn't matter because at last he could breathe! It was difficult to stay afloat at first because he coughed and spluttered so violently. Subconsciously, he registered the muted reverberations that signaled an enormous, but enclosed, space. Calmer, he swam long easy strokes in the still water. Rolling into a backstroke, he observed a distant circle of light far above him and gradually, as his eyes adjusted, he could make out the walls of a giant cavern, perhaps a thousand feet tall and a mile across. Ten minutes of slow but steady swimming brought him to a sandy beach and he flopped ashore, exhausted.

How long he had lain there, he couldn't be sure, but gradually his consciousness began to coalesce on two incredible thoughts. This discovery was even more amazing than the Tunnel of Atlantis on nearby Lanzarote island. The second thought, by far more disturbing, is that he had absolutely no idea how he was going to get out to tell anyone about it. Swimming back the length of the tunnel, against the current, was out of the question—he'd never survive it. Just glancing across the water where he had emerged was enough to make him shudder.

Gazing upward at the wide crater opening far overhead, Daniel also gave up any thought of climbing out. Where the broad beach met the walls was a steeply rising, tortured jumble of sharp volcanic rock. High above, great sea birds roosted in nests wedged into every crevice. It looked possible to climb the rockpile for perhaps a hundred feet, but then the glassy rock walls of the cavern leaned inward to such a degree that it formed more of a ceiling than wall. Dejected, he stole another glance toward the spot where the tunnel lurked beneath the water and again thought, *no way*. Somewhere else in this vast shadowy cavern, he had to find another means to escape.

After 10 minutes of trudging along the beach, he thought of Diego. What would he do after Daniel had failed to surface? If he found the tunnel and got swept in, Diego would never be able to hold his breath long enough to survive. Daniel pushed the thought away by assuring himself that Diego wasn't a strong enough diver to even get down the thirty or so feet to the tunnel entrance. Almost certainly, he would ride back to town for help. Of course, no one on the island was even aware that this cavern, entombed in the heart of a long-extinct volcano, existed. Though they would undoubtedly scour the seas, eventually they'd be forced to conclude that he had drowned. With sudden clarity, Daniel realized that if was going to ever see his friend or his family again, he would have to find his own way out.

Daniel paused to wipe his eyes, which had become watery, and as his vision cleared, he became aware that a few hundred yards farther along the beach a shadowy structure extended out into the water. He broke into a run that minutes later brought him standing atop a large rusty iron wharf, its far end having collapsed into the cavern's lake. His mind exploded with a kaleidoscope of thoughts. Clearly people had visited this cavern before—perhaps it was well known? Might they return? If there were heavy materials and equipment here—could there be a sizeable entrance somewhere? Find it, and he'd be home for dinner. Wait, this wharf hadn't been touched in a long, long time—maybe the entrance was sealed up?

His thoughts raced in a maelstrom of possibilities, until a sudden insight froze his thinking in place. This place was strangely familiar. Though he couldn't fathom how that could be, the certainty of the feeling raised the hairs on his neck. Rooted to the spot, his eyes roved the surroundings. The huge cavern in the heart of an extinct volcano. The birds soaring out the opening high overhead. The underwater tunnel. The ancient pier. Suddenly he made the connection and nearly let out a laugh. Of course, this all reminded him of Captain Nemo's secret underground base —just as Verne had described it.

As that thought registered, his every muscle tensed as if to instinctively protect him from any physical harm that might be manifested by his mind's obvious slip into insanity. Forcing his breathing to slow through a still wide-open mouth, Daniel carefully constructed each next thought into a deliberate truth. *Twenty Thousand Leagues Under the Sea* was just a book. A *fiction* book. Any resemblance to this place had to be pure coincidence.

He fought back the chaotic doubt that began to intrude. Perhaps he could allow the possibility that Verne's story might have incorporated a few distantly related real events—like *Treasure Island*. But with this admission, Daniel sensed control of his logic might be slipping and he fought back. It's just a wharf. In a cave. Under a volcano. For his summer reading assignment to really be true, there would have to be coal mines, machines for extracting sodium, and stockpiles of stores. Shaking now, Daniel pivoted around slowly. There, in the gloom, not more than fifty yards away, he could see an immense stack of cylindrical drums and the faint outline of a chimney rising behind them.

In a trance, his body responding robotically, he placed one foot in front of the other. Slowly he backtracked from the wharf and then onto the beach, his eyes fixed on the drums as if to pin them in reality. Approaching, he reached out with his hand and then drew back, suddenly gripped with the absurd notion that touching might cause it to disappear. *But was that any more absurd than what it meant if all this was real?* His fingers made contact with the container.

Whatever the implications, there could be no doubt that what was in front of him was real. Three-foot-high casks were stacked in two rows on top of each other and at least six rows deep. Behind this stash a low steel platform stood on pilings sunk into the sand. Some sort of chemical production plant had been built upon the platform. At the center stood a steel tank perhaps six feet in diameter and twenty feet tall that bristled with a forest of pipes that ran everywhere and, like a mechanical vine, appeared to engulf an adjacent hopper. Daniel couldn't guess what the apparatus produced, but nearest to him sat a mechanism obviously intended for filling the casks. Everything on the platform was so corroded it looked unsafe and so rather than cross it, Daniel remained on the sand and circled, gazing up in awe.

On the far side of the platform was a structure he recognized instantly as a blast furnace. Constructed entirely of brick, its chimney seemed to reach up toward the inward sloping wall of the cavern overhead. On the black sand beach closer to the shore, there were several neat circular piles of a rocky material that were blacker still. Clearly, here was the coal to feed the furnace. Assuming Verne's story accurately reported its source, then somewhere in the inky depths beyond the wavelets lapping these mounds, must be rich seams of anthracite.

Beyond the furnace, rose another steel platform. A tank mounted on the near end was a boiler for it had a brick firebox beneath the platform. Pipes ran from the lake to vessels on the platform, leading Daniel to conclude that it was a distilling apparatus for making fresh water. But at the far end of the platform was another tank, this one taller but narrower, with small pipes that extended from the domed lid to rows of what looked like ancient gas cylinders set in racks on the sand. At the base of this columnar tank, thick electrical cables, supported on short poles, ran across the sand toward the cavern wall. These were different than the wires strung on the two platforms to service the strange looking light bulbs, so Daniel decided to follow them. They led to a cave excavated in the side of the cavern wall. Inside, he could just make out a vast, corroded heap of what must have been battery cells and so he decided against entering.

Daniel headed back toward the wharf along the cavern wall so that he passed behind the platforms. Here, he found another cave filled with crates and barrels, all covered with a fine layer of black grit. A few were empty, and from their interior arrangements and the prodigious weight of the other sealed crates, Daniel concluded that the majority contained machine parts.

By some good fortune he uncovered two crates of milky glass bottles that contained water of dubious quality, but by now he was so parched he barely cared, and drank deeply. A less pleasant surprise were the barrels, which contained an unusual oil and a rancid spongy mass whose odor drove him from the cave.

Almost back to the wharf now, the final cave contained a sizable workshop. Along one side, machine tools of every description littered the tops of long, heavy workbenches. On the opposite side, beneath an oilcloth cover, stood a treadle-powered sewing machine. An ordinary table held tailoring tools, but underneath, five long, narrow crates caught Daniel's attention.

He grabbed a crowbar from the workbench to pry open the lid. Inside, wrapped in paper which crumbled in his hands, nestled a large roll of the most exquisite cloth he had ever felt. With full recollection of the novel—make that history book—now, Daniel knew this must be the Byssus cloth, or sea silk, made from the secretions of a unique Mediterranean mussel and worn by the crew of the Nautilus!

Several hours later, Daniel lay slumped on the sand against the decaying wharf. His explorations complete, he might have been amused by how quickly this most amazing of fantasies had become just another element of his grim reality. But he was tired and hungry, and his head still throbbed from his fateful dive.

Despite his earlier convictions, he had forced himself into the water when the tide had started to ebb in order to attempt swimming to freedom. The current, though not as strong as before, had foiled him. Long before he could see the exit to the ocean, he had felt the rising panic, and doubted whether he'd be able to either reach it or regain the cavern. With this fresh reminder, he had once again dragged himself up the beach in defeat. Swimming was not an option.

He dozed.

Hours later, Daniel woke, groggy, stiff, and cold, and noted that the feeble light was gone. He crawled in complete darkness away from the water's edge until he found the workshop cave. Banging his already sore head more times than he could count, he found the five-foot wide roll of Byssus cloth and wound some around him like a cocoon. Then he flopped on the floor and fell back into slumber.

When he opened his eyes, he could tell it was morning because a faint light once again illuminated the cavern. Wild dreams had come to him in his sleep of Captain Nemo and his crew tramping about on the beach, hauling coal from the sea, and tending the machinery that made their fuel. Daniel imagined building a submarine to drive out of the tunnel. Then, he conjured the fantasy of harnessing the great sea birds he had seen roosting where the jumbled walls met the inclined overhead, to fly him out of the crater opening and back home.

A sudden question startled him awake. For several minutes he fought to extract himself from his Byssus bedding. Despite his frustration, he now took great care not to damage the lightweight cloth. Once freed, he found a pair of shears to cut a small square of the fabric. Then, he grabbed a wrench and a hammer from the workbench and ran to the racks that held the gas cylinders.

Selecting a cylinder valve that looked like it might turn with the least amount of persuading, he tied the silk cloth into a pouch and fitted it over the valve. It took several whacks from the hammer before the wrench began to open the valve, but then gas hissed into the pouch, blowing it off the valve. As it shot away, Daniel watched the silk slowly rise, then hang in the air, until finally deflating and settling like a leaf. *Yes!* There was gas in the cylinders, and it was lighter than air.

Daniel realized that the distilling apparatus he'd seen on the second platform supplied water, which the electrolytic cell separated into hydrogen and oxygen. Captain Nemo must have bottled the two gases to use in their diving suits, because there was no way to perform the extended, deep, dives described in the book on compressed air alone.

For a moment, Daniel contemplated whether he could use the oxygen to swim out through the tunnel. But hope faded quickly as he realized even one cylinder was much too large to swim with, and no smaller container existed. So, he reverted to his original plan, to launch a small balloon out of the crater with a message.

Excitedly, he set about the task, laying out a quantity of Byssus silk to form the balloon, trying to keep at bay the doubts encroaching on his mind. His crude balloon was unlikely to travel very far. And what were the odds of someone finding his message on the slopes of a volcano on the remote end of an island that contained one small town? And if the balloon did travel beyond the mountain slopes, wasn't it just as likely to come down in the ocean as on land? How would he know? How long might it be before someone found it?

Daniel tried to focus on the vexing problem of the message. The only paper he had found had been wrapped around the Byssus cloth, and that had disintegrated at his touch. He might be able to write on the silk with a piece of charcoal but that seemed unlikely to remain legible. The more he thought about his plan, the more frustrated he became. On the verge of tears, he wished his balloon could just carry him, like the characters in his latest book, directly out of the cavern.

At this, he paused and said aloud, "Why not?"

The question hung in the air and the indifferent coo of the birds far above offered no challenge. Energized by the prospect of securing his escape, he threw himself into the work. Each bolt of Byssus cloth unrolled to nearly forty feet in length. Joined side-by-side and folded lengthwise on itself, Daniel could create a pocket about twenty-foot square. Would it be enough? He could only hope that, for once, his skinny frame would be an asset.

Sewing was his next challenge, and the 19th Century sewing machine he'd uncovered earlier proved to be a formidable adversary. Back and forth he stitched the fabric, breaking thread and needles apace, until satisfied the seams—irregular and rough as they were—might hold the gas. *After all,* he reasoned, *it only needed it work for a few minutes.*

Then he had another idea. Foul as it was, he dug out the spongy, white, oily substance, which he now suspected may have once been spermaceti, from the barrels and rubbed it into the cloth. Trying not to vomit, Daniel blew hard against the oil-impregnated cloth and was pleased his breath didn't pass through.

From the wharf he scavenged a short length of hemp rope. He took great care in attaching the ends to the silk pocket because this loop would serve as his harness.

It had taken four days to create the balloon, during which time Daniel had had little to eat save for what he assumed was century-old dried jellyfish, he had found packed in cans. So, when at last it was time to fill the balloon, he was eager to proceed.

One after another, he emptied the hydrogen cylinders into his crude silk envelope, and it began to come to life. He had tied it to the platform, but when the balloon reached the point where it started to rise from the sand, he slipped his head and arms through the harness. This complicated the process of adding additional gas; but more importantly in Daniel's mind, it guaranteed that if the balloon went, so would he.

In under an hour, the fabric envelope was looming overhead, straining against its tether. It had assumed the shape of a fat, four-pointed star and Daniel began stealing troubled glances at his stitching as it stretched under pressure. Already he could hear the faint hiss of gas escaping from his crude balloon. It was time to go.

As he slipped the silk off the filling pipe, Daniel cinched the balloon shut with a piece of rope. Then he untied the knot at the railing that held the balloon captive.

The balloon shot up a foot until the harness caught Daniel under his arms. It lifted him to his toes, then slowed. Frantically, Daniel untied the tether from the balloon and tossed the rope to the ground. Would that make any difference?

Now, his feet hung above the cylinders. The balloon took its time gaining momentum but slowly, inexorably, it drifted upward. Daniel was elated. He stole a moment to enjoy the view from what now had to be a height of at least fifty feet, when suddenly, the balloon lurched.

He looked up, seeing nothing but the silk bag, but he knew he was near the cavern wall where it sloped steeply in his direction. It was agonizing to feel and hear the balloon bump along the glassy rock, his roughly sewn seams catching and scraping every sharp projection.

As it crept upward, the balloon was forced by the rock toward the center of the cavern and now Daniel dangled four hundred feet over the vast lake. He was glad the scene below was becoming lost to view as the light from above grew brighter.

Nearing the center under the crater opening, the sound of scraping diminished, replaced by the hiss of escaping gas. To his horror, the sound grew louder. Only a short distance from freedom, the balloon was stalling out!

Daniel felt the cold sweat of panic as he imagined a fall from this height only seconds away. His eyes searched wildly—there was nothing he could release to lighten the load—then locked on the knot that sealed the balloon just inches above his head. Before a flicker of doubt could form, Daniel held his breath and jerked the knot free.

The effect was immediate. The gas blasted past him. As the balloon shot upwards, Daniel's harness was wrenched over his head. Only a fingertip-catch of the rope saved him from plummeting.

Hanging by his hands onto what felt like the tip of a bull whip, he was blinded when his head popped above the crater rim. As soon as his feet were clear, he let go of the balloon and dropped to the ground, tumbling head over heels down the steep, barren side of the mountain.

Released of its weight, the balloon soared in a few convulsive jerks before it collapsed and drifted far down the slope. When he came to stop, Daniel jumped up and shouted with pure exhilaration. He ran with abandon down the mountain—he was alive, he was free, and what a story he had to write about! As the wind rushed through his hair on his carefree descent, the title came to him instantly: *Five Minutes in a Balloon.*

Leviathan

Michael D. Winkle

The leviathan's subsonic grunts echoed away and returned, striking his great plow of a snout and rippling through spermaceti to form an image of the schooner, the long hollow shell that housed the scrambling four-limbed creatures.

He heard the slap of waves against barnacle-encrusted wood and the rush of the ship's keel through choppy seas. Around the vessel smaller hollow casings floated, longboats dropped like calves by this unliving-yet-moving object.

The leviathan lifted and lowered his flukes, shoving tons of water aside as he sent his cylindrical body forward, faster and faster. Eddies and cross-currents, visible to his senses like strands of kelp, exploded before him. He rocketed toward the schooner, his path as straight as the metal stingers used by the land dwellers.

Silver fans broke over his head and spine as he breached the surface. He divided the sea into two high palisades, one port and one starboard.

The gray-brown belly of the ship loomed before him, a wall of low-pitched noise. Gulls rose from the masts and gunwale.

The cachalot's spermaceti-lens rang with false images upon impact. He cupped thousands of gallons of salt water beneath him as he worked back out of the bark's side.

He sensed a huge gash in the wooden hulk. Small objects plunked into the sea around him—the four-limbed parasites abandoning or flung from their host.

He lowered his heavy snout, dove beneath the vessel, and rose again in a shallow arc. He sensed one of the lesser boats above. He yawned wide his long, narrow jaw and caught it up. It cracked and splintered as his conical teeth sank in, and he recalled the taste and texture of a floating log he bit once out of curiosity.

He also felt a squirming, which ceased when he crunched again. He tasted hot blood and flesh, not unlike that of harbor seal.

A dull sting behind his dorsal hump reminded him of the other wooden vessels and their barb-wielding parasites. He spewed out the geyser of his breath and inhaled. He sank and beat his flukes angrily.

He tilted his head to port like a rudder and glided in a vast circle through the Pacific depths. He rose between two boats, knocking one high in the air with his snout. He arched his back, scooping up the other with his flukes. He caught another land-dweller and crunched it down.

The schooner listed now, mortally wounded. More surface dwellers scrambled to and fro on its decks. The leviathan rammed the ship on the starboard side, just below the forecastle. The tattered sheets on the masts shuddered. Planks popped and cracked. He left the ship heaving sickly over, sensing death in an object not alive.

The encounter with the whaler stoked the leviathan's appetite. He spent a day and a night plumbing lightless canyons, miles deep, until he found something substantial enough to assuage his hunger.

Substantial but uncooperative. The squid's tentacles swept over the whale's head, its hook-lined suckers biting into skin and blubber like a thousand lampreys. The cachalot shook the giant mollusk, sawing yellow ivory over pale pink arms. The squid's two longest tentacles slapped their diamond-shaped tips against his wrinkled back, grating and tearing through a field of rusty harpoons. Clouds of ink obscured his vision and numbed his tongue, but the squid could not escape his hold.

The leviathan jerked, opened his crooked jaw, and crushed. A stalagmite of a tooth punctured a porthole-sized eye. He jerked and bit again, and the mollusk's subdermal shield splintered. The cachalot thrashed and squeezed the brain within the squid's body. The many arms coiled snail-shell tight and loosened.

He tore and bit and gulped down the enormous squid. A fifty-foot arm drifted away like a sea serpent. He swallowed the main body hastily, chased after the gristly tentacle, and gulped it down as well.

He rose out of the squid's canyon off the coast of New Zealand, and swam idly south with the East Australia Current. He caught the distant burbles and baleen-rattles of right whales. That was soon joined by the higher-pitched chatter of dolphins, as they chirped about the numbers of pilchard and flying fish around them and found something significant in the answer.

He heard the clicks and rumbles of his own species, twenty miles to the north. A large pod, thirty or more. The leviathan angled away with a twist of the tail. Once he battled other males with impunity, the ordinary cachalots proving no match for his great size and strength. No longer did he fight for females, however. They fled with the defeated males as they might before a titanic orca.

Everything feared him, the sharks, the orcas, the other sperm whales. He in turn feared nothing. The ocean's inhabitants were mostly humble creatures that avoided him.

Mostly. Once a cold, welling cone of bioelectric charges and scent molecules billowed out of a deep black trench off New Guinea. A huge, hoary sound signature, like a Great White Shark's, only much larger, issued from the darkness.

The *Megalodon* struck as soon as it noticed him, its hollow jaws and gill slits deceptively frail looking, its eyes deceptively dead.

It took two days to kill the ancient shark. Some of the crescent-shaped scars on his sides and tail still throbbed in Arctic currents. That encounter was the closest he had ever come to death—yet he felt an odd exhilaration—a jolt of memory—whenever he caught sight or echo of a normal Great White.

His own kind shunned him. He preferred battle to utter isolation—but nothing else lived that could challenge him.

The leviathan swam alone.

He drifted just under the surface, as near to dreaming as he ever came, the waves breaking over him as over an atoll. Gulls wheeled above, their squeals audible to his tiny ears.

It was not his ears but the vast store of spermaceti in his forehead that caught the echoes of his own voice, the sight-sound more important than eyes. The reservoir of oil channeled low-pitched noises to his brain, not only his echoes, but the crash of waves, the roar of storms, and the bloops and grunts of fish; the rumbles of marine landslides and sea-quakes; and the songs and booms of other cetaceans.

The Tokelau Pod dolphins chirped and squeaked among themselves as they always did, unable, seemingly, merely to float and rest. The leviathan knew their language. They spoke now of the four-limbed land-dwellers they called *men*, who rode in the hollow wood. Their ultrasonic chorus rose to spires of admiration for the cleverness of the land creatures.

When he was younger and less surly, the leviathan had listened to the words of the old dolphin philosopher Kik-Kik-Eet. The men of olden times had merely ridden on hollow logs to brave the Mother of Waters, said Kik-Kik-Eet, but eventually with their fingers that curled like crab legs, they attached two, then three logs together. Now they assembled hundreds of wood pieces to create these "ships" of theirs, some of which were larger than the greatest whale.

"And employed to hunt and kill us," the leviathan had grumbled.

"I do not know how they make their vessels air-tight, but it would not surprise me if one day they started following us into the depths," Kik-Kik-Eet had said.

"I can think of no development more horrible," the young whale had retorted.

"If men could see the kaleidoscope of coral and fish and sea-comb, hear the songs of the Finned Folk and gilled things and of the Mother of Waters herself, *experience* as we experience, perhaps they would be more...sympathetic."

"And perhaps we shall spread our fins and sail over the dry land to visit them in return," had been the sperm whale's last word.

The leviathan shook himself back to the present as excited squeaking began within the Tokelau Pod. Apparently, they had seen more of men's magic: smoke-spewing ships that moved against all currents and all winds.

The leviathan emitted declarations of displeasure at both ends of his digestive system and dove.

A few timeless days later a new vibration disturbed the cachalot's noonday sleep. It was not loud but it was steady. And strong. Secondary echoes reached him from islands on both sides of the Hilgard Deep.

The leviathan spewed out air and inhaled deeply several times to flush and fill his fleshy grottos of lungs. He sank head first, slapped his flukes on the surface, and propelled himself down at a sixty-degree angle.

The ocean deepened from brilliant blue to cobalt green to somber violet. He located the strange rumble welling out of a gorge ahead.

The huge whale swam deeper, between peaks wrinkled up by tectonic collisions. An echo signature reached him, a form reminiscent of a marlin's, only colossal—larger than he.

Then vast yellow eyes glared up out of the gorge.

The unknown creature slowly approached the cachalot, its great luminous orbs studying him coldly, their burning gaze infinitely more unsettling than the black dots of shark-eyes. Its back was ragged with vicious spines. Sawfish teeth edged its pointed beak. With a powerful stirring of abyssal brine, it swept toward him.

The leviathan bellowed without air, an explosive challenge of shock waves in liquid. He worked his flukes furiously, his twenty-fathom form rippling like a worm's. He charged the monster head on for a few seconds, then he swerved aside. The beast swung its sulfurous eyes to follow him, but it was not as swift or as limber as he. The cachalot swept silty masses of water under his tail as he braked and twisted about.

The gorge-creature turned. The whale charged again, his blunt axe-edge of a head aimed for the base of its skull. He bellowed and crashed through his own echoes.

Krooomph. The beast from the depths hung heavy with scales, thicker than those of a basking shark. They scarred his snout even as he hit the thing. The creature shuddered and rolled onto its side; the leviathan shook himself and slammed his tail against its flank before swimming away.

While the creature righted itself, the leviathan rose over it. He twisted again and shot straight down in a slip stream of kelp and bubbles.

Another impact. Pain! The spines on the beast's back punctured the barnacle-encrusted skin of his brow. The enemy's tail drooped; it raised its head high. The whale passed it to starboard, scanning for any vulnerable point. Weirdly, the creature possessed a third glowing eye on this side.

The leviathan gazed into the abyssal monster's large yellow orb. A black spot passed across the golden glow: Its pupil? No. It was an outline—a silhouette.

It was a man.

It is no monster, thought the leviathan, *but a ship—a vessel made of something much stronger than wood. A ship that can follow us into the deeps, just as Kik-Kik-Eet predicted.*

A man dwells within the monster-ship's skull as the part of me that is "I" dwells within my heavy, barnacled head. The land dweller is the "I" of this beast, and the beast is the body for the man. It is something new in the sea. A Man-Whale.

A chill colder than the abyssal water crept along the leviathan's spine. This was worse than any monster. Men could harry him anywhere. There would be no escape from them. Indeed, if man and ship could become one—it was as if mere annihilation were not enough. They meant to replace the Finned Folk with themselves.

A feeling of camaraderie, of pride in his species, a social instinct he had not felt in decades, burst within the huge cachalot. He churned the water and gave his silent battle cry. He fought for all whales—for all Finned Folk—even for the foolish dolphins who would welcome the land dwellers into the Mother of Waters.

The Man-Whale had to be destroyed—here and now.

The land dweller in the glowing eye stood balanced on its hind legs, its upper limbs crossed over its chest in a stance that suggested supreme confidence—and supreme arrogance.

And the best way to destroy this Man-Whale is to destroy its brain, concluded the leviathan.

The huge cetacean changed course with a speed few living creatures would have anticipated. He calculated where the eye would be in three seconds and churned his flukes as never before.

The man broke his haughty stance and stumbled away.

Let us see how air-tight you are, Man-Whale.

As the leviathan shot through the water, however, the bright eye began to close. At least, the sun-bright orb shriveled to a point.

The sperm whale struck anyway. The undersea vessel rang, an oddly musical chord. His echo-hearing told of many shards of something scattering through the water, some casing his assault had shattered. The leviathan sensed that this glowing eye would not open again.

As the artificial whale swept by, the leviathan opened his eighteen-foot jaw and clamped hard on its tail. It shook and shuddered in his grasp. He bit and released and bit again, ivory cones cracking against rock-hard scales.

A distressing sensation rippled through his teeth, along his jaws and down the bundled muscles of his hundred-ton body. He convulsed like an injured eel; his bioelectric sense shorted, and his sight and hearing momentarily faded. Flashes of light specked the sea around him.

Not since he was a calf, running afoul of a Portuguese man-o'-war, had anything stunned him so completely. What venom did this unliving, unnatural thing possess?

The man-whale yanked itself free. Its wash rippled over him as it swam away, unscathed.

The leviathan fought his own unresponsive muscles, spewing barrel-sized blobs of stale air from his S-shaped spiracle. His tail flicked, lashed, and beat the water into myriad eddies. He grunted in rage and swam unsteadily after his enemy. Curtains of its rumble-voice slid over him. The noise dopplered into a higher pitch as it came about in a vast circumference, and once again the molten eye-lights glared out of the darkness.

The leviathan would not be cowed. He roared again, his voice bouncing off undersea peaks, multiplying, becoming an invisible pod to cheer him on.

He beat his flukes ever faster. He remembered the unliving creature's beak, long and pointed like a narwhal tusk. He angled flipper and head to avoid it, but the strange venom slowed his actions.

Agony tore into the whale's side, ripping worse than a coral reef. The scaled thing's larboard fin plowed through blubber and muscle, laying him open from eye to fluke.

He drifted. He struggled. He sank.

Gray silt clouded up around him, tasting of centuries-old plankton.

The undersea vessel settled near him, its eye-lights still cold and staring, its body black save for a sharp-edged mottling where the line of mouth would be on something alive.

The whale lay in pain and confusion. Dark objects, dotted with lights like fish of the deepest chasms, dropped from the beast like remoras and walked over the sea floor toward him. Walked, because they were four-limbed creatures. More men.

How—how could the land dwellers do this? They could not, to his experience, hold their breaths long at all beneath the surface. Yet they marched through the silt toward him undistressed. Did they breathe like fish on top of all else?

The whale could not move without body-wide spasms of agony and clouds of dark blood jetting into the water. He could not remain submerged forever without renewing his air.

Perhaps it was for the better. He had often seen what land dwellers did to whales they immobilized with their metal barbs, and now these water-men drew strange tools and cables from their glowing-eyed vessel and hauled them toward him.

The water-men arranged themselves around him, and then the darkness closed in.

…Yet the light returned, hours or days later. The leviathan heard and felt his own typhoon breath blasting out over the sun-heated Pacific surface, and even more amazing, cool morning air and mist hurricaning into his cavernous lungs.

Enormous bladders of some sort, like jellyfish, crowded him. He moved, feebly at first but soon aggressively. Finally, he realized a huge net held him, and he thrashed angrily.

There was a multiple *bang*, and the jellyfish-bladders mounted to the sky like strange clouds. The net dropped away below him, and the leviathan sank.

He planed out his fins and beat his tail. The pain of his hundred-foot gash was gone. Only a sort of tightness remained, as from a healed wound. He tasted no blood in the water. He could not see it, but he sensed the gash had somehow been sealed.

All that happened now was pure magic to the leviathan. He came slowly about—

And found the man-whale, the undersea vessel, sitting still on the ocean's surface.

A man stood on its back, tall (for a land dweller) and straight. The cachalot had no doubt this was the one in the glowing eye, the brain to the vessel's body.

The man and the whale exchanged regards for a long moment. The man-whale and the water-men had conveyed him to the surface and sealed his wound somehow. He would never understand such magic, but he knew it to be true.

The four-limbed being entered an orifice on the man-whale's head, the vessel's equivalent of a spout. A vibration filled the waters, and the vessel started to move.

The leviathan did not know what to think. Instead of killing him, the man-whale had saved him. Why?

He could just imagine Kik-Kik-Eet spouting one of his crazy ideas: "Having essentially become whales, they know now what it is to *be* whale. Perhaps they even see the Finned Folk as their people now."

The leviathan grunted and dove. It was beyond him. He could never understand what transpired here, any more than he could understand the sharp etchings on the beak of the man-whale, the printed symbols spelling NAUTILUS.

Last Year's Water

Nikoline Kaiser

"I looked at his intelligent forehead, furrowed with premature wrinkles, produced probably by misfortune and sorrow. I tried to learn the secret of his life from the last words that escaped his lips."

~ Jules Verne, *Twenty Thousand Leagues Under the Sea*

Nilak took a piece of fresh plantain and put it on her tongue. She was too tired to go out today, but she had to. Her mother would yell at her if she did not go help her sister. Even though the wind was too cold.

"Now, come now," her mother said, door already open. She always yelled when Nilak opened the door and let the cold in; but it was alright for her mother to do it, because she was mother, and this was her house. It had been her house since Nilak's father had died, six years ago when Nilak was twelve and remembered him best as the large man who smelled like the dogs and laughed through broken teeth. He had always smiled with his mouth closed, because of those teeth, but his smile was beautiful. Nilak's mother had always told her that, that the men here, the men of Kalaallit Nunaat had the most beautiful smiles. The women too, Nilak's father had said, and then he'd kissed her mother, and her mother had laughed.

When she was thirteen, Nilak had been playing with her friends. She had been dodging snowy missiles, and jumped, but she'd miscalculated, and twisted her ankle when she landed, and she'd fallen face-first and chipped one of her front teeth. It could be fixed, but Nilak, thirteen and fatherless, had not wanted it to be fixed.

"Nauja, you can't laze around here all day!"

"I'm Nilak!"

"Yes, yes, go outside, now!"

Nauja was already outside, and had not heard their mother's cry. Nilak's sister was sitting by the dogs, throwing scraps of fish after them, letting them rumble and sit and play and obey to get the pieces of their breakfast. Nilak could taste the melting remains of plantain on her tongue.

"I don't need your help, go back inside," Nauja said. Nilak kicked snow at her, but she was too far away. "Go back inside, *lømmel!*"

"Mom said to help you out here!"

"I don't want your help! Go somewhere else!"

Nilak had already turned away. Nauja, older but more temperamental, had decided two years ago that her mother and little sister were not worth her time. Only the dogs were, the last remaining of the pack their father had tended so well. Nilak did not want to go back inside.

She walked instead. She had always been good at walking, could eat up kilometer after kilometer with her feet, could outpace the dogsleds not by speed but by sheer persistency. She had told their mother that her endurance was better than Nauja's, that standing on the sled was no trouble for her. She could walk until her feet bled and then keep on walking, but her mother had not listened, had let Nauja take over, because Nauja was older and had already started working with the dogs, when their father was still alive.

On days like this, when they were too busy ordering her around to actually make her do anything, Nilak walked until she was lost. She was not truly lost, of course—she had lived here for near two decades now, and she knew the snow, the cliffs, the melting ice better than she knew their tiny house. She could tell who else had walked here, if Nauja had taken the dogs around the bend by the shore, where the fishermen had moved to get a better catch. She could tell where the Danish meteorologist had set up equipment, oohed and aaawed at the ice, and then sighed in frustration because it was melting too fast for the sea to drink. In her mind's eye, Nilak could see it all, every shift from the wind, every foot and stave and sled that had been there. Nilak did not navigate by the stars, but by the lulling of the sea.

Today, as the sun moved across the sky, she could see a new path to tread; the snow had furrowed, as if something large had been dragged through it. It was curious—Nilak had never seen something like that happen before, had not seen sleds or dogs or humans make those tracks. Seals were not big enough, or intent enough to get that far inland. It could be the military, but they kept away from here, stayed on their air base.

Knowing it could be dangerous, or pointless, or even just foolish, Nilak followed the track until, at the middle of it, she found a man. He was covered in snow and ice, his clothes tattered, his beard whitened by the frost. He looked for a moment so much like the old men who sat at the bars each night and drank Tuborg-beer that she almost cried out familiar names, almost turned around and ran back to get help. But the man was not one Nilak had ever seen before. He was still breathing.

She walked over and touched his shoulder, shocked when he opened his eyes. His hand shot up and grasped her wrist, his eyes shot lightning with no thunder, and she screamed. It echoed over the ice and the water, and Nilak thought this was what death must look like, an old man frozen over, his eyes full of fire.

He opened his mouth and croaked out something she could not understand. Then again—was that French? He spoke German next, something she'd had at school but had never picked up properly. He was confused now, eyes roaming around. His grip had slackened, but now Nilak did not want to pull her hand away. The man tried again in French, then in English.

"*Jeg forstår engelsk,*" she said, but his eyes were confused still, so she switched. "I speak English. It's okay. Let me go, please, I want to help you. How are you still alive? It's so cold and your clothes are broken."

"In tatters," he said, and let her wrist go entirely, and Nilak thought, what an arrogant man, correcting her speech while he was half-frozen to death.

"Can you get up?"

"Help me, child."

She did, because this man no longer scared her, cold and confused as he looked. He had not understood Danish, but he spoke German and French and other languages too, ones she did not recognize.

He weighed almost nothing, and Nilak was strong, so she aided him easily. He was tall, though, towering over her. She could tell he wanted to stand on his own, but he couldn't, and instead he was forced to lean against her, almost clinging.

"My house is close by, we will have to walk…"

"No! No house, no cities." His teeth were clattering. "Forward, please. I shall show you the way."

"It's ice and snow ahead, nothing there…"

"There is," he interrupted. "My home lies ahead."

The man was clearly insane, but Nilak walked forward with him anyway. They walked for half an hour, and she only stumbled when she looked up and saw the giant metal monster, half-submerged in the snow. The man let go of her, and stumbled forward, towards it.

"Go home now, child, I thank you for your aid. Tell me, before you go, where in the world am I? What shores have I been cast upon?"

"You—you're on…What *is* that?"

The man ignored her question. "Where are we, child?" The fire was back in his eyes, but there was a blue tinge around his mouth. He would not be standing for long.

Nilak, knowing it was dangerous and foolish, pointed to the giant submarine. "Let me with you inside, and I will tell you."

The man looked thunderously angry, and she knew he would argue, but then he collapsed, crumbling on the snow like a pile of fallen leaves. Nilak sighed, and hoped the door was unlocked. Hauling him inside would be difficult enough already.

Nilak, piled blankets on top of the man after rubbing his torso and arms and legs until they were no longer blue. She found some foul-smelling brown alcohol, like the kind the old men drank when there wasn't any beer left, and she poured it down his throat and wet his lips when he wouldn't drink anymore. There was electricity down there, though the wiring and the furniture were all old. Not old like her mother's furniture, worn and used until it literally collapsed into nothing, but old like it had been bought in a different time and never replaced because that time had never been left behind. Nilak explored the submarine as far as she dared, the living-room and bedrooms and a library so big it had made her head spin.

She didn't want to leave her patient alone for too long, and she was unsettled by the vastness of the place, so she returned to the living-room where she had placed him. She dug through his pockets (empty save for keys), leafed through a book on marine biology that had laid on a plush chair (old and boring), and ate three plantains before the man woke up.

"Ah," he said, and then he noticed her and sprang up, tangled in blankets and with a face red with fury. "You! How did you enter here!"

Nilak, having expected a reaction quite like this, sat in perfect stillness and stared at him. "The hatch was open," she said.

"Lie!"

"I took your key."

"How dare you…"

"I saved your life," she reminded him, talking gently, the way mother talked to her and Nauja when they were sick, the way Nauja talked to the puppies, eager for attention and love. "You were freezing to death, and I could not drag you to my house or the doctor, and you said you wanted to go home."

His fury left him, but he still stared at her with hard eyes. It took every ounce of courage to meet those eyes, to not flinch. Nilak felt as if she might be staring into the vastness of the ocean, cold and unyielding, full of sharp teeth in a giant, gaping mouth.

"Of course," he said. "I thank you for your assistance. You may have done better in leaving me. Now I thank you to go from here, and tell no one what you saw here."

Nilak stared. "I won't promise you that."

"You…!"

"Tell me who you are, and I will tell you where you are and who I am, and I will also keep your secret. I will tell no one back home that you are here." Heart beating too fast, she continued. "I will also let you die, if you do, but first you have to tell me. And if you don't, I will stop you."

He scoffed. "And how, child, would you stop me?"

Nilak shrugged. "I have talked with old men before. They have been drunk and raving, and some almost walked off the ice and into the ocean. I dragged them home. I dragged you home too, and I can do it again." She faked her courage. She had seen her father do it. "I carried you here and brought you back to life once already, so who is to say I cannot do it again? But tell me everything and I'll let you go."

He laughed. It was a rattling sound, more a cough than a real laugh, but laugh he did. He gathered the blankets closer around him and wrung his hands through his long, scraggly beard. She could tell it had been a deep black-brown once, but it was not just the ice that had made it white and grey. He was older than she had thought.

"Am I your prisoner, then? How curious. How *ironic*." He held out his hand. "The book you are holding, would you hand it to me please? It is quite precious to me."

"Yes. But I don't know why it is; this Aronnax guy is boring."

He smiled. His teeth were perfect and white, and Nilak had to look away. His smile was not familiar at all, but she had wanted it to be.

"Tell me where I am and who you are, so I might thank my rescuer."

"You're in Greenland. You're lucky, you know. No one lives on the ice like this, or at least they didn't use to. It's by the other shores we've settled, but my parents moved here when they were young and set up with some other people who were tired of it all. They wanted away from the noise and the Americans and the nuclear weapons."

"Nuclear?"

"*Atomkraft*," she said, but he still didn't seem to understand. "Anyway, I get to ask my question now. Who are you?"

"I am no-one."

"Guy, that is unfair! You answer me, because I answered you!"

"No," he said. "I have answered. I am no one. Nemo, I called myself, and Captain when I had a crew. I am Outis, Odysseus, Ulysses. I am the giant narwhal that haunted the seas, from pole to pole. I have cast aside all identity save the one I made for myself, and even that I have now lost. Nemo, that is my name, but even the Nemo that was is now gone and forgotten. Truly, I am no one now—if I am even that."

Nilak peered at him. "Are you drunk?"

"Possibly. The taste of brandy is hot on my tongue."

"I gave you some brown stuff to heat you up."

"I thank you." He didn't sound completely sincere. "What is your name, then? And tell me more of these nuclear weapons, please."

"Well, maybe my name is no one too."

"It is not."

"How would you know?"

He sighed, deeply, and it struck Nilak that he must be a father, that there must be children running around here somewhere—she was so rooted in this thought that she looked around, expecting to see them. But there was no one there. She had to be right, though. She had only ever heard parents sigh like that.

"I was born with the name Dakkar," he said.

"See? Why was that so hard? I'm Nilak."

"Nilak." It sounded only a little odd when he said it. He spoke it better than most foreigners who came here. "Your mother named you?"

"Yes. It's proof she loves me more than my older sister, Nauja." He looked confused.

"*Nilak* means, um, something like…" Her English disappeared for a moment; he seemed amused at the wild hand-gestured she used to make up for it until its return. "Fresh ice water. It's good. *Nauja* means seagull. And she deserves it."

His lips twitched. "Truly a horrid bird."

"They're useful but they just screech and screech and steal your food and then they taste awful too. Do you know how to cook one?"

"I do not think I do, no."

"It's my mother's way of cooking them. You pluck it and boil it, then you take it out and pick the meat from the bones, then you boil it again, then once more with salt and then you throw the whole thing out in the garbage 'cause it's trash."

He laughed again. "I see. I am sure your sister is none too happy about that."

Nilak shrugged. "It also means she's tough, you know. She's very..."

"Hardened?"

"No, no. *Stædig*—stubborn!"

"That must be a family trait."

Nilak glared. "You sound like her!"

He failed to hide his smile behind his hand. Then his eyes landed on the book, and his face darkened.

"The weapons you spoke of..."

"The Americans put them here. And the Danish too, I guess."

"Nuclear means it is..."

"Bad. It's bad."

"Well, it is a weapon in the government's hands..."

"It's a weapon," Nilak said. And then, almost unbidden, they both looked up, and around, at the metal around them, hidden by rich carpets and tapestries.

"I've looked around your home," she said. It came out sounding more like a confession than an accusation.

"Without my leave."

"I saved your life. And I wanted to see if there were any others here."

His hands tightened around the book. "No. I am alone now. My crew is lost to me, forever. Only I remain, and I should not have."

"What happened to them?"

He pressed his lips together and shook his head. "Do you know how far it is to Lincoln Island?"

"Where?"

"I see. Forget it." He seemed determined, now. "If you give me the location of these weapons you speak of, then I will go there and destroy them. As my thanks for your services."

"What are you going to do?"

"As you have no doubt noticed, this vessel is one of a kind. The Nautilus was designed by me, and once, there was nothing more powerful in the world. I dare say she shall be sufficient for the task, though it may be her last."

He was hoping it would be, Nilak realized. She had only just met him, but pain shot through her heart at the thought of this suicide mission he had decided on. "What about your children?" she blurted out, so sure of herself, and so very unthinking.

She had been wrong before, it turned out; there had been no lightning in his eyes when she found him in the snow. It was there now, sparking a storm, shooting a bolt right through her. Nilak thought she would drop dead, right there on his carpeted floors.

"Get out of here!"

She was on her feet immediately, running for the hatch, for the exit. She was not even sure he had spoken, if he had shouted at her in anger or had warned her, or if she'd just thought he was about to shout before he could speak. But she had to heed those words, because not doing so would mean losing her life.

The hatch was closed and locked. She had done it herself, and then she had left the key on the table in the room she had just escaped from. She could not go back, and immediately, Nilak resigned herself to roaming this huge, strange place, hiding in the library, in the kitchen, doing her best to avoid Captain Nemo so he would not kill her for her transgression. She would live and die here, surviving on scraps and no sunlight, missing her mother and even Nauja, yearning for the snow and ice outside.

Nemo appeared behind her. The key was in his hand.

"You forgot this." He didn't sound angry any longer. Nilak stared at him. Her back pressed against the cold wall.

"I'm sorry," she said.

"You are young," he said. "You saw the picture in my private chambers?"

She shook her head, not sure what he was talking about.

"Then you know of Prince Dakkar, and what happened to him?"

Again, she shook her head. His hand with the key fell down to rest by his side.

"How did you know of my family?"

"You talk to me like my father did."

And there it was, laid bare. The real reason she had dragged him back here, and not run for help. The real reason she had stayed, waiting and watching. Wanting him to wake up.

He stood very still after she said that, like he was not real at all.

"You say 'did.' He is dead then, your father?"

"He drowned. I was twelve."

"I am sorry for your loss."

"I'm sorry for yours too. You did—I mean…"

"Yes."

"Is that why you want to die?"

"Yes." She could tell he wanted to say more, but he was too exhausted. His walk to catch her had tired him out.

"Nilak, I…" His shoulders slumped forward. He looked more ancient than old now, so grieved and burdened he was like to keel over like a tree covered in too much snow. "Would you, please, if you can— would you bury this vessel? The Nautilus, I will not let her sail again. She will not return to the ocean. But she must not be on land, no, not if any force in this world can help it. It would be best if you could sink her, but she has become locked in the ice, and cannot be budged from this place. You must bury her, so deeply and well that only centuries from now will any find her, and by then it will be when the British and the Americans, the French and the Germans have all destroyed each other, destroyed everything else too, as it must be. As it will end. Will you do this, Nilak? I can rest, then, if you do this."

In the hand not holding the key, he was clutching the book.

"If you give that book to me, I will," she said, bold and brave, and Nemo recoiled as if she had slapped him. "See? Just a stupid book, but you won't part with it. So, you don't want to die, really, not completely."

He sighed again, deeply. "So young, you are so young, to think that that is enough…"

"This place is still functional…"

"So much optimism, precious yet false…"

"You could sail again…"

"Soon, you will learn, there is only destruction…"

"And you could take me with you."

That stopped him short. Nilak went on before he could recover.

"Take me away from here, let me come with you! I want to see the world, travel. I don't want to be stuck here, with Nauja and the dogs and—I want to go! I've seen all there is here, and it bores me. It bores me to tears. It's all snow and ice, and I want to see the rest of the world!" Her voice rang through the corridors; Nemo almost smiled.

"Ah. But then you should not go with me. I am like all other men in this world, Nilak. I do not go and see the world. I only destroy it."

Slowly, so very slowly, he lifted his hand and held out the book for her. She wanted to refuse it, knock it from his hands and tell him he was a coward. She wanted to scream at him. And at the world.

She took the book. She took the keys too, when he handed them to her.

"I buried Prince Dakkar in a griever's grave," he told her. "And Captain Nemo was buried on Lincoln Island. I cared little for either burial, in truth."

She had no idea what he was talking about. Perhaps he meant he had died when he had changed his name, that his past self had gone and made way for a new one. "We used to bury our dead at sea." She told him, in lieu of something better to say.

"A wonderful place, yet my vessel will no longer go there, and I will not part from my vessel—ah, you cry. A bit of salt and water, then, to alleviate the horror of being buried on land."

Nilak wiped furiously at her eyes, nearly poking them out with the corners of the book. "Here," she said, handing it back to him. "Here, just take it. I don't want to bury you. I just saved you, you're not dead."

Nemo spoke; "I have been dead for many years now. My corpse has walked the bottom of the sea and claimed untrodden lands as my own. My decaying body has loved crew and companion, has felt betrayal and pain and hunger. But dead I was, still. Dead, and alone."

"I feel that too," Nilak said, though she knew she did not feel a fraction of what he did. "I feel—void, and alone. I want to go to sea with you."

"And yet..." he started, but she finished for him.

"Your vessel will not sail."

The key in her hand was heavy. "Okay," she said, sniffling between her tears. "Okay, I'll do it. Can I—can I ask, what were their names—your family?"

His smile was so threadbare it was a miracle it did not snap. "I do not remember their names. I told you, I am but a corpse, and corpses forget."

"Oh. Will you forget me as well?"

"Your name. Not you."

"Fresh ice water," Nilak reminded him, crying openly now, because she had given up trying to fight it. "It's like your watery grave. Think of that."

The taste of plantain on her tongue had turned rotten, but she did not stop for a drink. Shovelling snow was hard, hacking up ice was even harder.

But Nilak had promised to bury, and bury she would. It was lucky she was strong; she worked until her arms trembled, for many days and weeks, and she barely spoke a word while her work was yet unfinished. Her muscles grew, and she stood taller, too, did not slump like she'd used to. She was not absent-minded, did not wander any longer, though some of the old men with their beer said she had lost her mind. Nauja left her alone, perhaps scared; her mother hugged her tight, every morning, and did not ask her to do anything. The devil had taken hold of Nilak's mind, the others in the city said, and it was dancing on her shoulders until her task was completed. That is why her shoulders had become so broad, that is why she had grown taller and leaner; why she had grown stronger, too.

She finished her tireless task without fanfare or celebration. Snow had fallen heavy over the months, and it had aided her in her work. By the following week, she presented her sister with new hooks and rings for the dogs and the sled, made from fine, heavy iron. She refitted the locks on her mother's house, made them new and sparkling.

"Where did you get all that iron, Nilak?" her mother asked, and she told her it had once been keys to the doors that held behind them all the secrets of the world, of human pain and human minds, but now they were locked and buried forever. The keeper of the keys had been too grieved, and he had gone to rest now.

Farragut's Gambit

M.W. Kelly

*H*ank strode down Hilo's wharf to USS Daedalus which
had docked at the end of the pier yesterday. A week of
solid rain had left Hawaiians waterlogged and cranky, even those who
had grown up in the world's rainiest city. The outline of the formidable
ironclad appeared out of the mist shrouding the harbor. His mind
confused, Hank stopped short of the warship's bow. At first, he feared
the hull had capsized. Years as a clipper ship purser hadn't prepared
him for this ghost from the future.

The bow raked backward, sloping down to a long, menacing
ram just below the waterline. A metal gun port sat open in the center
of the bow housing a cannon with its muzzle exposed. Closed gun
ports lined the side of the ship's hull. Two masts dwarfed a centerline
smokestack. The sight of this unusual warship made it clear why King
Kamehameha had assigned Hank to act as a harbor pilot for the vessel, a
cover for his real assignment of intelligence gathering. In the aftermath
of the Civil War, the royal court worried that American imperialism
would add to the British threat to Hawaiian sovereignty. Emboldened
by the Union victory, America proclaimed a Manifest Destiny, their
ever-westward march over conquered lands.

Hank came up to the quartermaster standing watch pier-side.
"Henry Kahale, Naval Attaché to King Kamehameha."

"Yes, sir. I have you on the visitor manifest." He turned to a
folding table on which a telegraph sat and tapped a message. Hank's

eyes followed the wire up the gangway leading to the ship, along the bulwarks, and into the ship's bridge. The telegraph answered with an indecipherable series of clicks. "Permission to come aboard is granted," the quartermaster said as he unlatched a chain hung across the gangway entrance.

A man in a white, seersucker suit came from the pilot house and met Hank at the top of the gangway. Although the white attire was appropriate for the tropics, his frumpy appearance and silk ascot looked out of place on a naval ship. His wild, black hair and wry smile also gave a hint to a witty personality that lurked behind the twinkling eyes and the bushy mustache. "Samuel Clemens," he said in a Midwestern accent and offered his hand. "Happy to make your acquaintance, Lieutenant Kahale. Welcome aboard USS Daedalus, a marvel of modern masochism." His words were muffled by his thick mustache, so Hank wondered if he had heard him correctly.

"Excuse me, but where might I find the captain?"

"In the wardroom having supper. First, let us get you settled in your cabin. Hand me your seabag; it must have been a long walk from town. Damn this rain."

Clemens led Hank below to the gun deck. A familiar smell of oak and tar hung in the air. Clemens opened the door to a small stateroom opposite of the officer's wardroom. "The air in here can become a little stuffy in port, but this ship has many modern conveniences." He pressed a wall switch, and to Hank's amazement a light shone from orbs mounted in the ceiling.

Hank squinted at the ceiling lamp, amazed at its brilliance. "In what manner do you serve on the ship?" Hank asked.

Clemens chuckled and looked down at his coat. "You noticed my suit does not match the gilded uniforms of this ship's inhabitants. While roughing it in these splendid Sandwich Islands as a reporter for the Sacramento Union, I received an invitation from the captain to accompany him on a short excursion. I think he believes—or hopes at least—that I will write a glowing article about the Navy's latest and greatest gift to the altar of the god Ares."

"Her lines are most unusual, unlike any other US ironclad I've seen."

"She was CSS Stonewall before the Navy confiscated her after the war. Lacking our fleet strength, the rebels relied on ingenuity over quantity. But the captain can tell you more. Come, we best not keep him waiting."

They went aft to the wardroom where the smell of roast pork wafted from the galley. The ship's steward walked past them as they entered, his arms filled with dirty dishes and silverware. Alone at the table sat a uniformed officer whose face had graced many newspapers. The epaulets on his broad shoulders had lost their luster, tarnished green from many years at sea. He must have approached his sixties by now, but he had a younger man's intensity, all held in tight reserve. Although Hank had never met David Glasgow Farragut, he recognized the legendary man at once.

Farragut studied Hank, as if trying to remember why he was here. Insight flickered in his eyes and a quick smile creased his cheeks. "Mr. Kahale, please extend my thanks to your king for offering your assistance in navigating these waters. Our charts are worthless past the island of Ni'ihau. I hope you found your quarters satisfactory."

"Quite so, sir." Hank shifted uneasy on his feet in the sultry wardroom. The tight space reminded him of his ill-fated trips around Cape Horn. Having spent much of the last three years ashore, he had grown to like the comforts of life in the royal court. The thought of a three-month deployment left a sour hardness in his throat.

Farragut studied him with skeptical eyes and tossed his napkin on the table before rising from his chair. "In that case, let me take you on a ship's tour."

From the wardroom they went to the main gun deck, its dim interior lit by a row of overhead electric lanterns that spanned the passageway. "The rebels built better ships than us," Farragut said as he led Hank around a hydraulic capstan. "The three-hundred-foot hull is encased with two-inch iron plates, angled so that enemy cannon balls deflect off the freeboard. Her broadside gun ports house seven-inch Dahlgren guns, designed to swivel to meet the enemy."

Farragut stopped at an oval steel door. "We can isolate each of the twenty compartments belowdecks with these watertight doors. If we take a hit below the waterline and have flooding, the ship will not sink."

"The bow—it is a ram, is it not?"

"The ram is oak sheathed in iron over her entire bow, able to sink any vessel afloat, assuming we can get close enough."

"Let us hope our adversary is not better endowed below the waistline," Clemens said. He leaned his elbow on the nearest cannon, seemingly unaware he had rubbed a streak of gun powder on his suit. "I imagine all this technology might lead one to become too confident."

Farragut ignored the journalist's quip and motioned for them to follow him through a watertight door and down a narrow ladder to the engine room housing two enormous boilers amidships that ran two decks below to the ship's keel. This was unlike the open holds of the swift clipper ships. The captain continued his tour belowdecks, boasting about the ship's superior range, speed, and armament. Hank's mind filled with visions of the future, a future where machines rather than men determined battles, a time when weaponry might be beyond mankind's control. Just a generation ago, his ancestors had ruled the islands, armed with only spears and outrigger canoes. King Kamehameha had every right to fear American imperialism.

"This ship is very impressive, a wonder of technology," Hank said. "I do not doubt that other Confederate raiders were equally equipped. During the war, our economy collapsed after the confederacy raided New England whaling ships, the prime source of our welfare. The rebels-turned-pirates still trouble us. Our king has—"

"Yes, yes," Farragut said, holding his hand up. "We share your concern; I can assure you."

"Whalers have reported CSS Shenandoah is still on the high seas, blundering whaling ships, bankrupting our economy. We need your help to stop her."

"She is no longer your—or our—problem. Her captain surrendered her to the British in Liverpool six months ago. We have a bigger concern, one that could ravage both our fleets; starve our commerce and trade. Last July, this menace attacked ships here in the Pacific. Captain Baker of the steamer Governor Higginson struck what he first thought to be an unknown reef, but it sprouted air and steam from two blowholes."

"A blue whale?" Hank suggested. "They can grow to the length of a full-rigged ship."

"We thought likewise until the creature plowed into the Christopher Columbus three days later and 1,500 nautical miles away."

"Sounds like a whale of a tale," Clemens joked. "No whale can travel over such a distance in so short a time."

Farragut narrowed his eyes at Clemens before he added, "Last November, I took USS Lincoln to hunt this monster. After months of searching, we came upon a sinking ship in the South Pacific and were ourselves attacked. A Canadian aboard my ship attempted to harpoon it, only to discover its skin was metal, not flesh. It rammed our rudder, leaving us disabled while it escaped."

"A submarine, such as a sister ship to the Hunley?"

"No, this was no ordinary submarine. She is the Nautilus, a pirate submarine threatening all civilized nations. When she attacked us, I estimated her hull length at more than two hundred and fifty feet. Earlier this year, the Norwegian government reported that three men held captive aboard the ship escaped. They described the Nautilus as having unimaginable technology, able to steam the world's seas for months without provisioning. It can stay submerged for five days, farming food from the ocean, and distilling drinking water from seawater. Electricity provided by sodium-mercury batteries powers propulsion and auxiliary services."

"I doubt any country could keep such a ship a secret," Hank said.

"She sails under a black flag belonging to no nation. According to one of the prisoners, a French professor, the ship's captain is in self-imposed exile, steaming over twenty thousand leagues on a fanatical quest of revenge for the wartime death of his family."

"I recall an article in the San Francisco Chronicle reporting the Norwegian affair," Clemens said. "Eyewitness accounts claim it sunk in a giant whirlpool."

"I place no faith in those reports. The ship's hull was too long. Even if it did sink, it was a submarine after all. She could simply submerge and surface later using extra reserve buoyancy by blowing its ballast tanks. No, gentlemen. She still plies the oceans and was last spotted in among the outer western islands. Tomorrow, we sail to rid ourselves of this nemesis for good."

For a month after leaving Hilo, Daedalus patrolled the Hawaiian archipelago, a string of small islands and atolls stretching five hundred miles from Kauai to Midway. Hank's apprehension of being at sea again melted with days of fair winds and tropical sun. Not a single storm.

Clemens often engaged Hank with questions about his clipper days. He seemed satisfied with the veracity of Hank's sea stories, if not their fit for one of his articles. Clemens seemed more interested in Farragut. During the last two days, the captain's mood turned dark, dampening the spirits in the wardroom. He no longer bantered with his first lieutenant, played his fiddle, or shared sea stories from his Civil War victories. When conversation turned to the mysterious captain of the Nautilus, Farragut turned stoic or retreated to his stateroom. Like the infamous captain of the Pequod, Farragut seemed self-obsessed in his quest for a menacing denizen of the deep.

One morning Hank rose before dawn, unable to sleep in the hot and humid berth that masqueraded for a bed. After dressing and coming on deck, he saw the outline of a man sitting on the companionway hatch, glimmering white in the moon's light. Clemens no doubt. The tobacco smoke confirmed as much.

"I did not expect you up this early," Clemens said with his pipe at the corner of his mouth. "I thought Hawaiians lived the carefree life."

"Not this Hawaiian."

"You are just in time to see the morning launch."

Hank looked around but found no one at any of the boat davits. Clemens seemed to understand Hank's confusion and pointed to the quarterdeck. Pre-dawn purple light revealed a dark box festooned with a silk tarpaulin folded many times over to reduce deck space. A deckhand lit an oil lantern, its light shining on a wicker basket affixed to a pyramid tress of metal and wood, the sight of which revealed the meaning behind the ship's name.

"Is that a—" Hank struggled for a name of the contraption.

"An airship," Clemens said. "Last night the lookout spotted a ship's light on the horizon. In an abundance of caution, Captain Farragut has ordered the reconnaissance balloon aloft."

"I have never seen anything like this. A ship that commands the air as well as the sea."

"Farragut fancies himself a captain of the world's first aerocraft carrier. The airship carries bombs we can drop on any enemy."

The launch crew continued their preparations—rigging control lines, loading munitions, and inflating the balloon from a flexible tube led from belowdecks. As the airbag inflated, it filled the entire quarterdeck before rising above the mizzen mast. Its gray-blue silk blended with the sky, offering a degree of camouflage. Unlike any balloon he had seen in the newspapers, this craft had an oval, horizontal airbag tapered to a point at each end, giving it the appearance of a giant dart. At its stern, rigging suspended a long beam with a triangular, sail-like rudder. Beneath the beam a wooden-framed, long wicker basket hung, festooned with an array of sandbags, possibly used as ballast. Lost in rapture at this aerial wonder, Hank was unaware of the captain's presence until Farragut placed his hand on Hank's shoulder.

"Care to take a ride?" Farragut asked.

"You mean in the balloon?"

"I prefer to call it an aerocraft. Unlike a balloon, it's steerable. Tethered from the stern of the Daedalus, it can maneuver over an arc of forty-five degrees either side of centerline. The tether has a telegraph line, allowing the pilot to stay in constant communication with us. What you are seeing here," Farragut said while pointing to the growing airbag, "is coal gas from the ship's boilers inflating the envelope, making it lighter than air."

"Is it safe...I mean, what if it catches fire while aloft?"

"The pilot and observer can escape, using a parachute to break their fall. Here, let's get you suited up. Clemens will be joining you."

Hank hesitated, unsure at the wisdom of this attempt to defy gravity. But after seeing Clemens in a set of gray coveralls over his white suit with a silk parachute in his arms, Hank acquiesced. Clemens strode up to the crew cockpit, a big grin on his face, and a twinkle in his eyes like a young boy. "Join us, Hank, as we break the surly bonds of earth and sail in the clouds."

One of the deckhands helped Hank into his flying suit and explained the operation of the parachute. It was folded and rolled into a compact shape and secured with twine. The silk chute would open with a strong pull on a loop of rope he called a *rip cord*, an ignominious name by any regard. Once secured into the aerocraft's cockpit, an officer gave the command to launch and off they went.

As they rose in the air, the noise from the Daedalus' engines and wake receded, leaving them in lonely silence. The cockpit swayed in slight movements from the tethered line that reached back to the ship, giving the feeling of riding in a small boat afloat on the waves. The Daedalus shrank beneath Hank, and the sea's white-capped waves became small specks that drifted on an endless and flat ocean. The sun sent a metallic sheen across the water to the horizon. Never before had he conceived the three-dimension aspect of the sky, the multiple layers of wispy clouds that stretched thousands of feet above him and cast long shadows on the Earth's surface. The rarefied air cooled as they ascended, the sky a deeper blue, rays of sunlight all around.

The pilot took a reading from a barometer and announced, "Two thousand feet and steady on." He tapped a message on the telegraph, and the aerocraft lurched forward. "We will remain at this altitude for our reconnaissance." He took binoculars from a drawer in his desk, brought them to his eyes, and scanned the ocean for many minutes. Ahead, a cloud approached, or they approached it; Hank could not be certain. He gripped the handrail, his knuckles white, his mind in panic at the pending collision with the solid white cloud mass. Still absorbed in his watchstanding, the pilot must not have noticed the impending disaster.

"Sir, see here," Hank exclaimed. "You must draw your attention at once to the approaching cloud. We are on a collision course."

The pilot took his eyes from the binoculars long enough to give Hank a perplexed look before he faced aft and continued his search. Clemens winked at Hank and gave a knowing smile. His eyes wide, Hank gasped and braced for impact. The cloud dissolved into a diaphanous envelope of fog. Unbelievable. Clouds were not solid after all.

"How did you know?" Hank asked Clemens whose outline was obscured by the mist.

"Before you came aboard, I had taken a shakedown cruise and had the pleasure of a similar ride through the clouds."

Just as quick as they had entered the cloud, they broke free into bright sunlight in the azure sky. The wall of clouds stood behind them, its tendrils billowing into a great arch thousands of feet above them. Hank had never felt so alive, so free. Flight made all other earthbound ventures seem so pedestrian. He wished he could stay up here forever.

Hours later, the splendor wore off, giving way to quiet boredom. Hank sat on the cockpit bench; his chin tucked in the nook of his elbow resting on the cockpit railing. He peered down at the infinite expanse of water below him. His mind turned again to the captain of the Nautilus which sailed unseen beneath these waves. Why had he built such a lethal weapon? Surely, such advanced technology could be better served in the study of the oceans, to discover new minerals, to find new sources of food for a planet already swollen with millions of people. Despite the impression Hank got from textbooks, he still believed man's knowledge of the oceans resembled only a small island in the vast Pacific.

"Ship four points off the starboard quarter."

With a start, Hank snapped his head up at the pilot's urgent call. He handed the field glasses to Hank and went to the telegraph on his desk, his hand busy tapping a message to the Daedalus. Below them the ship changed course, its wake leaving a wide arc to the right. Hank felt the cockpit lurch forward with renewed speed. He brought the binoculars to his eyes and struggled to focus the lens. A clear circular image of the horizon emerged as if he were looking through a porthole. After some searching, he found the whaling ship. Although it was a tiny speck on the great ocean, the ship's sails cast long shadows over the waves even at this distance.

"I see a pod of whales nearby with waterspouts aplenty," Hank reported. The ship heeled over as if to change course, yet its wake held true. Perhaps a gust. No, its stern set lower in the water. "Wait. Something is afoul with the whaler. Here, look."

The pilot snatched the binoculars from Hank's hands and brought them to eyes. "She has run aground," he yelled. "Impossible. We have nothing but deep water in this area."

"Perhaps she was attacked by a whale," Clemens said. "Just such a mammoth cetacean fell upon the ill-fated Essex in 1820. Melville wrote about the incident, but I failed to get through his book. It put me asleep."

"You could be correct," the pilot said, his eyes glued to the binoculars. "I see a beast broaching astern of the ship." He ran to the telegraph and sent off another message.

Soon the cockpit surged forward, and Hank went to the rail. Below them, the Daedalus' wake grew larger. The pilot pulled a rope to expel hot gas from the airbag. They descended toward the ocean until the pilot poured sand from two ballast sacks, arresting their descent. He checked the barometer. "Five hundred feet. That should be adequate."

The Daedalus steered for the whaler. Several whaling skiffs dropped from davits and men from the stricken vessel climbed into them. They rowed clear of the sinking wreck and waited for the Daedalus to pick them up. The terrifying sight of the ocean swallowing the three-masted, full-rigged ship sent a sour taste to Hank's throat. Within minutes, the topgallant sails disappeared into a whirlpool of water.

While the Daedalus retrieved the stranded seamen, the whale swam in a long arc back toward the wreckage, gathering speed as it approached. Through the binoculars, Hank made out a metal structure with portholes in the bow and a raked superstructure that rose just a few feet above the waves. "That's no whale, all right," Hank shouted to the pilot before handing him the binoculars. "It is the Nautilus, I am sure."

The pilot confirmed Hank's sighting and went to the telegraph station. Hank followed the submarine's wake as it ran straight toward the Daedalus. "It is on a collision course with the ship. Tell them to abandon recovery operations and make flank speed!"

While the pilot tapped the message with a frenetic finger, Hank and Clemens leaned over the cockpit railing. The Daedalus moved away from the wreckage with agonizing sluggishness. The Nautilus altered course to hit the Daedalus amidships, but failed to account for the ship's acceleration, smashing the ship's rudder instead. "She struck the ship," Hank yelled to the pilot.

The pilot ran to the rail with astonishment in his eyes. "We must maneuver above the submarine at once," he yelled. He grabbed Hank's arm and pulled him to the front of the cockpit and picked up a bomb. "You arm the bombs by releasing this catch." He yanked on a metal latch and a spring-operated plunger popped out from the nose of the bomb. "This rod is a trigger that will compress when it hits the water, after which it detonates the explosive, following a short delay. The bomb explodes underwater, creating a concussion wave that will disable the submarine." Handing the bomb to Hank, he jumped to the airship's wheel and steered for the Nautilus.

Hank rested the heavy bomb upright on the cockpit railing. Clemens leaned away from him in a strained manner, his eyebrows dancing. "I pray it will not go off prematurely."

Clemens' eyes darted from the bomb as a series of loud pings and whistles resounded through the air. Hank peered over the rail and found the submarine directly below them. Three men stood on a narrow deck along its spine, their rifles aimed at the airship. Clemens brushed by Hank and ran to the pilot who sat slumped at the helm. "He is shot. What should we do?"

"Do you think you can steer this thing?"

Clemens stood beside the wheel and ran his hand along it. "Perhaps. I was a riverboat pilot for a few years on the Mississippi. I shall give her a try." He lowered the pilot from the helm station, then sat behind the wheel while looking over the railing. "I will endeavor to get her over that maritime menace to put you in a position to drop the bombs."

The aerocraft swung in a lazy arc behind the Daedalus until it flew above the target. Without its rudder, their mother ship steamed in a wide turn, forcing them out of position. Clemens tried to correct, but each time they came over the submarine, the Daedalus pulled them out of position again. Clemens' face glistened from his efforts to steer the craft. At intervals, Hank strained to look below them; yet always the surfaced submarine trailed the ship, and the ship in turn dragged the airship around in wide circles. This dance to the death left neither adversary in a good position to attack the other.

At one point, they swung over the submarine and stayed there long enough to break the stalemate. Hank estimated the lead angle and dropped the first bomb, forgetting to right it before launch. It fell below him, first tumbling in the air until its fins stabilized its flight path. The bomb smacked a few yards from the submerged Nautilus and exploded underwater less than a second later. A huge column of water sprayed up and over the submarine, rocking it on its keel. Its bow broached the surface long enough for the Daedalus to join the fight with its stern mounted seven-inch Dahlgren turret, sending a barrage of cannon fire. The Nautilus veered away and steamed to the east until out of sight.

The orange haze of sunset yielded to purple dusk. Soon, the sky was black, the clouds hiding the stars and moon. Hank lit a lantern that hung from a metal beam above his head, its light sending sharp shadows dancing in the cockpit, masking all else outside the aerocraft.

They wrapped the pilot's body in a square sheet of spare canvas and waited for the Daedalus to retrieve them. A heavy silence filled the cockpit until the telegraph came to life. Neither of them knew Morse code, so the message went unanswered. With a jolt, the aerocraft lurched downward, pulled by the tow cable. Hank doused the lantern and saw the clouds had cleared, revealing a moonlit ocean below them. He released gas from the airbag as he had seen the pilot do prior to the attack. Halfway down to the Daedalus, a green glow emerged in the ship's wake. It grew brighter as it reached the surface. Hank swallowed the rising panic in his throat and yelled to Clemens. "She is back. Take the helm again while I man the bomb battery."

Clemens sat behind the wheel with a wary posture, his shoulders slumped. The tow cable slacked, arresting the aerocraft's descent. Phosphorescence in the Nautilus' wake streamed below them. Hank lifted a bomb and waited for the exact moment for the lead angle to match the submarine's track. The bomb fell, disappearing into the darkness until a bright plume of orange light erupted next to the submarine's hull. A billowing cloud of gray smoke rose and obscured the target. Hank reached for the next bomb and waited for the smoke to clear. The Nautilus pulled ahead, as if it intended to ram the Daedalus' stern. Hank dropped the bomb, and through luck or Hank's practiced eye, it hit its mark. A loud explosion accompanied by shearing metal came from the submarine foredeck. In the diminishing light of the smoke cloud, the submarine slowed.

Men crawled out of a hatch with lanterns in hand and inspected the damage. Hank heard them yelling, but the distance was too great to discern their words. A brilliant light beam burst from the submarine's wheelhouse onto the foredeck. A man armed with a rifle looked up to the sky. Yet he must not have spotted the balloon from within the glare on the deck. By this time, the submarine had lost headway and wallowed in the heavy swells. A seaman lost his balance and fell overboard. His arms flailing above him, he cried for help.

Hank seized this distraction to drop another bomb into the water, careful to aim it away from the seaman in the water. With a great splash, the bomb exploded on the opposite side of the Nautilus, rocking it in violet motions. She seemed to have sworn off the fight and turned away from the scene, leaving the poor soul treading water to the fate of the circling sharks.

A lifeboat departed from the Daedalus and its crew recovered the abandoned seaman and bought him back to the ship. Underway again, the Daedalus steamed rudderless in a long arc, its guns firing on the retreating submarine. The aerocraft's tow cable snapped taut and pulled them back to the quarterdeck with no more incident.

Hank climbed out of the cockpit and took a deep breath. This would be his first and only ride in a balloon if he could help it. He assisted Clemens down the cockpit ladder, and they squeezed out of their coveralls. Captain Farragut ran over to them, his arms wide. "You did it! Great thinking, men. The aerial bombardment saved the ship."

Ignoring the captain's adulation, Hank made sure crewmen were recovering the dead pilot's body from the aerocraft, then staggered to the stern rail in slow steps. The ship's wake spread behind him, its phosphorescent froth stretching into the distance. Clemens had told him "War is a wanton waste of projectiles." And a wanton waste of science and ingenuity. Below the waves, the Nautilus might still lurk unseen, its next victim unknown, and its captain's identity still a mystery. A genius of naval architecture, an inventor without any peer, he could have done so much more for the world. What if he had dedicated his life to the peaceful exploration of the soundless depths rather than vengeful terrorism? One may never know.

Raise the Nautilus

Eric Choi

South Pacific Ocean
1,700 nautical miles east-northeast of New Zealand
June 1916

*T*he being that emerged from the depths of the sea was humanoid, but it did not look human. The creature's tough beige hide was the texture of elephant skin. The head was a heavy bronze sphere, its face a cyclopean eye crisscrossed by a metallic grate. A pair of thick tubes protruded below the glass eye, snaking back to a heavy cylinder on its back.

Commander Thomas Jennings watched as the diver was hoisted onto the deck of the research ship RRS Discovery. Two sailors helped the diver to a seated position on a wooden bench, where they began to disconnect the tubes and unfasten the helmet. A third man in a brown trilby and civilian attire, tall and gaunt with a sharp nose, started impassively at the scene.

Jennings turned and looked out to sea. A few hundred yards distant the grey bulk of his ship, the cruiser HMS Euryalus, drifted serenely on the sparkling waters. The tranquility was a welcome relief from the fierce storms that had delayed the start of the operation for days.

The sailors lifted the helmet off the diver, revealing the ruddy face of a middle-aged man with sweat-soaked dark hair. He closed his eyes, threw his head back, and inhaled deeply.

"Are you all right?" Jennings asked.

The diver, Jonathan Badders, nodded. "Yes, sir. Thank you."

The civilian, Donald McCabe from the Meta Section of the Directorate of Military Intelligence, stepped forward. "What did you see? Is she there?"

Badders nodded again, this time smiling. "She's there. I saw her. The Nautilus."

As the executive officer of HMS Euryalus, Commander Jennings was glad to be back aboard his ship. Both Euryalus and Discovery had been launched in the same year, but the latter seemed much older. Discovery was a wooden three-masted auxiliary steamship, the last of her kind to be built in the British Empire. The Admiralty had purchased Discovery from the Hudson's Bay Company, refitting the cargo ship to serve as a floating base for Operation Mobilis—the Royal Navy's attempt to raise the Nautilus.

Jennings, Badders, McCabe, and the divisional officers gathered around a table in the commanding officer's day cabin.

"What's the state of the Nautilus?" asked Captain Richard Powell.

"She's at a depth of 41 fathoms, with a slight list to starboard of about seven degrees," reported Badders. "Her stern is buried in about eighteen feet of hard clay, but otherwise she appears to be undamaged."

"When can the salvage operation begin?" asked McCabe.

"Weather permitting, as early as tomorrow," said Lieutenant-Commander Eugene Seagram, an officer from the Royal Navy Engineers who had been seconded from the Admiralty to support Operation Mobilis.

"About bloody time," said McCabe. "The Smith-Harding report was quite specific about the last known location of the Nautilus. I can't believe it took almost a month to find her."

Jennings, Powell, and the key divisional officers had been briefed by McCabe on the Nautilus file just before their departure from Auckland. Of particular interest to the War Office was a description in the Smith-Harding report, corroborated by earlier accounts from Aronnax, of "a destructive weapon, lightning-like in its effects" that could stun or kill men. His Majesty's Government was still telling the public that the Great War was going well, but military men like Jennings knew the terrible truth. McCabe's impatience was annoying but understandable. Such a weapon, in the hands of the British, could break the stalemate on the Western Front.

"Badders' report on the condition of the Nautilus is excellent news," said Seagram. "It means we can proceed with the original salvage plan with little modification." He spread across the table a schematic diagram of the submarine, copied from a trove of documents seized five years ago during a joint raid by the Directorate of Military Intelligence and the British Army on the ancestral palace of the late Prince Dakkar in the Bundelkhand region of India. "The five pontoons from the Discovery will be deployed as follows: Three above the stern, and two above the bow. For additional buoyancy, we will run two hoses down to blow the main ballast tank of the Nautilus. The biggest challenge will be the unforeseen need to tunnel the clay under the stern to place the harness and lifting chains for the aft pontoons."

"How long will this take?" Powell asked.

"Three weeks," Seagram replied.

Donald McCabe rolled his eyes and shook his head.

"Very well," Powell said. "Get some rest, gentlemen. We have a big day tomorrow."

There was one other aspect of the Smith-Harding report that had made an impression on Commander Jennings—the fanatical hatred of Prince Dakkar, later known as Captain Nemo, for the British Empire. How ironic it would be if Nemo's invention ended up saving it.

Donald McCabe's cynicism was vindicated. It actually took fifty days for Badders and his team of divers to pass the harnesses and lifting chains under the Nautilus, attach the pontoons, and connect the hoses to the main ballast tank. Just tunneling the clay under the stern took the entirety of the originally-estimated three weeks.

But at long last, everything was ready. Jennings, McCabe, and Seagram returned to the Discovery to supervise the operation.

"Proceed with blowing the stern pontoons," Seagram ordered.

Jennings watched as the pumps roared to life, the needles on gauges began to move, and the hoses snaking into the water stiffened.

"We're starting with the stern first," Seagram explained, "which will hopefully avoid any center-of-gravity issues that might arise if both ends were lifted at the same time."

Euryalus was anchored a few hundred yards away. She was joined by HMRT Rollicker, an Admiralty tug that had been dispatched from Auckland six days ago.

"There!" Yeoman Farley called out excitedly, pointing to a colored float that had bobbed to the surface.

"I see it," Seagram said. "That's good. It means the stern has been lifted off the sea floor. Stop the air to the aft pontoons, and start blowing the forward pontoons!"

The men scanned the surface of the water with binoculars, looking for the second colored float. It did not appear.

Seagram glanced at the pressure gauges and frowned. "The bow should be lifting by now." He shook his head. "It's taking too long. Start the tertiary pump. We'll try blowing the main ballast tank on the Nautilus."

After ten minutes, the second float finally appeared. Moments later, the surface of the ocean began to froth violently, like water in a saucepan brought to boil.

"Something's wrong," said Jennings.

Suddenly, both of the bow pontoons popped to the surface. The massive cylinders, twelve feet in diameter and thirty feet long, briefly cleared the water before crashing back down in a torrent of spray.

Seconds later, it was the Nautilus.

Jennings gasped as the bow of the submarine came up, smashing into one of the pontoons and tossing it aside. She rose like a giant breaching metallic narwhal, the armored steel spur that protruded from her nose glistening in the midday sun. Then, with a great splash, the Nautilus slipped back under the waves and quickly disappeared from view.

"What the devil went wrong?" Captain Powell demanded.

"It appears the center-of-gravity of the Nautilus is further aft than we expected," Seagram explained. "When we blew her main ballast tank, the momentum caused the bow to rise so fast it slipped out of its harness, separating it from the pontoons and sending everything to the surface. The impact with the pontoon dislodged the hose and opened the ballast tank vents, allowing water back into the main ballast tank and submerging the Nautilus again."

"How could you have not known the location of the center-of-gravity?" McCabe asked. "We have the drawings of the Nautilus."

"We have the *design* drawings, not the as-built drawings," Seagram explained. "The mass properties of the final build appears to have differed significantly from the original design."

"What do we do now?" Powell asked. "The damaged pontoon is beyond repair."

Jennings was in a glum mood. The Admiralty was demanding daily wireless reports and bristling at the delays and costs, even threatening to cancel Operation Mobilis. He thought for a moment, then said, "I have an idea."

"Commander?"

Jennings spread a nautical chart onto the table. "The only reason this operation was even feasible is because the depth of the ocean here is unusually shallow. There was an island here until it was destroyed in the volcanic eruption of 1882. We know from the Fessenden Oscillator soundings we took during the search phase that there are even shallower areas nearby." He traced a finger on the chart. "For example, just two nautical miles due east of our present location, the depth is only 16 fathoms."

"Yes!" Seagram exclaimed. "I see where the XO is going with this." He produced a notepad and began to sketch. "We can use the four remaining pontoons, not to bring the Nautilus to the surface, but to lift her just high enough off the sea floor for the Rollicker to tow her to the shallower area, and then we deliberately ground her there. Her ballast tank vents will have to be repaired, but it will be much easier and safer for Badders and his divers to work at the shallower depth. We'll then use the shorter hoses from the Discovery that we couldn't use before to blow both the main and secondary ballast tanks, and we can also use the trim tanks to compensate for the center-of-gravity issue. Taken all together, there should be sufficient buoyancy to bring the Nautilus back to the surface."

"You think this is feasible?" Jennings asked.

"I'll need to work out the details with my team," Seagram replied, "but yes."

"How long until we're ready for a second attempt?" Powell asked.

"Three weeks," Seagram said.

McCabe shook his head. "Is that your answer to everything?"

The preparations took almost triple the time. Just lifting the Nautilus off the seafloor took three weeks, followed by two days for the Rollicker to tow and ground her in the shallower water, and finally another five weeks for the divers to repair the ballast tank vents, reattach the pontoons, and connect the additional hoses and lines.

On the day of the second salvage attempt, it appeared as if every man aboard Euryalus had gathered along the portside railing to watch. For a moment, Jennings had the amusing and absurd thought that the ship might very well tip over.

Once again, the surface of the ocean started to foam and bubble, and then the great bulk of the Nautilus, this time with pairs of massive pontoons attached at deck level to bow and stern, burst through the frothing water. Pressure-relief valves on the pontoons and the submarine opened, sending up spray that shrouded the Nautilus in rainbowed clouds of vapor. Slowly, the Nautilus righted herself and settled onto the surface, her bobbing motion sending small waves towards Euryalus and Discovery.

For a moment, nobody could speak. The men of the Euryalus just stood there, mesmerized by the sight. And then, a massive cheer erupted through the crowd.

"About bloody time," muttered Donald McCabe.

The real Nautilus bore little resemblance to the version depicted in the popular press during Captain Nemo's infamous reign of terror in the late 1860s, with its ridiculous serrated fins, bulbous viewports, and outsized rivets. The real Nautilus was two hundred and fifty feet in length from the tip of the armored spur at her bow to the large propeller and fish-like rudder at her stern. A pilothouse protruded about a third of the way along her deck, below which were mounted large hydroplanes for diving control. She was a sleek grey war machine, in some ways a long-lost ancestor of the Royal Navy's new K-class submarines that were only now commencing sea trials.

Jennings turned to Seagram and shook his hand. "Congratulations!"

"Sir!"

Jennings made his way through the crowd to find Jonathan Badders and the divers, shaking each of their hands in turn. "Well done, gentlemen. Yours was the most vital and dangerous job. This accomplishment belongs to you."

"Thank you, Commander," said Badders.

It took a day to run the towing hawser between the Nautilus and the tugboat Rollicker, and the following day the flotilla commenced its long journey back to Auckland under the escort of Euryalus. The most difficult part of Operation Mobilis was over, but there was still one more task to perform.

Only one body had been found aboard the Nautilus, and what to do with it became a rather delicate question.

"Sir, you can't be serious!" exclaimed Jennings, sitting across the table from Powell in the captain's day cabin.

"I am quite serious, and my decision is made," said Powell. "Captain Nemo is to be reburied at sea with honors."

"Sir," Jennings pleaded, "that man was an enemy combatant. All those ships he sank. I would not be surprised if there are men right here on the Euryalus who knew some of the people he murdered."

"I'm aware of that," Powell said. "Nevertheless, Captain Nemo was a comrade of the seas, and arguably he was even a subject of the British Empire for a time. Like it or not, he is entitled to the honor."

"I don't like it, sir."

"Your objection is noted," Powell said. "However, if it makes you feel better, think of it this way. What better revenge could we exact than to bury him under the flag of his adversary?"

Jennings thought for a moment and decided that he had greatly misjudged his commanding officer's sense of humor.

So it came to be that Jennings, Powell, and the divisional officers of the Euryalus found themselves in dress uniform standing at attention before the Union Jack draped coffin of Captain Nemo. Jonathan Badders and five of his fellow divers served as pallbearers, lifting the coffin and slowly marching towards the edge of the deck.

"The sea is the largest cemetery, and its slumberers sleep without a monument," said Captain Powell. "All other graveyards show symbols of distinction between great and small, rich and poor. But in the ocean cemetery, the king, the clown, the prince, the peasant, the hero, and the villain are all alike, undistinguishable."

The pallbearers set the coffin down on a platform at the edge of the deck, and they removed and folded the flag. Badders pulled a lever, the platform inclined, and Captain Nemo returned to the sea.

Commander Jennings kept his face neutral and respectful, but in his mind's eye he was smiling. Captain Nemo had been taken from his beloved Nautilus, which in turn had been taken from him. His final resting place would be a remote and obscure part of the South Pacific, amongst the sharks, alone and far from the coral cemetery of his crewmates. The Royal Navy had given Captain Nemo exactly what he deserved.

It was a very British thing to do.

At full speed, Euryalus could have made it back to New Zealand in about four days. But after a week at sea, the flotilla was still more than three hundred nautical miles out from Auckland. The problem was the antiquated Discovery, which could barely manage eight knots under sail and steam. Jennings was still making daily wireless reports to his impatient masters in the Admiralty, and he knew that every additional day at sea was another day that something could go wrong.

On the eighth day, his fears were realized.

"What is it, XO?"

"We have company," Jennings said, handing his binoculars to Powell.

The captain looked out the bridge windows of the Euryalus to where Jennings was pointing. "Are we expecting any Allied shipping in this area?" Powell asked.

"No, sir," said Jennings.

"I'm not aware of anything either," said McCabe.

Jennings spoke into a voice pipe. "This is the bridge. Can we get a range on the target bearing zero-four-nine?" After a few moments, he bent his ear to the pipe. "Probably about thirteen nautical miles," he reported, "but it's hard to tell with the mist. Wait a minute." He held up a finger. "Lookout reports the target appears to be turning. The rangefinder will need a moment to reestablish coincidence."

"I don't like this," Powell muttered.

"The mist is clearing, and the target is no longer turning," Jennings reported. "Sir, the rangefinder has a new solution. Eleven nautical miles, and closing rapidly."

Powell turned to McCabe. "If that's a German warship, how soon until we're in range of her guns?"

"For their Pacific fleet, I would expect it to be a light cruiser like ourselves, with similar weaponry," McCabe said. "Main guns would have a range of around 15,000 yards."

After a few minutes, Jennings raised his binoculars again. "Target now at ten nautical miles, still closing fast. I can see a profile and battle ensign." He flipped through the pages of the silhouette book. "Confirmed, she's German sir! Most likely SMS Scharnhorst, an armored cruiser."

The klaxon sounded, and Powell spoke into a voice pipe. "All hands, this is the Captain. Action stations, action stations. Inbound hostile vessel. This is not a drill." He turned and called out to a young man. "Yeoman Farley!"

"Yes, sir!" said Farley, pad and pencil ready.

"Get on the wireless. Make to Rollicker and Discovery. 'German cruiser inbound. Euryalus engaging. Rollicker and Discovery to maintain current speed and heading.'"

"Yes, sir!"

"Make course zero-one-five to bring the target within the firing arc of the fore-turret," Powell ordered. "Prepare to fire when the Scharnhorst breaks seven nautical miles."

From the bridge windows, Jennings could see the turning of the fore-turret and the single barrel of the 9.2-inch Mark X gun beginning to rise. The approaching German cruiser was now visible without binoculars.

"Seven nautical miles!" Jennings called out.

At that moment, a flash and a puff of smoke erupted from the Scharnhorst. Seconds later, the unmistakable screech of a shell in flight could be heard, followed by a concussive boom and an explosive geyser of foamy white seawater a few hundred yards off the bow of Euryalus.

"Return fire!" Powell ordered.

The Euryalus trembled as her forward gun discharged. A plume of water erupted short of the Scharnhorst.

"Visual splash spotters, recalculate the solution," Jennings ordered. "Gunnery, open fire when ready."

Euryalus fired again, and this time, the shell found its target. On the Scharnhorst, an explosion blossomed amidships.

"Hit, sir!" a lieutenant exclaimed.

Jennings bent his ear to a voice pipe, then turned and peered through his binoculars. "The Scharnhorst is no longer closing. She appears to have stopped. However, her guns seem to be—"

A shell exploded a few yards off the bow.

"—very much intact, sir!"

Yeoman Farley returned with a piece of paper. "Message from the Rollicker, Captain!"

Powell read the telegram, his eyes wide. "Rollicker reports spotting another ship bearing three-four-nine, identified as SMS Gneisenau."

Jennings called into a voice pipe. "I need confirmation and range to the new target, bearing three-four-nine." Moments later, he said, "Second target confirmed, Captain! Range five-and-a-half nautical miles."

Suddenly, a massive explosion rocked the Euryalus, throwing the men to the floor. Powell got to his feet and staggered to the engine order telegraph. "Helm, make course three-five-zero, half speed. I want to engage with a broadside."

The helmsman rotated the steering stand, but the Euryalus did not turn.

"I have a report from damage control," Jennings said. "We've been hit astern, probably by a torpedo. Rudder and propeller are damaged. Helm will not respond."

"Bring the aft-turret to bear on the Gneisenau," Powell ordered. "Fore-turret, keep firing on the Scharnhorst." He looked around. "Where's Yeoman Farley?"

"Here, sir!"

"Make to Rollicker and Discovery. 'If Germans attempt to intercept or board, make no attempt at armed resistance.'"

"Sir?" said Farley, incredulous.

"Young man, we are in a terrible tactical situation," Jennings explained. "Discovery and Rollicker cannot run, and we cannot protect them against two cruisers. Their only chance is to stay out of the fight—and pray that these particular Germans are inclined to abide by the London Declaration." He jerked his thumb. "Now, go!"

"Wait!" Powell said suddenly. "XO, what's the depth of the ocean here?"

Jennings consulted a nautical chart. "About 880 fathoms."

"Yeoman!" Powell thought for a moment, then said, "Further message to the Rollicker. 'Cut pontoons. Scuttle the Nautilus.'"

Farley's eyes widened. "Sending this right away, sir!"

McCabe approached. "Captain, I assume you want me off the bridge?"

Powell nodded. "Get below, Mr. McCabe."

The fore- and aft-turrets fired simultaneously. Another explosion blossomed on the Scharnhorst, this time at the bow.

Moments later, a blast ripped through the Euryalus.

Jennings struggled to his feet. He touched his forehead and felt blood. "Captain? Lieutenant? Is everyone all right?" Mumbled affirmations drifted across the shattered bridge. Staggering to the smashed forward windows, he looked out and beheld a horrific sight. The fore-turret had been hit, reduced to bent and twisted metal from which smoke poured out of serrated holes.

Hearing a shuffle of feet, Jennings turned to see Captain Powell at his side. They looked at each other for a moment, and both knew what needed to be done. They could not run, and it was only a matter of time before the fire ignited the magazine of cordite charges. When that happened, the Euryalus would explode in a fireball.

"All hands, this is the Captain. Abandon ship. I repeat, abandon ship. All hands to the lifeboats immediately." Powell turned to Jennings. "Divide the decks between us. Check as many compartments as you can."

"See you at the lifeboat, sir!"

Jennings raced through the smashed and smoke-filled decks and compartments of the Euryalus, calling out and directing dazed crewmen, both able-bodied and injured, to external hatches and lifeboats. The men were afraid but not panicked, the evacuation carried out with a stoic British efficiency that Jennings would later recall with tremendous pride.

The last place Jennings checked was the wireless cabin. He had expected it to be already evacuated, but was surprised instead to find an unconscious Yeoman Farley sprawled on the deck. Relieved to find Farley alive and breathing, Jennings hooked his elbows under the armpits of the unconscious man and lifted him in a fireman's carry. His lungs burned from smoke and exertion, but finally he managed to stagger outside.

Captain Powell, Lieutenant-Commander Seagram, and the divisional officers of the Euryalus were already in the last lifeboat. With their assistance, Jennings brought Farley aboard and then hopped inside himself. The derrick swung the lifeboat over the side and down to the water.

"Is the crew accounted for?" Jennings asked. The pained, vacant look in Powell's eyes was the only response he got.

They began to paddle furiously, joining the other lifeboats in trying to get as far away from the Euryalus as possible. Suddenly, there was an explosion. The occupants of the lifeboat turned to watch an ominous mushroom cloud rise into the air. But it wasn't the Euryalus. It was the Scharnhorst.

Jennings knew Euryalus would soon share the same fate, but for now he took grim satisfaction in seeing the German ship go down first. For the moment, Euryalus was still afloat, as were the apparently undamaged Discovery and Rollicker.

And the Nautilus.

"Sir!" Jennings tapped Powell on the shoulder, and pointed.

The Nautilus was still on the surface, still attached to its four pontoons, still hooked up to the Rollicker. A short distance away was the second German cruiser, the Gneisenau. Jennings watched in stunned disbelief as a boatload of *seebataillon*, marines of the Imperial German Navy, came alongside the Rollicker and boarded. About twenty minutes later, smoke began to billow from the Rollicker's funnel and the tug began to move, with the Nautilus in tow and the Gneisenau following behind.

Under different circumstances, the men in the lifeboat might have shouted and cursed. But nobody spoke. Cold and in shock, and physically and mentally exhausted by the battle, the harrowing escape, and the imminent loss of their ship, they just sat in helpless silence as the Germans sailed away with their prize.

London, England
December 1916

A note on the menu reminded customers to limit their order to two items for lunch and three for dinner. Commander Thomas Jennings flipped through the pages but decided he wasn't hungry. He put down the menu and sat back, waiting.

Half an hour later, a tall man wearing a brown trilby exited the War Office Building across from the restaurant. Jennings stood, remembering to push his chair under the table, and walked across the street to intercept.

"Mr. Jennings," said Donald McCabe. "What a surprise to see you."

"You're a hard man to reach," Jennings said. "I've been trying to contact you for well over a month."

"What do you want?"

Jennings gestured. "Let's talk a stroll through the gardens."

The two men walked down Horse Guards Avenue, then turned to pass through the black wrought iron gates into Whitehall Gardens.

"The ocean is big, but the German Pacific fleet is not," Jennings said. "Yet somehow, we managed to run into two German cruisers less than a day out from Auckland."

"Perhaps the ocean isn't as big as you think."

Jennings stopped and turned. "And why was the order to scuttle the Nautilus not carried out? Or was the order never sent? I found Yeoman Farley unconscious in the wireless room."

"As I recall, we were being shelled and torpedoed by German cruisers. Men tend to fall down under such circumstances."

"This is all a game to you DMI people, isn't it?" Jennings hissed, his anger rising. "Let me remind you of the cost. The Euryalus destroyed. Ninety-three injured, many seriously. Twenty-eight missing and forty-four dead, including Jonathan Badders. The crew of the Rollicker taken prisoner. And the Nautilus in the hands of the Germans."

"Forgive the pun, Jennings," McCabe said with condescension, "but as a Navy man, you're out of your depth."

"Then explain it to me."

Jennings lit a cigarette. "Would it interest you to know that German war production is down almost nine percent from this time last year?"

Jennings was puzzled. "What does this have to do with anything?"

"Kaiser Wilhelm fancies himself a man of science," McCabe continued, "but in reality he is quite mad. He is obsessed with the Nautilus and her weapons. Well, let him have it. An armored battering ram is hardly impressive in the age of torpedoes. As for the large vessel-mounted *lightning* weapon, I suppose what the Germans would call the *groß blitzwaffe*..."

McCabe flicked ash onto the grass. "He can have that, too. Directed energy weapons are years if not decades away from widespread practical military deployment. This war will be won with more ships, more artillery, more guns, perhaps more aeroplanes—not with fantastical inventions from the realm of scientifiction. In the meantime, if it pleases the Kaiser to pursue this folly, every pfennig spent on this fantasy is a pfennig that is not being spent on real weapons that will make an actual difference to the outcome of this war."

Jennings was silent for a moment, contemplating McCabe's words. At last, he said, "I think you're wrong."

"I don't care what you think."

"Then maybe you should care that I know something about you," Jennings said.

"And what would that be?" McCabe asked.

"That your mother was born in India."

McCabe stared at Jennings for a moment, then threw the cigarette butt to the ground and crushed it with his shoe. "It goes without saying that everything I've told you is sensitive and privileged information. I should remind you that the penalties for disclosure under the Official Secrets Act are rather severe."

"So are the penalties for treason," Jennings hissed.

A thin smile crossed McCabe's lips. "We each have to fight the war in our own way." He tipped his hat. "Goodbye, Mr. Jennings. God save the King."

The man from the Directorate of Military Intelligence walked away. Commander Thomas Jennings made no attempt to follow. Alone amongst the greenery of Whitehall Gardens, he wondered when the history of the Great War is written whether Operation Mobilis would be remembered as a success or failure. And by whom.

About the Authors

Mike Adamson holds a PhD in archaeology from Flinders University of South Australia. After early aspirations in art and writing, Mike returned to study and secured degrees in both marine biology and archaeology. Mike has been a university educator since 2006, has worked in the replication of convincing ancient fossils, is a passionate photographer, a master-level hobbyist, and a journalist for international magazines. Short fiction sales include *Weird Tales, Abyss and Apex, Mind Candy, Daily Science Fiction, Compelling Science Fiction* and *Nature Futures*. Mike has placed over a hundred stories to date. You can catch up with his writing career at *The View From the Keyboard*, at http://mike-adamson.blogspot.com.

Alfred D. Byrd has a bachelor's degree in Medical Technology from Michigan State University and a master's degree in Microbiology from the University of Kentucky. He's worked for more than thirty years as a research analyst in a plant genetics laboratory at the University of Kentucky. His short stories "The Earth-Shaker's Answer" has appeared in *Quest for Atlantis*, "Natural Law" in *Warrior Wisewoman 3*, "Dead Man Stalking" in *Past Future Present*, and "Bhailgeth's Ransom" in *Death's Sting—Where Art Thou?* He's published several works of fantasy, science fiction, theology, and Appalachian regional fiction available from Amazon https://www.amazon.com/Alfred-D-Byrd/e/B001JSFFDE, Smashwords https://www.smashwords.com/profile/view/adbyrd54, and other on-line booksellers.

Demetri Capetanopoulos credits *Twenty Thousand Leagues Under the Sea* for inspiring his career as a nuclear submarine officer and deep submersible pilot. In his creative work, Demetri combines precision and technical knowledge with the wonder and possibility of imagination. A meticulous re-examining of the most famous submarine in literature was the impetus for his first book, *The Design and Construction of the Nautilus*.

In an upcoming graphic novel, *Rage Runs Deep*, Demetri weaves the tragic backstory of Captain Nemo through the seminal historical events of the 19th century. Fact and fiction are blended in a more lighthearted way in *Ned the Nuclear Submarine* and *Hadley the Lunar Rover,* two books written and illustrated by Demetri for children and all those who remain young at heart. To connect with Demetri or learn more about his creative projects, visit http://PreciseImagination.com.

J. Woolston Carr currently lives in Dallas, Texas. He works for the Dallas Public Libraries in the Youth Discovery Center for children and teens, is an avid reader of 19th century history. He is a member of the North American Jules Verne Society. Mr. Carr is also employed as a fencing instructor for the Fencing Institute of Texas, teaching modern Olympic style fencing, and is president of the Victorian Fencing Society for the study of the martial art of fencing as it was practiced in the nineteenth century. Mr. Carr has a blog for the Victorian Fencing Society with articles on nineteenth century fencing at http://victorianfencingsociety.blogspot.com/.

Maya Chhabra is the author of the middle grade historical novel *Stranger on the Home Front* (Jolly Fish Press), dealing with Indian immigration and the Indian independence movement. Her short fiction and poetry have appeared or are forthcoming in *Daily Science Fiction*, *Cast of Wonders*, and *Strange Horizons*. Visit her online at https://mayareadsbooks.wordpress.com/, or on Twitter as @mayachhabra.

Eric Choi is an award-winning writer, editor, and aerospace engineer based in Toronto, Canada. He was the first recipient of the Isaac Asimov Award (now the Dell Magazines Award) for his novelette "Dedication," which was published in *Asimov's Science Fiction* magazine and was later reprinted in Japanese translation in the anthology *The Astronaut from Wyoming and Other Stories*. With Ben Bova, he co-edited the hard SF anthology *Carbide Tipped Pens*, and with Derwin Mak he co-edited the Aurora Award winning Chinese-themed anthology *The*

Dragon and the Stars. His short fiction has appeared in more than 25 publications including the horror anthology *Re-Terrify: Horrifying Stories of Monsters and More* from Pole to Pole Publishing. In 2009, he was one of the Top 40 finalists (out of 5,351 applicants) in the Canadian Space Agency's astronaut recruitment campaign. Please visit his website www.aerospacewriter.ca or follow him on Twitter: @AerospaceWriter.

Corrie Garrett is an indie author of more than 10 science fiction and romance novels. She went to school in the Piney Woods of East Texas, earning a degree in Political Science, with a minor in Computer Science, since she mistook her love of dystopian novels for a career path. Corrie's favorite authors include Asimov, Niven, and Wells, and she enjoys writing science fiction with an old-school feel. Her Alien Cadet series is in this vein, following the choices of a group of young adults coming of age under the (arguably benevolent) despotism of an alien race. Corrie lives in Los Angeles with her husband, four kids, and a surprising number of coyotes.

Andrew Gudgel has always loved words and playing with words. His fiction has appeared at Writers of the Future, *Flash Fiction Online, Escape Pod, InterGalactic Medicine Show* and other publications. He lives in Maryland, in an apartment slowly being consumed by books.

Nikoline Kaiser is the pen-name of Nana Nikoline Boller, a Danish student with a BA in Comparative Literature, currently located in Aarhus and aspiring to make it big, or at least medium, in Literature. Most of her work is focused on queer and feminist issues. She can be found online at https://nikolinekaiser.wordpress.com/ and Twitter: @NikolineKaiser.

A born and raised Chicago Southsider, **James J. C. Kelly** is a veteran who served eight years in the U.S. Marine Corps. The geek in him is happy to have fifteen years in Information Technology. He's been writing stories since his young fingers learned to hold a pencil and tablets were fantasy devices unique to Star Trek *The Next Generation*. He comes from a large family, which includes seven sisters and a mother who often called on religion to keep the household together. Today, he's happily married and a proud father to four girls. His life has been diverse and a product of powerful women. As a father to five children, he wants to weave together stories enriched by his life's experience and cast women in a powerful light. Doing so, he seeks to give his daughters and others, male or female, dynamic examples of heroines who change the world.

M. W. Kelly became hooked on science after Neil Armstrong took an epic stroll one Saturday evening in July 1969. Kelly later served as a submarine officer based in Scotland and New England. He is a graduate of the U.S. Naval Academy, Bryant University, and Swinburne University. After leaving the Navy, he spent two decades teaching college physics and astronomy. A member of Rocky Mountain Fiction Writers and the Hawai'i Writers Guild, Kelly loves reading and writing mind-expanding science fiction. His debut novel, *Mauna Kea Rising* came out in 2019 and his articles and short stories have appeared in *Pilot Mag*, the *Torrid Literature Review*, and *Latitudes*. Visit him at his Web site at www.mwkelly.com or on Facebook at www.facebook.com/MW-Kelly-Author-211404242868188.

Jason J. McCuiston has been a semi-finalist in the Writers of the Future contest, and has studied under the tutelage of best-selling author Philip Athans. His stories of fantasy, horror, and science-fiction (and even a few crime dramas) have appeared in numerous anthologies, periodicals, websites, and podcasts, including Pole to Pole Publishing's *Dark Luminous Wings* and *Not Far From Roswell* anthologies. *Project Notebook*, his first novel, will be available from Tell-Tale Press in June of 2020. You can find most of his publications on his Amazon page at https://www.amazon.com/-/e/B07RN8HT98 or follow him on Facebook at https://www.facebook.com/ShadowCrusade.

Gregory L. Norris grew up on a healthy diet of creature double features and classic SF television. His work appears in numerous national magazines, fiction anthologies, novels, and the occasional script for TV or film. Norris novelized the classic made-for-TV Gerry Anderson movie *The Day After Tomorrow: Into Infinity* (which he watched at the age of eleven), its original sequel *Planetfall*, and is at work on a third release for the franchise. Norris lives and writes in the outer limits of New Hampshire's North Country in a beautiful old house called Xanadu, where he helps run an outstanding writers' group. Follow his literary adventures at www.gregorylnorris.blogspot.com.

Allison Tebo is a Christian writer committed to creating magical stories full of larger-than-life characters, a dash of grit, and plenty of laughs. She is the author of the *Tales of Ambia*, a series of romantic comedy retellings of popular fairy tales and her flash fiction and short stories have been published in *Splickety, Spark,* Inklings Press, and *Rogue Blades Entertainment*. When not creating art with words or paint, she enjoys reading, baking, and defending her championship title of GIF Master. Visit her author web site at https://allisonteboauthor.com/, or find her on Facebook: https://www.facebook.com/allisonteboauthor/.

Stephen R. Wilk is a physicist and optical engineer who has been publishing nonfiction for over 40 years. His love of the offbeat began with his first published piece, "The Physics of Karate" in *Scientific American*. Since then he has written on edible lasers, the mythology of lightning bolts, the 1727 trial of an American Indian chief in New Jersey, the physical origin of the Myth of Medusa, and the 1906-1910 history of a Revere Massachusetts amusement park, among other things. He has been publishing genre fiction (science fiction, fantasy, horror, and mystery) for the past decade, including three stories in *Analog*. He's published two books through Oxford University Press, with a third coming out, and has recently published his first novel, *The Traveler*. You can see more of his stuff at https://srichardwilkcom.wordpress.com.

Michael D. Winkle was born in Tulsa, Oklahoma, many years ago. He marks important life events mainly by the books he has encountered. High school in the small town of Bixby coincided with his discovery of science fiction literature, Lovecraftian horror, Andre Norton's fantasy, P. J. Farmer's pulp-hero meta-fiction and Marvel Comics. After receiving a B.A. in English from Oklahoma State University, Mike worked as library assistant, bookkeeper and in the usual array of *writer experience* jobs, from car washer to postal worker. He is the author of thirty-plus published stories, including: "Wolfhead: Tales of the Witch World 3;" "A Wondrous Portal Opened Wide," published in Illumen 13:2; and "After the Matilda Briggs Went Down," published in Orson Scott Card's Intergalactic Medicine Show. He also has seven ebooks available on Amazon Kindle. Visit Mike's web-site, *The Fantasy World Project*, at: http://www.fantasyworldproject.com/index.html.

About the Editors

As a teenager, **Steven R. Southard** read Jules Verne's Twenty Thousand Leagues Under the Sea, and it inspired much of the rest of his life. After graduating from the Naval Academy with a degree in Naval Architecture, he served in the submarine force aboard USS Bluefish (SSN-675). During his professional civilian career, he worked in several Navy submarine program offices.

Like Verne, Steve turned to writing fiction, creating characters who grapple with new technologies in far-off places. His short stories have appeared in over a dozen anthologies, most recently including *Not Far from Roswell, Re-Terrify, and Quoth the Raven*. Fourteen of his stories form the *What Man Hath Wrought series*. He's written science fiction, alternate history, steampunk, fantasy, and horror. He wrote the upcoming sci-fi collection titled *The Seastead Chronicles*.

The book you're holding is Steve's first foray into editing, and he's been delighted to work with Kelly A. Harmon on this project.

Order your engines to ahead full and submerge into Steve's website at https://stevenrsouthard.com, where he's known as Poseidon's Scribe. Or steam over to his mysterious islands on Facebook and Twitter.

Kelly A. Harmon used to write truthful, honest stories about authors and thespians, senators and statesmen, movie stars and murderers. Now she writes lies, which is infinitely more satisfying, but lacks the convenience of doorstep delivery.

She is an award-winning journalist and author, and a member of the Horror Writers Association and the Science Fiction & Fantasy Writers of America. A Baltimore native, she writes the *Charm City Darkness* series—a dark, thrilling adventure through the streets of Baltimore, Patterson Park and below the Pulaski Monument at Eastern Avenue. Find her short fiction in many magazines and anthologies, including *Occult Detective Quarterly; Terra! Tara! Terror!* and *Deep Cuts: Mayhem, Menace and Misery.*

Ms. Harmon is a former newspaper reporter and editor, and is now the senior editor for Pole to Pole Publishing, a small Baltimore publisher. She is co-editor of both *The Dark* series and *The Re-Imagined Series,* and now *20,000 Leagues Remembered.*

For more information, visit her blog at http://kellyaharmon. com, or, find her on Facebook and, occasionally, Twitter: http://facebook.com/Kelly-A-Harmon1, https://twitter.com/kellyaharmon.

Available in The Re-Imagined Series

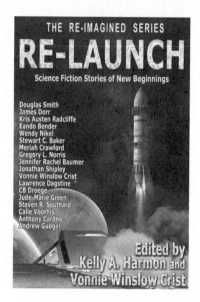
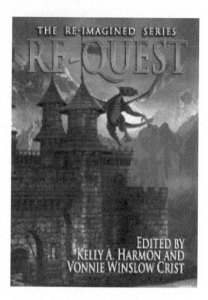

Re-Launch
Science Fiction Stories of New Beginnings

Re-Launch reminds readers that new beginnings rarely go as planned and danger waits for the unwary on all worlds.

http://poletopolepublishing.com/books/re-launch/

Re-Quest
Dark Fantasy Stories about Magic and the Fae

Re-Quest takes readers on fantastical quests filled with adventure, magic, and danger.

http://poletopolepublishing.com/books/re-quest/

 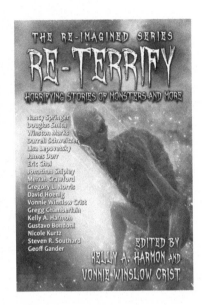

Re-Enchant
Dark Fantasy Stories of Magic and Fae

Re-Enchant takes readers down twisted walkways to discover strange and magical places, people, and creatures.

http://poletopolepublishing.com/books/re-enchant/

Re-Terrify
Dark Fantasy Stories of Magic and Fae

Vengeful undead. Demons. Hungry rats. These creatures and more haunt city streets, unlit hallways, deep space, and the corners of your imagination in Re-Terrify.

https://poletopolepublishing.com/books/re-terrify/

Re-Haunt
Chilling Stories of Ghosts and Other Haunts

Murdered. A possession mislaid or stolen. An unmarked grave. The dead refuse to leave for many reasons. Meet the spirits who still move among us in Re-Haunt. Feel the hairs on the back of your neck rise as you read 16 ghostly tales from an international roster of authors.

https://poletopolepublishing.com/books/re-haunt/

Available in the Dark Stories Series

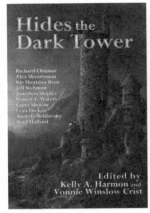  

Hides the Dark Tower

Dark Stories #1

Mysterious and looming, towers and tower-like structures pierce the skies and shadow the lands. Hides the Dark Tower includes over two dozen tales of adventure, danger, magic, and trickery from an international roster of authors. So step out of the light, and into the world of Hides the Dark Tower—if you dare.

http://poletopolepublishing.com/books/hides-the-dark-tower/

In a Cat's Eye

Dark Stories #2

Egyptian cats. Victorian cats. Space Cats. Cat stories in pre-history Mexico, grim magical worlds, during the zombie apocalypse, and a typical neighborhood give a glimpse into the mysterious lives of felines. And each cat, whether friend or fiend, believes in this truth: In a Cat's Eye, all things belong to cats.

http://poletopolepublishing.com/books/in-a-cats-eye/

Dark Luminous Wings
Dark Stories #3

From Icarus to Da Vinci to tomorrow's astronauts, humans have dreamt of flight. Feathered wings. Mechanical wings. Leathery wings. Steel wings. Stories of winged creatures set in graveyards and churches, bustling cities, fantastical worlds, alternate histories, and outer space reveal the shifting nature of Dark Luminous Wings.

http://poletopolepublishing.com/books/dark-luminous-wings/

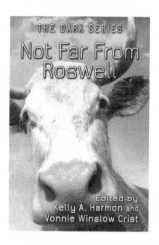

Not Far From Roswell
Dark Stories #4

Strange lights. Alien visitations. UFOs. Implanted technology. Unexplained disappearances. And cows. Roswell, New Mexico, a crossroads of extraterrestrial encounters, is the starting point for 18 dark tales which take place Not Far from Roswell. Though aliens haunt these pages, at their heart, these stories are about people and the choices they make when confronted with beings from beyond our world.

https://poletopolepublishing.com/books/not-far-from-roswell/

Coming Soon from Pole to Pole Publishing

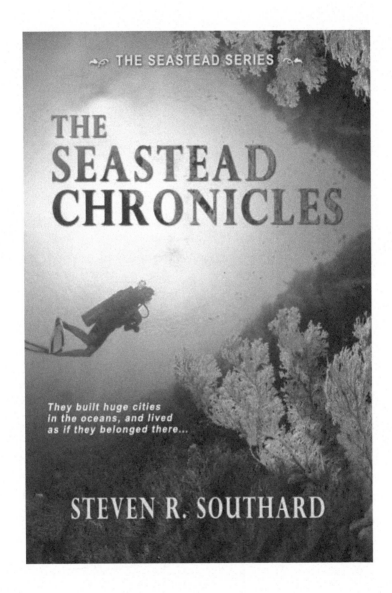

Join the

North American Jules Verne Society

If you'd like to read more Jules Verne, by the author himself, we invite you to read The Palik Series that we published from 2011 – 2018. The series features novellas, short stories, and plays that were translated and appear in English for the first time. You can find out more here:

http://www.najvs.org/palikseries.shtml

In 2002 we published the first English translation of the play "Voyage à travers l'impossible" (Journey through the Impossible). You can find out more here:

http://www.najvs.org/publications.shtml

We also welcome you to join us; you can find membership information on our website:

http://www.najvs.org/

You'll also find us on Facebook, just search for "NAJVS - (North American Jules Verne Society)."

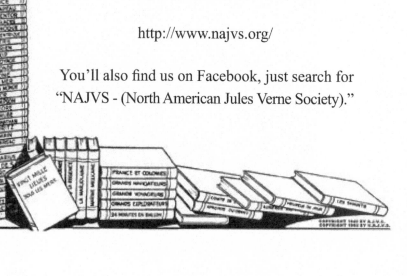